CANCELED

THE STORY OF AMERICA'S LEAST WANTED

Canceled:
The Story of
America's Least Wanted

by

Michael D. Britton

For Jean

Acknowledgements

I'm grateful to my First Readers, mentors, encouragers, patrons, financial backers, writing buddies, family and friends. This includes my wife & son; Dottie Lima, David Schibi, Ryan Pitt, Mom & Dad, Maria DaCosta, Dan & Mel Scarbrough, Wynn Clayton, Dean Wesley Smith & Kristine Kathryn Rusch, and the OWN "New York Publisher's Editorial Room" who shook their heads, smirked nervously and said "are you crazy?" You know who you are; and yes, yes I am.

PROLOGUE

Studio executive Dave Kohler leaned back in the black leather high-back and swiveled toward the tall plate glass windows overlooking downtown Los Angeles. He ran his fingers through his short salt-and-pepper hair and sighed.

"All the focus group data showed it was going to be a huge hit, Tom, but it's just not going to fly. I'm sorry."

"Remind me of the problem," said Tom Highgate, President and CEO of FBC, the Federal Broadcasting Corporation.

Tom, a stocky man in his early sixties with a shock of white hair and a barrel chest that filled his classic navy blue three-piece suit, stared longingly at the unlit cigar between his fingers. His chair sat at the head of the small glass-topped conference table in his office. He too, turned to the window and gazed out at the shimmering late summer heat rising from the roofs of buildings below.

"Well unfortunately," Dave said, "we gave ourselves just enough rope to hang ourselves with this one. ACLU has fought tooth and nail against *Death Row: Mercy or Justice* ever since the pitch was leaked. They say it's illegal, and unconstitutional, and all that other bleeding heart crap. They've tied it up in the courts, and there's no end in sight, now that they've got an injunction ordered. It could be on hold indefinitely. We need to move with something for the fall season, and we can't pin our hopes on a judge ruling in our favor at this point."

"But the idea is perfect," said Tom, boasting of his own creation. "Each season, sixteen death row inmates are selected from a pool of applicants, we follow them around each week – a real chance for America to see what life is like on the inside – and then each week one is voted off the show, off death row, and back to the general prison population. For the season finale, the last man standing gets an up or down vote – a commutation of sentence and conditional release under electronic monitoring – mercy – or immediate execution on live television – justice. We'd have got a thirty-five share with something like that."

Dave shook his head slowly. "Yes, yes we would have. But it is not going to happen – at least not for the 2031 season. So, we need an alternative. Something just as explosive, but impervious to lawyers."

Tom could see the gleam in Dave's eye. "I'm listening."

"I'd like to bring in Jake Granville to pitch it to you."

"I suppose you have Granville waiting outside."

"Matter of fact, yes. I know Jake rubs you the wrong way – and I don't even know why – but he's a great VP of New Network Programming with one hell of a track record for high-return ideation. Just give him a listen. Five minutes."

Tom raised his eyebrows and sighed heavily. "Bring him in. Five minutes."

Tom got up and poked his head out the large double doors of rich dark wood and in came Jake Granville. He was only about thirty-five, with a strong jaw line and slick black hair combed straight back in long shiny lines and brushing the top of his collar. He wore a high-dollar deep green suit with a glossy sheen, and onyx cufflinks on his cream colored shirt. A classic striped-pattern tie in gold and teal finished the ensemble.

Jake smiled a big, white-toothed grin as he stepped in carrying a slim valise. "Thanks, Dave. Good to see you Mr. Highgate."

Dave and Jake sat down opposite Tom, who sat back in his chair across the desk, seeming uninterested.

"Okay," said Jake, "here's what we have. A young woman. Beautiful, of course. Between twenty-four and twenty-eight. Single. She's pregnant. Just found out – in fact, we capture that on video – the discovery, that is – not the conception."

Jake chuckled, but Tom remained stoic.

"Anyway," Jake went on, "we'll need to, of course, start with a pool of girls who suspect they're pregnant, film all of them taking the test, so on and so forth. We select the one we want – one who is pregnant and unsure how to proceed – and then she is the star of our show. For the duration of the extended season – thirty two weeks – we follow her around and experience her life as a young, troubled pregnant woman."

"And the point?" Tom interrupted, impatient for the payoff.

"Every week, Americans call in and vote: should she keep the baby, or terminate the pregnancy? A simple up or down vote. Carry to term, or go see Doctor Ian. The season finale will result in either a live abortion or a live birth. And either way, the woman walks away with a big chunk of cash."

Jake stared at Tom. Tom stared back.

A standoff.

Tom mulled it over in silence for the length of a prime time commercial break.

"Abortion Idol," Tom finally said.

Then his face changed.

He lit up and grinned.

"I *love* it. It's truly sick, disgusting, repulsive and revolting. It's absolutely horrible. And it will tear this nation apart at the seams – disrupt the very fabric of our culture – well, if we're lucky. And damned if it won't make us *billions*." He looked at Jake like he'd swallowed a bitter pill that would make him crap gold bars. "Granville, you are a freaking genius."

Jake smiled and nodded as Tom shifted in his seat, as if one of those gold bars was already working its way out.

"And no legal troubles with this one," Dave said. "It's all a contractual relationship, consensual, et cetera. With termination up to full term now legal in California, we're all set. I've already vetted it with the studio attorneys. We're on solid ground."

Tom continued to grin.

"Who's Doctor Ian?" Dave asked, turning to Jake.

"Oh, he's an abortion doctor I hired. I wanted to get a head start on casting, because I know we're in a crunch to hit the season premiere deadlines. He's fantastic on camera. You'll really like him."

"All right," said Tom, "get a casting call out. We don't have time to scour the nation for the girl next door. So, we'll just look *next door*. I'm sure L.A. has plenty of sexually active single girls who've been careless recently. Get on it. Oh, and one more thing – what are we slugging it?"

Jake smiled and rubbed his strong chin. "The show is called *CANCELED*."

CHAPTER 1

FOUR WEEKS EARLIER

Kaylie Adams had a hangover the size of . . . her misgivings about that guy – what was his name?

Yeah, he was charming, and handsome, and had some kind of slick job in Burbank. And he knew how to make her feel very, very good. For most of the night.

But now that was just a blur of music and candlelight and flesh and heat – and snoring.

The snoring was gone now – along with old what's-his-name.

Kaylie slowly sat up in bed, her head banging like a drum. The sheets and covers were mostly on the floor, just one corner of the linens near the red painted toenails of her right foot clinging on to the mattress for dear life, ready at any moment to lose traction and join the rest of the pile on the hardwood floor.

A stream of white light split the room through a gap in the blackout curtains, illuminating the normally invisible dust particles that gently tumbled in the stale air of the apartment.

Kaylie glanced to the clock radio on the nightstand, but its thin blue numbers were too blurry for her to read without her lenses. She'd obviously lost both contacts in last night's activities, so she fumbled for her rimless corrective glasses and slipped them on.

Twelve-twenty nine.

She flopped back on her pillow and let out a foul-tasting puff of air.

This had to stop.

She'd been living this life of mayhem and unaccountable pleasures for nearly six months now.

Since a week or two after she'd kicked out her roommate Erin – for the same exact behavior.

Now she had become Erin Two – the Sequel. Your standard Sunday night movie fare – good girl moves to the city to get "discovered" and become a film star. Good girl meets a girl who used to be just like her – only has been knocked around by the big city for a couple of years. The two become friends, the more seasoned girl gets out of control and gets kicked out, and before long, good girl is now the bad girl. Rinse and repeat.

It's a story that's been rinsing and repeating though Hollywood's streets for generations.

But Kaylie felt she'd finally hit rock bottom. She was ready to break the chain of failure and fatigue, to make a fresh start.

To stop living this way and get back to the reason she came here in the first place.

And besides, she'd been raised better than this. If her parents could see her now, they'd be sick.

Sick.

There's a thought.

Kaylie leapt from the bed, nearly tripped over the sheets on the floor, and stumbled into the bathroom with just enough time to throw the toilet seat up before the muscles in her belly and throat seized up, ejecting a thick stream of yellow vomit into the water below.

She coughed and sputtered, pulled some toilet paper off the roll to dab the drool off her mouth and chin, then heaved again.

And again.

Once more, but this one was dry. Just her stomach making sure it had expelled all its unwelcome contents.

She coughed again, her throat stinging. She moaned to herself as she pushed her long brown hair back out of the toilet, and sat back on the little furry yellow rug from the squatting position she'd been in.

And then she sobbed.

Now she had hit rock bottom.

Kaylie surfed the forums looking for a casting call she could audition for this week. Orange rays of light cut through the cracks in the blinds as the sun dipped low in the sky, setting the room in a warm glow.

As she sat at her tiny desk in the corner of her apartment browsing the newest listings, she felt a little queasy and lost focus as her mind wandered.

She hadn't been feeling right for the last three weeks, since the morning she'd hit the wall of personal despair and resolved to change.

She wasn't sure if she'd caught something, or if maybe it was psychosomatic – the physical ill-feeling that can accompany a mental and emotional burden.

Either way, she was starting to wonder.

But trying not to wonder *too* much.

That is, she was over a week late, and kept pushing the thought away from her mind.

She consciously avoided even *thinking* the word.

Pregnant.

No – no, no.

That would not do at all.

Not unless some soap opera was looking to cast a girl with a motherhood story arc.

Which would mean her audition options would quickly begin to diminish.

Okay – no more thinking about it. No use trying to plan and fret over something that wasn't even happening.

No use living out a feared future, instead of focusing on the real present.

Feeling weary, she shut down the computer and decided to take a nap.

✧

Twelve days late.

This was getting ridiculous.

Kaylie was tired of feeling like this – ready to cry at the drop of a hat – and tired of waiting for her period to start.

This was turning into the worst case of PMS of her life.

She was scanning the casting calls again, this time determined to make it to an audition this week, and get around to changing her life for the better.

And then she saw it.

She couldn't quite believe it at first, and had to read through it slowly a second time, just to make sure she'd read it right.

It seemed like a custom-made casting call – as if someone, somewhere was speaking directly to her – *looking* for Kaylie Adams.

The ad read:

Kaylie stared at the screen.

How many girls could there be who fit her exact description?

It was bizarre. Unreal.

And she would surely be a shoo-in for this show. It was probably one of those shows where they stick a group of people in a room to debate a hot topic.

Kaylie knew from her limited experience that "very significant" money was code for a huge chunk of cash in this industry.

She was at once convinced and committed to trying out for this gig. She didn't know what she was in for, but a job was a job, and giving it a shot would go a long way to getting her out of this funk.

She had nothing to lose, and at least a "small stipend" to gain for taking the test.

She jotted down the audition location, flipped her laptop closed, and got to work on looking her best.

CHAPTER 2

"Wow."

Jake Granville shook his head in amazement as he stared down at the crowd from the production booth. Below in the sound stage area, which consisted of a large riser in front of about five hundred theater seats, young hotties lined up to take their shot at being the next big reality TV star.

"More takers than you expected?" asked Hal Urich, the casting director, who also gazed down at the throng, peering over the top of his glasses and scratching at his trim white goatee.

"Uh, yeah. I figured – for some crazy reason – that people had a little more shame. Sometimes I forget this is Hollywood."

The line of attractive women wound its way off the stage and out the door, ending somewhere in the parking area. As girls got checked in and received their information sheets, they sat down in the theater seats, filling up the auditorium.

Jake noticed that a handful of them were visibly pregnant – obviously too dumb to read the announcement properly, or figuring they could somehow game the system. A few others were plain, and some were just plain ugly – girls whose friends didn't have the heart to be honest with them.

"This is my least favorite part of running realities," said Jake. "Call me after you've got the short list."

Hal gave a nod and a grin. "I love my job. This is my favorite part — beautiful women everywhere I look, the chance to decide all of their fates. Gives me a rush, man. A quick and easy cut of the obvious pregos, the uglies, and the transsexuals, and then I get to ogle babes to my heart's content."

Jake shook his head and left the booth, headed for Dave Kohler's office.

He passed one of the young administrative assistants in the hall and gave her a smile and a nod, checking her out as she passed. Then he chastised himself.

Did he really want to end up like Hal when he was fifty?

Jake had already gained quite a reputation as a ladies' man over the past couple years at FBC, but the truth was, he was growing tired of the lifestyle.

Something strange about hitting the mid-thirties mark. He was starting to feel the yearnings for something deeper than one-night stands with nameless bimbos. It scared him a little to think that he was growing up enough to want to – he hated these two words – *settle down*.

But he couldn't deny it any longer, either. It was time to rein things in. If not for his emotional future, at least for his career. His big mistake was sleeping with Tom Highgate's daughter, Tawny. Everyone knows you don't sleep with the boss's daughter. Certainly not the boss's boss's daughter. It could be career suicide.

Jake was pretty sure Highgate was clueless about it, but you just never know.

Of course, that brief relationship had to end when Tawny had spent one drunken evening spilling her guts about her daddy's inclinations for little girls – namely herself. That was just too weird – and the girl clearly had issues as a result of her past experiences in that realm.

Better for Jake to just cut and run.

That was, after all, his specialty.

He arrived at Dave's office and gave a quick knock before letting himself in.

Dave was on the phone.

"Yeah. Yes, I know. Mm-hm. And that's why we're starting shooting tomorrow. That's right, just one day of auditions and we'll pick our winner. No, no I hadn't heard. How many? Wow. Well, Hal can handle it. We'll have our gal by the end of the day. Okay, thanks Tom. Talk later."

Dave hung up and swiveled his chair to Jake. "S'up?"

"About five hundred chicks who think they might be pregnant."

"Well, if you hadn't used your *whole* little black book for the casting call," Dave teased.

"Nice."

"We'll get through them. And we'll find our perfect little Pregnant Polly. This is gonna rock, buddy."

"I know it," said Jake. He strolled to the window and looked down at the parking lot, watching the rejects leave the sound stage one by one. "I've met with Doctor Ian again, provided him some scripts and rundowns. I'd like you to meet him, too. You open for dinner?"

"Lemme check." Dave scrolled through his Blackberry calendar. "I'm good all evening. Tony's?"

"Okay. I'll pick you up at seven."

◈

After Jake left Dave's office, he headed out to the gym and worked out for about an hour. Then he went home and changed into something more appropriate for the evening – a dark brown silk suit, white dress shirt, no tie – and hopped into his AC Cobra, taking off with the low rumble of the huge V8 echoing through the parking garage of the upscale Galaxy Apartments complex in Brentwood.

He swung back to Dave's office, knowing he'd find the workaholic still at his desk, on the phone, lining up details for the big show's debut.

Dave gave him the index finger to indicate "just a sec."

Jake flopped down on the black leather sofa, knowing he'd be there for a while.

After about ten minutes of scrolling through industry articles on his device, he looked at Dave and tapped at his platinum Longines watch.

"Okay, yes, thanks Justin. Yeah, we'll talk in the ayem. I gotta go – yeah, an appointment. Sorry. Chat later." He hung up. "Sorry, man."

"Don't apologize to me – Doctor Ian's the one sitting alone at Tony's."

The two headed out and managed to arrive at the restaurant ahead of schedule, thanks to Jake's judicious use of third gear and a keen knowledge of L.A.'s traffic patterns.

They were seated, and within minutes were joined by the doctor.

Ian R. Chaitanyanam-Burke, M.D. (yes, there was a reason he went by Dr. Ian) was a thirty-two year-old New Delhi-born man educated in London. He was about five-nine, deep bronze-skinned, with short black hair and a trim goatee. He was slim in body with a round face set off by narrow-lens black-framed glasses. He wore green slacks and a light-blue shirt with subdued Hawaiian pattern.

"Hello Jake. And you must be David. Very pleased to meet you, yes." He extended his hand and smiled, revealing a set of bright white teeth with a small gap in the front.

Before they could order food, Jake's cell buzzed in his vest pocket. He pulled it out and glanced at the screen.

"It's Hal Urich. I gotta take this." He tapped the screen and said, "Jake Granville."

"*Jake, I've found her.*"

"Already? I expected you to be there all night."

"*I did too. It wasn't looking good. But then SHE appeared. She's perfect. You're gonna love her.*"

"Name, stats?"

"*Kaylie Adams.*"

"Sounds familiar. Very all-American. I like it."

"*She's twenty-five, single, five-eight, long brown hair, green-eyed, nice skin, actor wannabe with no credits, great personality, passed the background check – and she's pretty sure she's about five weeks along, but hasn't tested yet.*"

"Perfect."

"*Of course, she may not be pregnant, so I've got a pool of twelve women. We'll shoot all the candidates taking the test in green screen tonight. Will let you know results.*"

"Keep me posted."

Jake hung up.

"Do we have our girl?" asked Dave.

"It's looking good. Just need to do the pregnancy test screen tests and we'll know within an hour or so."

"Forgive me," said Dr. Ian, "but it was my understanding that the show was going to include the pregnancy test experience in the pilot, yes? How will that work if it's supposed to be 'reality' TV, yet the girl is taking the test at a TV studio?"

"The magic of television, my friend," said Jake. "Tonight, we shoot the girls testing on a green screen. Then we'll send a crew to her home tomorrow at sunrise. We'll get her waking up, throwing up, and starting to take the test. Then we'll splice it with today's test footage, placing her on location through digital manipulation. The rest of the season will be all natural, of course, but we'll need to bend the truth a little to make the premiere work."

"Ah, I see. The magical deception of the digital age, yes. Fascinating," said Dr. Ian without looking up from his menu. "I suppose one should never really trust what one sees on television, eh?"

"Never," said Jake. "Especially not when it's labeled 'reality.'"

CHAPTER 3

Kaylie pondered this change in her life as she scrubbed down the cream-colored Formica counters in her dim little kitchen.

She couldn't believe it.

She'd been gobsmacked by bad news and good news, all at once.

The positive pregnancy test was a shocker – sort of. She'd been suspecting she was pregnant for long enough that the result wasn't a total surprise, but the reality of a positive confirmation brought her to her knees (an on-camera reaction that the director, Justin Mitchell, absolutely loved).

Then, just thirty minutes later when she was told she had the part – that she - Kaylie Adams from Medford, Oregon – had beat out all those hundreds of women and was going to be the star of a big network reality show – the amazing news mixed with the news of the pregnancy in another on-camera moment that overwhelmed her.

She was going to have to get used to every aspect of her life being an "on-camera moment."

But finally, she was getting her break – and all she had needed to do was get off her butt and decide to make it happen.

The casting director, Hal Something, seemed pretty nice – at least when he wasn't checking out her body. But then, that was his job, right?

He seemed really excited, and eager to get started right away. So, a production crew was coming first thing in the morning!

She was just about done cleaning the apartment. She'd done the laundry and the dishes, vacuumed, dusted, and even swept and mopped the bathroom and the tiny kitchen. She pulled out a couple of old glamour shots and hung them on the living room wall – partly as self-promotion, partly to cover some water-damage stains. The pictures were great – her long brown hair teased to the extreme, her perfect pale skin, slender nose, big dark green eyes, and the ideal sultry look accentuated by her voluptuous lips.

As she went back to the kitchen, the smell of the cleaning solution struck her with a sudden bout of nausea – so sudden that she didn't quite make it to the bathroom and upchucked all over the hallway.

Glamour, indeed.

Hormones raging, she broke down and cried before mustering the motivation to clean up her mess.

Once she was cleaned up, she considered the money she would be getting from this new job (a stipend in addition to the prize money), and decided to go out to treat herself to dinner tonight.

She didn't realize it as she grabbed her purse and headed out – but this would be the last time she would dine out in public for a very long time.

She made her way south to her favorite Chinese hole-in-the-wall, Dynasty Dragon, and ordered more food than she could ever eat in one sitting.

Eating for two.

After a final piece of the orange chicken, she pulled out her phone, trying to decide whether to call her parents to announce the news.

And which news to announce.

She cracked open a fortune cookie, looking for some random guidance.

YOU WILL SOON FACE A CHOICE THAT COULD LEAD TO RICHES.

A little late, there, fortune cookie god. Already signed on the dotted line for this job. Choice made. Riches on the way.

Hoping for some true inspiration, she opened a second fortune cookie that was sitting on her receipt.

YOU WILL LOSE IT ALL BUT GAIN EVERYTHING.

Nice. Completely vague, ambiguous and contradictory – she could think of a hundred ways that could come true. Actually, it kind of fit her mood.

She put her phone away, deciding to wait until she'd had a chance to learn more about this show, so when the inevitable questions came, she'd have some answers.

Maybe the pregnancy wouldn't play into the show that much, and she could procrastinate having to break that news until after the show was underway and her newfound success had gained some good will with the family.

They'd parted on not-so-good terms.

Mom and Dad had said that she shouldn't go running off to L.A. based on a few local modeling jobs and a couple of good runs in small productions at the Craterian Theater.

They said she should go to college, like her brother Bruce and sister Amanda had both done.

But Kaylie had rejected those suggestions. She'd said she had a feeling – something good was just over the horizon.

So, at age twenty, she'd loaded up her belongings in her 1998 Toyota Corolla and flown down Interstate 5, seeking the greener pastures and ripe opportunities of the world's entertainment capital.

That was five years ago.

And she'd only been home five times since – each year at Christmas.

The family kept in contact with occasional calls, but mostly by email and Facebook, and the calls had slacked off a lot the last few months, since Kaylie started walking on the wild side.

In fact, she hadn't had any contact with Mom, Dad, Bruce, or Amanda since before the summer – on her twenty-fifth birthday, May 15th. At that time she'd got a new phone and neglected to inform the family of her new number.

Kaylie boxed up her Chinese leftovers and returned home.

She was going to need a good night's sleep tonight.

Tomorrow – her first big job as a Hollywood star would begin. This show – and the exposure she would get from it – could lead to all kinds of job opportunities – especially if she could find a way to stand out from the other people on the show and take center stage.

As one of her favorite old Tom Petty songs said, "The future was wide open."

Excited, she turned out the light and dreamed strange, confused dreams of leering casting directors, her family – and tiny newborn babies emerging from fortune cookies.

She awoke to urgent knocking.

It was still dark.

She slipped on her glasses (she still hadn't found those blasted contact lenses, despite the deep cleaning fest yesterday), and looked at the clock.

Five twenty-six.

What was *wrong* with these people? They'd *said* "first thing in the morning," not "middle of the freakin' night."

She threw back the covers and slipped out of bed, and shuffled to the front door in a pair of green fuzzy slippers. A quick look through the peep hole showed a view of Justin Mitchell with his too-black hair, titanium spacer-filled earlobes, and already-large nose distorted by the peep-hole lens.

She unchained and unlatched the bolts to let him in.

"Mornin' love," he said in his West London accent. He was followed in by about ten people, all carrying some kind of equipment – boom mics, makeup kits, cables, two monitors, lights, cameras – all that was needed was the *action*.

"All right people," Mitchell said, pointing this way and that as he spoke. "Let's get the baseline — I want standard shots of all rooms first. We'll do a sound check in fifteen, and we roll at six. Go to it, then."

"Uh, um – is there someone I can talk to?" asked Kaylie, her arms crossed, trying to hide the braless bosom in her loose "Crater Lake, Oregon" t-shirt.

"I'm right 'ere, love," said Mitchell.

"No, I mean, yesterday when I signed my contract, it was all a bit rushed, and Hal — the casting director – he said I'd have a chance to meet with the producer to go over some details. Is he coming today?"

"Hal? Uh, no."

"No, the producer – I think he said his name was Dave Kohl."

"Oh, Kohler, yeah, Dave Kohler. He's the man, all right. Works odd hours – all over the place, really. Bloomin' workaholic if you ask me." Mitchell grinned, revealing a set of teeth so perfect they may have been fake. "Me, I like to get in early, finish by about three in the afternoon. Any night-time work will be directed by my A.D. She's great – I know you'll like her. You better – she's me fiancée!" He grinned again.

"Dave Kohler – how can I get a hold of him – you know, to meet?" She looked around at the crew, scurrying about her apartment setting up lighting and white-balancing cameras.

Mitchell pulled out his phone and scrolled through the menus. He handed her the phone. "Here you go – that's his secretary's number – she can set you up."

Kaylie was about to make the call, but realized it was still before six in the morning, and that she was about to have her first shoot.

"Um – shouldn't I get changed? Is there a wardrobe person or something?"

"This is reality TV, love! We want you just as you are. We'll deal with wardrobe changes later. This first scene needs to be *au naturel* – well, not, you know, *au naturel*, as in *nude*, ha ha, no. Um, just natural, is all. Unless of course you sleep nude?"

"No. What you see is what I was wearing when you knocked on the door. Minus the slippers."

He looked her up and down. "Right then. We'll be shooting in fifteen. You got any coffee?"

Kaylie handed the shiny silver cell phone back to Mitchell and led the way to the kitchen. She looked in her cupboards. "Uh, sorry. How about some hot chocolate?"

Mitchell screwed up his nose and shook his head. "No worries, love. I'll just send someone out."

"So, what do you need me to do – when we start shooting?"

"Well, the nature of reality TV is – well, it's all about the editing, really. We will need to shoot twenty-four-seven, then those magicians in the editing room do their thing and put together one hour of compelling television from one week's worth of footage. Today will be the easy day – we'll only be here through the morning, getting our set up shots and so on. Tomorrow, the real work begins. By then you'll have had a chance to speak with Dave and get oriented."

Kaylie raised her eyebrows and sighed. "Okay. Well, just let me know what you need – I can stay out of the way if you just need interiors of my apartment, or you can shoot me getting ready for the day – whatever."

"Perfect, love. I'll let you know. You and I are going to get to know each other pretty well over the next few months! Oh – and you may want to stock up on some coffee."

By noon, the last of the crew and equipment were gone. Kaylie was exhausted.

She flopped down on her sofa and immediately remembered: Dave Kohler.

Mitchell had left before she'd had a chance to call Kohler's secretary.

As she slumped down in the cushions, she heard her cell ringing in the bedroom.

She jumped up and ran to it, answered it.

"Hello?"

"Kaylie Adams?"

"Yes."

"Dave Kohler, producer at FBC. You available for lunch today? We can go over any questions you have and talk about the expectations of the network in more detail."

"Oh yes, yes. Um, lunch. When, where?"

"Oh, I'll just send a limo around. Say, twenty minutes?"

"Sure. I'll be ready."

The call ended and Kaylie looked in the mirror. "Shoot! I need to get ready!"

She scampered around the apartment, changing in and out of three outfits before settling on a simple black blouse and blue jeans with red pumps. She threw on her short red leather jacket just as a long black limousine showed up in the street below.

She teased her hair, touched up her makeup, and grabbed her purse.

Down below in the street, a capped driver opened a rear door for her and she slid into the back seat. Seated across from her was a man in his mid-forties with graying temples, tanned skin, and a light gray suit. His light blue eyes shined as he reached forward to shake her hand.

"Dave Kohler. Pleased to meet you. Hal and Justin have spoken highly of you."

Kaylie blushed a little when she smiled and said, "Oh thank you – I mean, pleased to meet you Mr. Kohler."

"Call me Dave. You like sushi?"

Kaylie had tried sushi one time since arriving in L.A., and didn't like it at all. "Love it." Then she had a brainstorm. "Uh, but, I probably should avoid raw fish right now," she added, patting her belly gently.

"Ah yes, of course. Well, is Italian okay?"

"Fantastic."

Dave pushed a button near his armrest and the tinted glass divider between the back of his head and the driver's seat slid down with a quiet mechanical whirr. "Il Pastaio."

Kaylie gulped as the car slid out into traffic. She'd heard of that restaurant, but only dreamed of ever eating there.

"So," said Dave, "I imagine you have a lot of questions. Yesterday was done in a bit of a rush – we have a very tight production schedule this fall – some things had to be done last minute. Eh, what the hell – I won't kid you, it's just another crazy fall season in Burbank, you know?" He chuckled.

Kaylie felt uneasy. Dave was nice, but it felt like he was holding something back – as if his efforts to put her at ease were really an attempt to calm himself down. As if he had news to break that he didn't want to deliver.

Great. They probably decided their decision was rushed and they're going to go with someone else. The fancy lunch is a way to soften the blow and hope Kaylie won't cry foul on a contract breach.

Well, there is no *way* she was going to let them back out of this deal.

She started to dig in her heels in her own head, all based on an imagined situation. She decided she was probably being silly, but thought she would test the waters.

"Well, now we have a little time this afternoon, I'd love to go over the contract – a clause at a time – just to make sure I understand everything. I'd have my agent do that, but she's out of the country right now."

Lie. Kaylie almost had an agent six months ago, but forgot to call back one hungover morning, and missed her chance.

"Oh, sure – that's perfect – just what I had planned," said Dave, looking like he'd accidentally swallowed a cigarette but was trying to hide it.

After a few minutes of small talk, the driver was opening the door. Until that moment, Kaylie had assumed the stop was just another red light – she'd totally lost track of their location during the trip.

They entered the restaurant and were led to a table next to the front window that looked out at the busy Beverly Hills intersection.

All through the meal, Kaylie's mind was on the contract, but Dave spoke little of business until the cappuccino came.

"So, about the contract you signed yesterday. We had a lot of dotted lines and a number of 'initial here and here' lines – but when it comes down to it, we didn't really have a chance to explain to you even the basic premise of the show – what will be expected of you. And what you can expect in return."

"All right," said Kaylie, trying her best to sound like a seasoned pro. "Hit me with the good news first."

"Three thousand a week stipend. Complete maternity medical care. End-of-season contract completion payment of nine hundred thousand dollars. Strong possibility of a book deal and maybe a movie deal coming out of it. Great exposure – it's going to be the number one show in America – guaranteed."

Kaylie felt her heart leap when he mentioned the payoff money. Nearly a million dollars! Wow. Wow wow wow.

She tried to stay cool and suppress her excitement. "Okay, what's the downside?"

"Well, it's not so much a 'downside' as your end of the deal. The job. First, today – this morning – was nothing. That initial setup shoot was non-invasive and brief."

Brief. They were there for over six hours!

Dave continued. "Starting tomorrow, you will have at least one camera, usually two, in your face around the clock. For the next thirty weeks or so, you will not have a single moment of privacy. No alone time. Ever. Standard reality TV stuff, really. But don't worry – if you're in the shower or taking a crap, it'll be a female photog. But I'm serious when I say that there will be zero off-camera time. Every second of your life will be documented and edited. I hope you're ready for that kind of exposure."

Kaylie nodded. She tried to imagine what the next few months would be like. It sounded tolerable enough.

"Then there's the voting aspect. We've got it set up like the talent programs, where each week the viewing public uses our app to make a decision as to the outcome of the uh – situation."

Kaylie picked up her tiny china cappuccino cup and sipped at it. "I don't understand. What are they going to be voting about?"

"It's going to be an up or down vote."

"You mean, like voting me off the island?"

"Like voting your fetus off the island."

"Huh?"

"Look, one of the prerequisites for the audition was that you be single, believe yourself to be pregnant, and that you be unsure of what you were going to do." He dabbed his mouth with the cloth napkin. "America is going to decide for you. It'll be a life or death vote – each week they will make the call and choose your destiny – whether you'll continue to carry the baby to term, or whether you'll go visit one of your costars, the very nice Dr. Ian – an abortion doctor."

Did he just say abortion?

The little cup slipped from Kaylie's suddenly weakened grasp and crashed against the saucer, cracking and spilling a little of the strong brew on the white tablecloth. A number of heads turned briefly in her direction.

"You — you have got to be kidding me."

Dave looked down for a moment, then looked into her eyes with his dead serious, piercing blue eyes. "It's all in the contract, Kaylie. This is what you signed up for. And it will make you the most famous person in this country."

Kaylie gulped and tears rose up in her eyes. "You're serious? You're *serious!*" her voice started to break. "A bunch of freaking couch potatoes are going to determine whether the baby lives or dies? That's – that's reprehensible! Preposterous! It's - crazy!"

"It is a kind of repulsive concept, when you first think about it," Dave conceded, reaching over to mop her spill with his napkin. "But when you really examine it – well, look at it this way. First – you are going to get top-notch free medical care, so you know you'll be taken care of no matter what. Second, you're an out of work actor trying to make ends meet – and once again, you'll be taken care of on that front with the stipend – not to mention the final prize money. Further, you yourself have already admitted you don't know what you're going to do with this pregnancy. Now, under another circumstance, you may ask a few friends or relatives for advice. But now you get to get advice from millions and millions of people – every week. What an opportunity!"

Kaylie just stared at Dave, the wet track of a tear glistening down her left cheek. "What if I come to my own decision, and America has different plans for me? How can I be expected to – to do what they say?"

"It's in the contract. And it's all perfectly legal. *Roe v Wade* and all that. The contract is a consensual agreement between two parties to carry out, or not carry out, a perfectly legal act."

"I didn't realize what I was signing!"

"Unfortunately, that would never hold up in court. A contract is a contract, Kaylie. You know you should never sign your name to something without reading and understanding it first. Oh, one more thing – the season finale will consist of either a live abortion or a live birth. We got the funding green-light to run an extended season – thirty two weeks – so that we can have either outcome in the finale. Since abortion is now legal in California up to full-term, we can go all the way to the end and then go either way. With America so evenly split on the issue, each week will be a real cliff hanger, a toss-up. Very compelling television, Kaylie."

"What if they vote for me to end the pregnancy on, like, week three?"

"I don't think they will. Too much morbid curiosity – too much hunger to see what will happen week to week. But they might do it. And if they do, we've written some contingencies into the rules – ways around it – we do have sponsor contracts to satisfy, after all. Those details are not important right now. The main thing is, I want you to know that although this will be very emotionally grueling, and a tough schedule to keep, and so on – we are on the same side here. FBC wants you – *I* want you – to know that we're here for you. One of the show's characters is even a therapist – to help you if you're struggling with anything."

Kaylie was still in shock, but her hands had quit shaking and the tears were gone. "Okay. Well, okay. Can you, uh, take me back to my apartment? I'm suddenly really tired. Must be the pregnancy thing."

Looking relieved that this meeting was over, Dave said, "You got it."

Dave paid the bill with a corporate card and they returned to the limo. On the way back through town, Kaylie stared out the window and said little. When they arrived at her apartment, she climbed out and said through the open door, "Thanks, Dave. What's next?"

"Full crew arrives at five thirty tomorrow morning. Justin will be there – the director from this morning. They'll set up their positions and just start following you around on a normal day. Next week, we bring in the rest of the cast. Monday, we'll get you in for your first exam with Dr. Jennifer Cho, your new OB/GYN. Tuesday we'll get you into the therapist, Dr. Len Hamlin – nice guy – in fact, he was my therapist for a couple years. Tomorrow we should have an itinerary for the following week or two, and get a final rundown to you some time during that time. This stuff is a blend of very well-planned and totally spontaneous. Sometimes we even plan the spontaneity – sometimes we surprise even ourselves. But overall, the demands on you won't be too great, other than the constant observation. Oh, and the weekly vote. For that, we'll have you in studio. Also for the premiere, of course."

Kaylie was feeling overwhelmed. She just nodded, said thanks and closed the limo door.

When she got back into her apartment, she flopped down on her bed.

What in the world was she getting into? Was this really the path to stardom? Or the road to hell?

The silent walls of her lonely room offered her no answers, and she cried herself to sleep.

CHAPTER 4

Jake Granville sat in his office looking at the
production schedule. He almost never sat at the big
rosewood desk by the plate glass window overlooking the
street, but instead would undock his laptop and sit
slumped in the cushy brown leather couch on the adjacent
wall.

He kept the blinds turned almost closed to block the
brilliant late September sun and let his Bose speakers
ooze a low and steady stream of mellow blues and jazz,
giving the office the atmosphere of a Chicago club's back
room on a quiet Monday night.

The production schedule was preposterous.

How they were going to cram three weeks worth of
pre-production and establishing video into four days was
a mystery.

Dave had said the director, Justin Mitchell, was a
miracle worker and the crew extremely dedicated, and
assured him that everything would look great for the
premiere.

Jake didn't want this to look rushed – he had a lot riding on this. He'd received an email from Tom Highgate containing a thinly veiled threat. It said that this idea was hot, but if the execution was lacking and the network didn't see appropriate numbers (a very vague condition) – Granville would be looking for work elsewhere, carrying a bad reputation.

Lately, Highgate was acting more and more like he knew about Jake's indiscretion with his daughter Tawny.

If that was the case, Jake wished Highgate would get off his high horse and just let it go. It was a short-lived thing between two consenting adults. No one else's business, really.

Jake closed his laptop and listened to the song that was playing – a heart-wrenching guitar solo and something about wasting life and losing love, chasing satisfaction and finding death. Real uplifting stuff.

It got him to thinking about his own life. He'd done well for himself professionally, but his twenties and early thirties had been, so far, a wash in the personal department.

Yeah, he was never in need of sex – that came easily enough.

But what about a connection that really mattered? Something longer term than eight or ten hours?

Maybe even something permanent.

His playboy days had fulfilled their purpose – got him through the lonely times while he built his career.

But now he was lonely again, and these flings were not filling the void.

He was maturing, and learning something new about himself.

He hated to admit it, but he needed love.

It was time to grow up – to stop playing.

Used to be that the end of playing sounded like the end of fun – the end of really living.

But he'd spent some time around a few of his married couple associates the past few weeks – Dave Kohler for one – and realized these people still had plenty of fun. More fun than Jake had been having lately, since these couples had more than one day's worth of shared memories to enjoy together.

Some were also bonded by children.

Jake had actually been feeling something inside that he couldn't identify – something he'd never felt before. When he spoke of it to Dave last night, Dave nailed it in two words: baby hungry.

Jake denied it at first – seemed ridiculous. But as he considered it more, he realized it was true.

A son to play with, to teach, to carry on his genetic legacy.

Of course, he realized also that this was all romanticized.

Kids also meant sleepless nights and responsibility.

Eighteen years worth.

And a lifetime of worry.

Not fun *at all*.

A knock came at his door and shook him from his reverie.

A moment later, Dave Kohler stuck his head in. "S'up?"

"Come on in."

Dave stepped in and closed the door, and took a seat on the other end of the couch. "So, I broke the news."

"What news?"

"You know – our star. We ran her though the system pretty quick last night, so I had to help her process the – uh – full extent of what this show is about."

45

"How'd she take it?"

Dave shrugged. "She seemed a little upset. But then she calmed down. Either she's a good actor or she's cool with it. Either way, it's going to be an incredible season, my friend."

"Yeah – about as incredible as this schedule," said Jake, reopening his laptop. "You see this crap? All the pre-prod finished by next Wednesday, and the premiere live on Thursday night?"

"No worries, man. We're recycling a bunch of the set pieces we had produced for the Death Row show that was a no-go. It'll come together. Trust me."

"I hope so," said Jake, thinking of Highgate's email. "I really hope so."

CHAPTER 5

It was time.

Kaylie had to face the music and make the call she'd been dreading.

She sat on the edge of her bed, cell phone in hand, just staring at the address book on the screen, where *Mom & Dad* was highlighted.

Waiting to hit SEND.

She knew she had to do it – it would absolutely suck for her family to find out she was pregnant – and on a reality TV show – from watching the TV.

She at least owed them a call.

It didn't help that the camera crew – albeit a pared-down crew of only two cameras – was right there in her bedroom with her, waiting for her to make her decision.

Bit of a Catch-22, really. Have the family find out by watching TV, or have the family find out *as part of* the show.

Ugh.

She took a swallow of water from the glass on her nightstand, then pressed the button, and raised the phone to her ear, sliding it behind the strands of brown hair falling from her loose ponytail.

One ring.

Two rings.

Three – CLICK.

"*Hello?*"

"Mom?"

"*Kaylie?*"

"Hi, Mom."

"*Kaylie! I was just thinking about you! Are you all right, honey? You sound – tired or something.*"

"Uh, yeah – I'm okay. How are you and Dad? And everyone else?"

"*I'm fine. Dad's doing okay. We've missed hearing from you – worried about you.*"

"Sorry. So, what's new?"

"*You know Dad retired last month? Now he watches a lot of TV.*"

"Oh, no!"

"*Oh, it's not that bad, I guess. I just think he needs to pick up a hobby. Maybe several hobbies. Tell the truth, he's beginning to drive me a little crazy. Ha ha.*"

Mom's laugh was more nervous than jolly.

"And everyone else? I mean, Bruce and Amanda?"

"*Bruce just landed a big web developer job in Portland, so he's moving up there in two weeks. He got engaged at the beginning of the summer to a gal named Cynthia. They're going to try to have a long distance relationship. I think she should move up there, too, but she's really tied to her job at Channel 12. She's a reporter for them.*"

"Oh."

"*And Amanda seems to want to be a lifelong student – she's starting another Masters Program at SOU in the fall. Ancient Micronesian Women's Studies. How's that for a niche? Dad told her good luck finding a job in that field when she gets out of school. I told him I don't think she plans on ever leaving school.*"

"Ha ha," Kaylie offered half-heartedly. She was feeling very meek and unsure if she could break the news.

But she had to.

She simply couldn't make them find out on Thursday night. Dad would fall out of his La-Z-Boy and the family would never forgive her. They'd disown her for sure.

But as much as she didn't want to be disowned, she hated even more the thought of causing them any more pain. She'd already hurt them enough.

She took a deep breath and exhaled.

"Mom, I called because I have some news. Are you sitting down?"

"*Did you get a part? A theater job?*" Mom butted in.

"No. I mean, yes, well, I did get a job. And that's kind of part of the news."

"*There's more? That's wonderful!*"

"Mom, I'm pregnant."

Silence.

More silence.

Excruciating silence.

Kaylie could hear Mom breathing on the other end, so she knew the line had not gone dead, and that Mom had not passed out.

"Mom? Say something."

"*Uh-h-how? How did this happen? Well, no, I mean, I know how it happens, but I mean —*" she sighed heavily.

"Who's the father? Are you in love? When are you going to be getting married?"

"Mom, I don't know."

"You don't know what?"

"I don't know the answer to any of your questions. Well, I know I'm not in love."

"How can you not know who the father is? My goodness, Kaylie! What kind of life have you been living down there?" A pause. *"I'm sorry. I'm sorry. The last thing you need right now is a lecture. That's not what you called for. Besides, I'm sure your father will have plenty of lecturing for you. How 'bout I just take a deep breath and be there for you, instead, huh?"*

Tears streamed down Kaylie's cheeks.

The cameras caught every one of them.

"Oh, Mom!"

Kaylie began to sob.

The cameras rolled on.

"Mom, there's something else I have to tell you," Kaylie said through ragged breaths. "That job I got. Well, it's a reality TV show, and right now, they're filming everything. I mean, the cameras are right here, and they're recording our conversation."

"What? Are you kidding me? Why would you let them intrude on your – on OUR privacy like that?"

"I – I have to! It's in the contract. They record every moment of my life and put it on TV – from now, until – until it's decided."

"Until WHAT'S decided? Oh my gosh! Are you – no, say it isn't so, Kaylie! I saw on TV the other night when Dad was watching AMERICA'S GOT WEIRDOS, I saw a promo for a new show that said they'll be following around a pregnant woman and – and America will be making a 'life or death' decision! Is that – is that you?"

Kaylie sniffled, then sobbed again. "Yeah! It's me!"

She heard the phone drop, and some shuffling around. "*Sorry, honey. Turns out I wasn't sitting down. I am now, though. Ha ha!*" This laugh wasn't nervous – it was near-psychotic.

"Mom?"

"*Honey, you have to get out of this. You can't let a bunch of strangers vote whether or not you keep your baby. It's ridiculous. It's sick and wrong. It's just horrible. That is a most personal issue!*"

"It's supposed to be the highest-rated show ever. They say it's gonna be bigger than the Superbowl."

"*Who cares about ratings! What about right and wrong? What about the life of that little child – MY GRANDCHILD – inside of you? Did you ever stop to think about THAT when you decided to become Little Miss Fame and Fortune?.*" Another pause. "*I'm sorry – I'm SORRY. I don't want to lecture you. But Kaylie! Oh, dear.*"

Kaylie heard her mother begin to weep quietly on the other end of the line.

"Mom? Will you please tell Dad? I don't think I could take it right now. I want to talk to him, but I know he'll yell when he first finds out, and I just can't take that right now. Please?"

Big sigh from Mom. "*Okay. I'll tell him. And I'll tell Bruce and Amanda, too. Can't have them find out from the TV.*"

"Thanks, Mom." Kaylie let out a deep breath she hadn't realized she was holding. "It'll work out. I don't know how, but it will, somehow."

"*Yeah. Well, you know how your father and I feel about this subject. I mean – you know. Abortion.*"

"Yes, I know. I'll go to hell if I kill my baby. Which means America may in fact vote me into hell. How crazy is that?"

"Are you making light of this?"

"No. Just trying to wrap my head around it and finding that it's making me a little loony. I know it's not funny, Mom. Believe me, I know better than anyone. I'm the one in this mess."

"There must be some way out of the contract."

"I suppose I could find a lawyer if I really wanted out. But I'm not so sure I *want* out. That would forfeit nearly a million dollars and I'd never work in Hollywood again."

"A million dollars? They're paying you that much money?"

"Yep. Plus generous living expenses and full medical care for me and the baby."

"Huh. I can see where that would be a good thing, if you were sure that the vote would be in favor of the baby. But you can't be sure. This is gambling with a life!"

"Mom, one of the reasons I got this job is because – is because I am not sure if I want to keep the baby."

"Well, Kaylie, it's not a choice. You made your choice already. I mean, you can decide to give it up for adoption, but I think we taught you better than to think that a life can simply be 'chosen' out of existence! Abortion for convenience is WRONG. Abortion for entertainment is absolutely reprehensible. Kaylie, what has happened to you? Since when did you start dithering on fundamental issues and dabbling with moral relativism?"

Kaylie rolled her eyes. "Mom, you're slipping right back into lecture mode again. Look, I can't help it if I don't know what I want to do. I mean, I have my whole life ahead of me, and -"

"*And so does that little baby.*"

"And I want to have my career. I want to maybe get married one day – who's gonna want a washed up actor with a kid? I know I have lots to think about – but one of the things I have to think about is myself."

A long pause. "*Sorry – I was just biting my tongue. No more lecturing – at least not today. Well, dear, I think I should go talk to your dad. Is this number you called from a number we can reach you at?*"

"Yeah. It's my new cell."

"*Okay. Well, we'll talk soon. I love you.*"

"Love you too, Mom. Bye."

"*Bye.*"

Kaylie ended the call and flopped back on her bed, dropping the cell beside her. She opened and clenched her right hand repeatedly, working out the stiffness that had developed from clenching the phone so hard.

And then she broke down again, burying her head in her pillow and trying in futility to cry in privacy.

CHAPTER 6

"Everything is ready," said Dave, walking into Jake's office and dropping into the soft couch. "We're on in thirty minutes."

"So, the band worked out?"

"Yeah – for this week anyway. Strangely, it's been a little tricky to get a wide variety of big names to commit to each week. They obviously have no idea how huge this is going to be."

"Or maybe they're just too image-conscious. I mean, I know this whole thing was my idea," said Jake, standing to decant some ice water into a tumbler, "but you gotta admit, it may be a little too hot to touch for folks who don't want to get smeared with the old 'exploitation' paint brush."

"Eh. Everyone can set aside those little quibbles when the dollar signs get big enough. By week four, we'll have everyone from Coldplay to Shakira knocking down our door for a spot on the show. Regardless, the musical number is just a small part of the candy. The meat is going to be that girl next door agonizing over her day to day life, with America agonizing right along with her."

"True. The gut-wrenching factor will completely outweigh the ick factor on this one. People love pain." Jake drank down his water and set it on the glass-topped end table with a click. "They also love power – the ability to choose the destiny of others. Throw in politics and religion, and nobody will care about the musical entertainment or how many commercials we cram into the show."

"You got that right."

"So, you wanna watch on the big screen or go sit in the booth?"

"You know it's a tradition to sit in the booth opening night, man."

"Then we better hit it."

The two left the office and wound their way down the corridors, then out to the parking area, where they got in Jake's Cobra, which took off out of the lot with a low growl.

Minutes later they were walking through the back halls of the studio and entering the dimly-lit production booth.

The smell of the booth – a kind of warm plastic smell that came from having too many monitors crammed into a small space and surrounded by soundproofed walls – reminded Jake of his early days in TV – as a sound board technician.

He had worked his way up from studio floor camera operator, then into the booth, then up to technical director and director before moving to editorial.

It all seemed like so long ago – but it was only about fifteen years.

Fifteen years – now *that* made him feel even older than his thirty-five years. But he'd gotten an early start on his TV career, working at KTLA through most of his college years.

These thoughts inevitably led Jake back to his conundrum: what's the use of a successful career if you have no one to share the success with? Rich and alone is poor indeed.

"Hey, snap out of it man," said Dave, waving his hand in front of Jake's face. "Grab a seat. We're on in one minute."

Jake sat in a cushioned swivel stool at the back of the tiny booth. From here he could see the backs of the sound man on the left, the technical director next to him, then the director, Shane McIntyre; and to the right of McIntyre sat the chyron operator, a script supervisor, and a digital specialist. Sitting next to McIntyre but slightly behind him was the line producer.

Immediately in front of this casually-dressed, headset-wearing crew was a wide board like a sloping dinner table covered in a bank of dials, sliders, buttons, switches and lights, with built-in computer interfaces.

In front of that sat the wall of monitors and the speakers.

Jake counted twenty-six monitors of varying sizes, the two largest of which sat side by side in the middle of the group: the preview monitor on the left and the live ON AIR monitor on the right. Whatever appeared on air first appeared on the preview monitor, until the director said "take" and the image switched to the live screen.

For now, the preview monitor was switching between cameras as they finalized their positions and shots; the air monitor showed the commercial that was airing as the lead-in to the show.

"And in ten," said the director, relaying the time count from the Master Control room. As the Master Control operator counted down the final five seconds, McIntyre started speaking his commands into his headset. "Standby to roll open, roll open. Take open."

The open was a pre-produced graphic introduction to the show, complete with dramatic music.

"Standby camera one, and dissolve to camera one."

The intro blended into a gliding boom shot that flew over the heads of a large studio audience and eventually came to rest on a medium close up of the show's host, a dashing young man named Troy Tanner.

Troy was about thirty, looked about twenty-three, and had been a successful radio deejay for nearly twelve years. His good looks had got him featured on the cover of GQ and a handful of teen girl magazines over the past couple of years. And he did look great in that dark suit with his spiky blond hair.

"Welcome to *Canceled*, ladies and gentlemen," he said with a huge, flashy grin. "This is the one you have all been waiting for."

What a nice bunch of B.S. Nobody even knew about this show's existence until a couple of weeks ago.

"Tonight, we'll meet a woman you are all going to get to know – intimately." His smile disappeared. "And you'll begin an odyssey with her that will redefine television."

Very nice.

Back in the booth, McIntyre said, "Standby camera six."

Camera six was the Green Room camera. In the preview monitor, a very nervous looking young woman appeared, sitting on a bright green couch, dressed in a conservative dress, with her long brown hair resting on her shoulders. She looked beautiful.

"And, take camera six."

Troy continued. "This is Kaylie Adams. Twenty-five years old. Single. And pregnant. Tonight, we'll take a look back over the last week of Kaylie's life – from the moment she discovered she was pregnant, to this very night. And then we'll meet her, live. It all starts – after the break."

"And standby Master Control, bring up music, take camera one, zoom out, and fade."

"Whatcha think?" asked Dave, grinning.

"It's a great start," said Jake. "Weird. That Kaylie girl. She seems *really* familiar."

"Well, didn't you check out any of the pre-prod, or review her file?"

"Actually, no. I didn't."

"Oh. Well, it's great that she seems familiar. That means America will relate to her better – she'll seem like everyone's friend, everyone's little sister, everyone's daughter, everyone's girlfriend."

Everyone's one-night stand?

Jake looked at the preview monitor, where Kaylie was staring right into the camera.

No – it couldn't be.

"Hmm. Weird. I'd like to meet her after the show."

"You bet," said Dave.

McIntyre spoke into his headset, "And we're back in five, standby camera one, standby music, and – bring up music, dissolve to one. Cue Troy."

"Welcome back to *Canceled*, everyone. Minutes ago you got your first look at Kaylie Adams, the star of our show. Kaylie Adams, who will, over the course of this season, grow in your hearts as you, America, become her most trusted advisors. Let's take a look at the last seven days in Kaylie's life."

"Standby HD-one, roll, and take," said McIntyre.

The image on the preview screen moved to the live screen – a shot of Kaylie Adams walking down a city street wearing blue jeans, low-heeled brown leather shoes, and a pink blouse. She carried a purse and a small shopping bag.

A quick shot of her sliding her key into the lock on the door – with great natural sound — then a cut to her coming in – shot from the inside.

Kaylie places her purse on the table and sits down, staring at the bag. It dares her to touch it – to open it. To remove its contents.

She takes a deep breath, squirms a little.

Then she grabs the bag roughly and storms down the hall to the bathroom.

The camera, of course, follows her in. Every private moment is now the most public of all.

A few close ups of her taking out the home pregnancy test. Cut to her face, extreme close up.

Some clever editing and digital magic.

The stick has two lines.

Kaylie's reaction – the real one from the day of the audition – fills the screen.

Tears fall.

The music swells.

She drops to her knees.

"And standby camera six, dissolve to six."

Jake looked on as Troy Tanner leaned in to Kaylie, sitting on the same couch, about a foot away from her. Kaylie sat with perfect posture, her slender body turned toward the host. "Kaylie, how are you feeling right now?"

She looked like a deer in the headlights for a moment, then she seemed to compose herself – fall back on her actor training – and said, "I'm excited to be here, Troy." A tiny smile flitted across her red lips. "I mean, it's obviously not the most ideal of circumstances that has led to this moment, but, I think this is going to be a real groundbreaking show."

"Groundbreaking" was one of the key words. Dave had supplied her with a list of terms that she was to try to work into her dialogue, in an effort to help sell the show, sensationalize this premiere as much as possible.

"It most certainly will be," said Troy. "Tonight is the beginning of a fantastic journey for you and for America. Well, the beginning of the journey was actually a few weeks ago, wasn't it, Kaylie? Why don't you tell us about that?"

Troy had likewise been given a list – a list of controversial "surprise" questions designed to throw Kaylie and get unrehearsed reactions.

"Uh, well," she started, choking back a nervous laugh, and doing a pretty good job of maintaining her actor composure, "that's the thing, Troy. You know what they say about kiss-and-tell."

"Based on results, I'd say there was more than kissing going on."

Audience laugher.

"Well, my mom did teach me about the birds and the bees — but I can't seem to figure out — which bee stung me."

That one caught Troy off guard, and the audience loved it, breaking into applause and whoops.

"Well, anyway," he said, "How do you feel about leaving the safety of the Green Room and coming out and meeting everyone?"

"Everyone?"

"Yeah, all at once – we don't have all night."

Kaylie nodded, Troy stood and offered her his arm, and she took it. The camera followed the two out of the Green Room, down a dark backstage corridor, through another doorway, through a second door, and out onto the stage.

The crowd let out a roar of appreciation – egged on by the stage direction for applause.

Kaylie's knees visibly buckled very slightly, but she caught her balance by relying on Troy's strong arm, which she clutched a little tighter as they crossed the stage to the center and took their places on two stools.

As the applause died down, Troy said, "Thank you. Kaylie, over the past week, we've gotten to know you just a little, and we want to share some of that with America. We've put together a little vignette – some discussions we've had about your background, along with key moments from the past week. And we'll take a look – right after this break."

"Cue music, camera one pull out – and fade."

Jake stared at the preview screen, in which the camera was zooming in on Kaylie to get a focus.

"This is gonna drive me freaking crazy," he said.

"What? Oh, I know – always with the commercial breaks. Our sales boys sold twenty-three minutes of this hour to some very big players."

"Well, that's exactly what we want – that's why we do this. But I'm talking about Kaylie. I just *know* I know her from somewhere."

"Like I said, we'll have you meet her after the show, and you can ask her yourself."

Jake stood and stretched his legs, strolled around the cramped booth. It was really bothering him that he couldn't place her. And something about that uncertainty gave him a most unpleasant sensation in the pit of his stomach. Jake liked to be in control, and this question was dancing along the edge of his grasp in a way that seemed to taunt him.

Who is Kaylie Adams?

"Back in five."

On screen, the camera zoomed across the audience and settled on the two seated center stage.

"Welcome back, everybody. Just a reminder – tonight's show will include no voting. Don't worry — we'll tell you all about how it will work – but voting won't begin until week four. For now, we're just getting to know each other – take a look at this."

He turned to the large screen at the back of the stage, and the lights dimmed. An image appeared on the screen, and McIntyre had the technical director dissolve to the source video full screen.

It showed Kaylie sitting in her apartment, browsing through a photo album. Family pictures. A voice-over of her speaking about her initial move to Los Angeles in search of a dream, followed by some interview footage with her and some highlights from her week. Standard montage stuff.

Then there was the phone call to Mom.

It played well.

Finally, the segment ended and they went to break again.

A final segment introduced some of the other key players who would be featured prominently during the season: Dr. Ian, Molly the Midwife, the OB/GYN Dr. Cho, and the show's counselor Dr. Len Hamlin.

Some fluff that teased upcoming material, another long commercial break, followed by a brief explanation of the voting system, a cliffhanger style promo for the next week's episode, and the show was over.

The booth erupted in a small cheer – they'd run a flawless episode – no technical blunders – and could count Week One as complete.

"Nice job everyone," Dave called out. Then to Jake, "Ready to meet our star?"

Jake watched as the monitors blinked out one by one, and the lights came up in the booth as the crew started their post-production meeting. "Sure. Let's do it."

CHAPTER 7

Kaylie sat in the dressing room of the studio, a large mirror before her, surrounded by bright bulbs. She did her best to avoid looking directly at the sole video camera being held by a young female photographer standing in the corner of the room.

She looked into the reflection of her own face, examining her features. She actually looked pretty hot.

At least for now.

Soon she'd start packing on the pounds.

Ironic that she was now sitting in the chair she'd dreamed of – on her way to stardom – yet totally miserable and scared.

This was not the way she had planned on hitting the big time.

She started to take off her earrings when a knock came at the door.

"Come in," she called out.

The door opened to reveal Dave Kohler in his gray suit, no tie, and a genuine smile on his face. Behind him was another man.

Was that who she thought it was?

That one guy?

"Kaylie – fantastic job tonight!" said Dave, walking toward her and patting her gently on the shoulder. "You were stunning – amazing! And that sharp wit – you really kept Troy on his toes! Sensational! Oh, by the way, I'd like you to meet Jake Granville. He's our executive producer and one of the VPs here at FBC."

Kaylie's jaw dropped and she scrutinized the handsome man standing before her. He had a quizzical look on his face – as if he was wondering the same thing as her. On auto-pilot, she stuck out her hand to shake his.

"Pleased to meet you," she said robotically.

"And you," he replied. "Um, are you – do I know you?" he asked, frowning a little and staring at her intensely.

"I'm pretty sure we've met," she said. Then it hit her and her hands flew up to her mouth and covered the lower half of her face as she gasped. "It's you! You're him! We – we uh. Woah."

"A couple of months ago? We danced at a club?"

She glanced away. "We did more than dance."

Dave got a look of dawning understanding and said, "Well, that puts a new spin on sleeping your way to the top."

"It's not like that!" Kaylie and Jake said in unison.

"I had no idea she was the one," said Jake.

"And I had no idea this was his show," Kaylie protested.

Dave held up his hands. "Okay, hold on, hold on. Let's not get carried away. It's just a crazy coincidence."

He chuckled. "No worries. However, we'll want to avoid the appearance of impropriety or favoritism." He turned to the camera girl. "Hey, let's kill that, okay. And the last five minutes never happened, capiche?"

"But, my orders are to shoot all the time, not miss anything."

"And I'm the producer – who do you think handed down those orders, honey? Now shut it off."

The girl clicked off the camera and stood there waiting, looking like an artist who'd had her canvas taken away mid-brush stroke.

"Okay, now take five. We'll call you back when we're ready to resume shooting," said Dave.

She left, and the room was silent for a few moments after she shut the door.

Then Jake spoke. "Well, this is a little awkward, eh?" He smiled at Kaylie and Dave.

"Right. Awkward," said Dave. "Listen, if you two are cool with it, I'd just as soon move forward and forget about this."

"Works for me," said Jake. "You okay with that, Kaylie?"

Kaylie looked down for a moment and took a deep breath, then exhaled. "Sure. Whatever. I can deal with it."

For nearly a million bucks, Kaylie figured there was a *lot* she could deal with.

"Good then," said Dave.

"It was nice to er, meet you – again," said Jake as the two men left the dressing room.

"Yeah," said Kaylie. A moment later the camera operator was back in the room with her, and she picked up where she left off, taking off her earrings and getting changed so she could go home.

CHAPTER 8

George Adams lifted the remote from the arm of his dark brown leather La-Z-Boy and pressed the power button, switching off the seventy-inch flat screen hanging on the opposite wall.

For a full minute, he stared at the now-black screen, saying nothing. Then he turned to his left, where his wife sat on a well-worn loveseat, dabbing at the corners of her eyes with a crumpled tissue.

"What are we gonna do, Ellen? What are we going to do about this – this insanity?"

Kaylie's parents had watched the season premiere of *Canceled* from start to finish without saying a word until this moment.

Ellen sighed. "I don't think there's much we *can* do. Kaylie is an adult. I think all we can do is support her – show her love."

George frowned and pondered for a moment, then realized he wasn't powerless in this situation. He realized the show itself had a built-in way to affect the outcome. "I think we need to do more than that. I think we need to start getting organized. She may have her head up her butt and not know what she wants to do regarding that baby, but you and I both know what's right. It's up to us to make sure the viewers don't kill our grandchild! We need to start contacting everyone we know – begin networking – and get people voting to save the child!"

Ellen brightened a little. "You know, you're right. We don't have to take this lying down. Maybe we can get Bruce to build a website to promote our cause. And Amanda can talk to all her friends – oh, maybe we can make a difference, George!"

The phone rang.

"Maybe it's Kaylie," said Ellen rising to grab the cordless off the oak coffee table. "Here, you answer it." She held the handset out to George.

"I – I don't know, I'm not ready yet. I'll just end up yelling at her," he said, shrinking away into his plush chair.

"Come on."

Unable to bear the continued ringing, he grabbed the phone from Ellen's hand and answered it. "Hello?"

"Dad, it's me, Bruce. Did you see that crap? I can't friggin' believe it! What is wrong with that girl?"

George glanced toward Ellen, "It's Bruce." Then into the phone, "Yes, Bruce. We watched. It is pretty unbelievable. But it's real, and your mother and I were just talking about how important it is that we do whatever we can – anything possible – to make sure this situation doesn't end with our unborn grandchild – your niece or nephew – getting killed on national television. We need to do what it takes to get out the vote to save that baby."

"Right. Uh, what do you have in mind?"

"Well, word of mouth, of course. Email. Phone calls to everyone we know. Facebook. And we were wondering, can you build a website for the cause? Some way to get more attention?"

"Well, Dad, I can certainly build a website, but I think that if this show ends up being as big as it looks – like bigger than American Idol – anything we do will be like peeing in the Mississippi River, if you catch my drift."

"Huh. Yeah, well, we should still do something. We have to. It's like voting in the elections – sometimes it feels like your one vote won't count, but all the votes matter, because together, they make all the difference."

"I guess there's a reason you served two terms in the state legislature, Dad. You're passionate, and you still believe individuals can make a difference. I'm a little more jaded, personally, but I'll do whatever I can to support you and the family."

"Good. We'll talk more tomorrow. There's no time to waste. Soon they'll start the voting, and we'll need to beat the opposition every single week. Talk to you later, son. Love you."

"Love you, too, Dad. Bye."

George hung up and looked at Ellen. "This is going to be one hell of a fight, Ellen."

"Yeah. The next thirty weeks are going to make my pregnancy with Kaylie look like a walk in the park."

Ellen had nearly lost Kaylie at six months, and George had nearly lost Ellen the day Kaylie was born. It was a very rough pregnancy, and was the reason Kaylie was their last child.

"Just like then, we'll make it through," said George. "I know we will."

The phone rang again. It was still in George's hand.

"Hello?"

"Dad! Oh my gosh, did you see Kaylie?"

"Yes, Amanda, we saw her."

"She looked terrific! I mean, I know the whole concept of the show is totally screwed up and all, but I thought she looked fantastic, and did a great job!"

George didn't say anything at first. It was true; despite the awful situation, his little girl had held up remarkably well on national television, holding her own with the host, and looking very pretty. He had been too angry and concerned to take notice at the time. "Yeah, she did well. Listen, can you swing by on Saturday morning? We need to talk."

"Uh, sure. I can even come tomorrow night after my last class. That is, if you don't mind me staying in my old room."

"Of course. You know all you kids' rooms are always available. I haven't turned them into a playground, yet. But when one of you three gets married, I'm putting in a pool table!"

"Aw, thanks, Dad. Okay, see you tomorrow night. Say hi to Mom. Bye."

"Bye, honey."

"She's right, you know," said Ellen, who had inferred the other end of the conversation. "Kaylie did do a smashing job. Despite it all."

George took a deep breath and nodded. "Yeah, she did." He placed the phone on the arm of his recliner and stared at it. "Somehow I think our phone is going to ring a lot more times tonight – and from now on."

CHAPTER 9

Kaylie sat outside the office of her new OB/GYN, Dr. Jennifer Cho, scrolling through Facebook.

Oddly enough, she kept seeing her own face popping up in article link after article link.

The headline for a link to *Variety* read, *Kaylie Adams – America's New Sweetheart and Star of CANCELED*. At least they were withholding judgment. For now.

The waiting room was much like any other in L.A. – rows of red fabric covered chairs, quiet murmurs, a gurgling aquarium filled with tropical fish.

And, of course, the two camera people sitting nearby, trained on every move Kaylie made.

This would be her first appointment with Dr. Cho – a basic getting-to-know-you session plus a little of the standard exam stuff.

Regardless of how Dave had played it up as a casual affair, Kaylie felt inexplicably nervous. As if the doctor was going to tell her something she didn't already know.

Since she knew she was pregnant, it was hard to imagine what that might be.

No, it must have just been the smell of the office and the ever-present cameras that were putting Kaylie on edge today.

"Dr. Cho will see you now," said a smiling blonde nurse younger than Kaylie who seemed to appear out of nowhere.

Kaylie stood, pocketed her phone, and followed the petite nurse in pastel blue scrubs down the hall and to the left.

The two camera people followed.

Strangely, no one but Kaylie really seemed to care. It was as if everyone in the place was a paid extra, instructed to act naturally and ignore the film crew.

Maybe they were.

For all Kaylie knew, half the stuff she encountered in her life from now on may be part of some elaborate entertainment construct. She was no stranger to the term "the magic of television" and the nuanced deception it entailed. Having seen the amazing final version of her pregnancy test moment, she knew editors and computer geeks basically defined "reality" and ruled the world through their technology and creative means of obfuscating.

At least they ruled her world.

For the next several months.

A quick weigh-in on the standard medical scale with the balancing arm and sliding weight revealed that she had already put on five pounds from her typical weight.

Must be all the extra eating lately.

Blood pressure was a little high – but that was to be expected with a camera crew watching your every move.

Kaylie eyeballed the nurse. So young. It irked her a little that someone younger than her was already grounded in a successful career. She tried not to resent the nurse – she was just a person doing her job – but part of her felt she'd wasted the last five years, when she could've been putting her life together like this smart young girl, instead of following her far-fetched dreams.

Of course, those dreams were at last starting to come true – in a nightmarish sort of way.

Another five minute wait in the consultation room, and in walked Dr. Cho.

Jennifer Cho was a slim, tall Asian woman with a wide face and long black braid. She wore a white lab coat over a pair of designer jeans. She smiled warmly at Kaylie and extended her hand. "Hello, Kaylie. It is a pleasure to meet you. How are we feeling today?"

"Hi. Uh, I'm feeling fine, I guess. Other than the nausea, the crazy appetite, the headache, and the fatigue – I find myself wanting to go to sleep at all kinds of weird times of the day. So, yeah, doing pretty good."

Dr. Cho smiled. "All par for the course, I'm afraid. But cheer up. You've got – at most – another 30 weeks of this. And it will get easier. Well, it'll also get a lot harder. I mean, it'll change, but you'll get used to it. I'm making a lot of sense, aren't I?" She chuckled and made a facial expression that only Kaylie could see. Her eyes darted to one of the cameras and she did a mini-shrug that told Kaylie the doctor was a little nervous about being captured on video.

Kaylie gave her a tiny, brief smile. A good connection. It felt nice to have a little secret that the cameras were not privy to. Like she was able to hold onto a tiny piece of her privacy – a fragment of her life that no one else could touch. She decided she liked Jennifer Cho.

"Just so you know what you're in for today," said the doctor, "I'm going to start with some questions for you, then do a little poking and prodding – sorry – and then give you some information. Okay?"

"Sure. Thanks."

Dr. Cho sat down at a little well-lit desk and grabbed a tablet, tapping the screen. "Okay, family history. How's your parent's health?"

"Good. They're both healthy. Dad has a little bit of high blood pressure, but otherwise they're doing well."

"No known history of heart disease, cancer, anything like that?"

"Nope."

"Good. And the father's health history?"

"I guess you didn't watch the show. Um, I don't know who the father is."

"Ah, I see," said Dr. Cho. "Well, that is important information. Do you have a short list?"

"I could narrow it down to three or four guys. Why?"

"We're going to want to run paternity tests."

"No we're not."

"Well, you may not *want* to, Kaylie, but it's in the best interests of the baby to have all the information we can get about his or her genetic makeup."

"Well, okay, I guess. But, I really don't know these guys personally. They won't have to be part of the baby's life, will they?"

"I'm a doctor, not a lawyer. I'll deal with the biology – someone else will have to handle the sociology, okay?" Dr. Cho's tone was not harsh – she kept it light, but clearly didn't want to go into the legal stuff.

"Okay."

"Now, we'll also need to take a urine sample and a blood sample today – we can take care of that when we're done here. So that means the pelvic exam is next. You'll need to strip down below the waist and get in the stirrups."

That was the male camera operator's cue. He left the room and the female photog stayed on as Kaylie slipped her shorts and panties off and got up on the exam table.

Dr. Cho slipped on a pair of latex gloves and dipped into some KY jelly. She spoke as she began the exam. "This is just to check and see if everything is normal – make sure you don't have any STDs and that your uterus is in the right position, size and shape. Gotta make sure that little apartment will make a good home for the next few months!"

The humor of Dr. Cho's well-meaning banter did little to assuage Kaylie's discomfort.

But a moment later, the doctor stood up from her stool and snapped off the gloves. "All done!"

"And?"

"Everything looks perfect." She turned and picked up the tablet from her desk and typed in a few notes while Kaylie slipped back into her clothes. "Okay, lastly, some education. Don't worry about trying to remember everything I say – we'll be sure to send you home with plenty of literature."

Dr. Cho then recited a list of conditions that could befall Kaylie through the pregnancy, from sore hips to gestational diabetes, told her the kinds of foods she should eat and what to stay away from, and talked about activities to do and to avoid.

"Any questions?"

"Nope."

"And now for the fun part: would you like to know your due date?"

Kaylie gulped. She hadn't even thought about it. "Yes!"

"Okay!" Dr. Cho pulled up a chart on the tablet and turned it to show Kaylie. "Well, based on my calculations, using the date of the first day of your last period – since you're unsure of the date of conception – we're looking at . . . May 21st."

Perfect for the May rating sweeps.

"May 21st."

"Yep. A Gemini."

Oh gosh, no, not twins.

"Huh."

Dr. Cho looked at Kaylie's ashen expression and said, smiling, "Or, if you prefer Chinese astrology, your child will be born in the year of the rat."

Kaylie's mind was still stuck on the overwhelming thought of having *two* babies, when she could barely wrap her head around the idea of having *one*. Then she suddenly switched gears and said, without thinking, "If it's born at all."

"Oh," said Dr. Cho. "Yes. Well, right. I almost forgot – that will all be up to the viewers, won't it?"

"How do you feel about that?" asked Kaylie, genuinely curious.

"Between you, me, the camera people, and all of freaking America," said the doctor, turning to look directly into the camera (in violation of the network's instructions), "I think it sucks. It's contrary to all that is decent in this world." She turned back to Kaylie. "But you needed a doctor – someone who would care for you and treat you with respect, and give you and the baby the best care possible. To be honest, I signed on for this as my way of protesting this abomination called *Canceled*.

By treating you and your baby with honor, maybe I can help offset the hideous nature of this show."

Kaylie liked her even more now, and she found a tear welling up in her left eye.

"Tell me, Kaylie, what possessed *you* to sign up for this?"

"I needed a job."

"McDonald's wasn't hiring?"

"I wanted a job in show business. And when I signed up, I didn't really understand fully what I was getting myself into. But I'm glad I'm here, and that you're my doctor. Thank you, Dr. Cho."

"Call me Jenn."

"Thanks, Jenn."

CHAPTER 10

"Paternity tests!"

Jake Granville was pacing around his office like a mad scientist on the verge of a mental breakthrough.

Or, in this case, break*down*.

"Isn't it great?" said Dave, grinning from ear to ear and sitting back on the couch sipping a diet cola from the can. "It'll be awesome. It'll be like those old daytime talk shows, only with much broader viewership. And classier and a lot more exciting."

"For who, exactly?"

"Whaddaya mean?"

"I mean, I'm not sure I'm comfortable with this."

It suddenly occurred to Dave that this could be a sticky situation. "Crap. I forgot you're a potential candidate, here. Yeah, that's not going to look so good, Jake-man. Huh." He exhaled and puffed out his cheeks while bugging out his eyes. "I'm not sure how we're going to angle this. I mean, it just seems a little tawdry to have a station executive involved in this. Kinda blurs the ol' lines, if ya know what I mean."

Jake finally took a seat and let out a sigh, relaxing every muscle in his tense body and sinking into a slouch, like a man who knows he's been beaten. "It's reality TV, Dave. Emphasis on the *reality*. We can't deny the reality. If I'm on the list, I'm on the list. We just need to be honest – keep everything out in the open – make it clear that Kaylie was chosen by our casting director without my knowledge. If we keep it transparent and tell the truth, they'll believe us. Heck, they believe us when we lie – why not when we tell the truth?"

"Because truth is stranger than fiction – it's usually harder to believe than the crap we make up. But yes, I agree. That's how we should proceed."

"Has the research department tracked down the other guys?"

"Yeah, we have a lineup. Paternity can be determined as early as week eight of a pregnancy using an enhanced CVS test – cutting edge stuff. That means we can put it on the air next week! I guess you'd better check the promo shooting schedule. You may be needed for a ten-second tease."

"Great. Just great."

"Hey Jake." Dave's face went dead serious. "You ever stop to think – what if you *are* the father?"

"No, of course not. I'm uh, responsible – when I'm being irresponsible. There's no way it's mine. Guaranteed."

"Famous last words."

CHAPTER 11

George Adams sat in his place at the head of the oval, light oak table. To his right, Ellen; to his left, Bruce and Amanda. An empty chair at the other end represented the wayward baby of the family, Kaylie.

The Adams kitchen looked much the way it did in the late nineties when they bought the house, with country-style colors and patterns on the curtains, oak furniture, and oak cabinets. The only updates were the tile floors and the stainless steel appliances.

Tall oaks outside the window, their leaves fluttering in a light autumn breeze, cast dancing shadows on the dining table and floor.

"Well, I think I should go down there and be with her," said Ellen. "Help her out – give her some support. Heaven knows she could use it right now. The only company she has is a camera crew following her around twenty-four seven."

"I'm fine with that," said George. "But for how long?"

"As long as she'll have me."

"Whoa, wait a minute, I don't know if I want to be a bachelor for seven months!"

"Why don't you both go?" said Amanda. "I'll stay here and commute to school – look after the house for you for as long as you need."

"That could work," said Bruce. "I think you'll be able to do a lot more good there than you can from here."

George slowly nodded. "All right, then. We'll go. I have a former business associate who owns some rental properties near Hollywood. We could probably get a good deal on a place to stay for a while. I'll make some calls."

George, a decisive man of action, stood immediately, pulled out his phone, and strode to the living room for some privacy.

"He's taking this whole thing *really* hard," said Ellen quietly. She stood to turn the rod on the vertical blinds in front of the sliding glass doors that led to the back yard, blocking out some of the late morning sun.

"Which part is the worst for him?" asked Amanda, getting up to refill her glass of water at the dispenser in the refrigerator door.

Ellen sighed and sat back down. "I think he's really disappointed to learn that his baby girl has been promiscuous. I'm not happy about it either, by the way. But it's really hurting Dad."

Amanda looked down and said nothing.

Bruce spoke up. "What did he think, she'd be a virgin till she eventually got married, some time in her damn forties?"

"Bruce!" scolded Ellen. "As a matter of fact, that was exactly our expectation. That's the way we were brought up, and that's how we brought you kids up."

Amanda choked a little on her water and coughed for a few seconds. Bruce looked over at her and smirked.

"Anyway, the other hard part," said Ellen, "is this whole abortion thing. You know how we feel about that, in general. And then when it's your own family, well."

Amanda returned to sit at the table. "I, uh, agree. It's a terrible thing when it's so close to home."

Bruce nodded vigorously. "Oh yeah, one hundred percent. This is just wrong. I can't even believe they're doing this show – I wonder who thought up this disgusting idea – to put the life of an innocent in the hands of a bunch of TV viewers. It's crazy."

"I don't know or care what Hollywood idiot came up with this. What's done is done. I just know we need to band together as a family and take this on," said Ellen. "We need to organize. We need to draw on all of our resources to save this child." Her voice broke on the last word and she put her hand to her mouth and tried to stifle her tears.

"Oh, Mom, it'll work out," said Amanda. "We'll make it work out. Don't worry."

George walked back in. "Good news. We have a place to stay in L.A."

Ellen brightened instantly. "Wonderful! Is it close to the TV studios and everything?"

"Actually, yes," said George. "It's right in Brentwood, which is pretty near to Burbank. A twelve-hundred square foot apartment in a very nice complex called Galaxy Apartments."

"Sounds expensive."

"It is. But my friend Conrad Bell is giving us a deal. He understands the nature of the situation, and is letting us have an 'emergency for friends' rate. Basically, we'll just cover the utilities."

"Oh, George, that's great."

"I also put a bug in his ear to start spreading the word. He's pretty well-connected. I'm sure not everyone in his address book is pro-life, but they are loyal people and will help out a friend – or a friend of a friend – in need."

"And that's what we all need to do," said Bruce. "I'll get to work on the website right away, and I'll post ideas there for ways to get the word out."

"I'm not sure if there's much I can do to help," said Amanda. "My roommate Clara is the editor of the newspaper. But a pro-life editorial won't go over too well on a college campus."

"Well, you have to try something," said Bruce. "Surely there are *some* conservatives at SOU."

Amanda shrugged. "Okay, I'll see what I can do."

"We all have things we can do to make a difference here," said Ellen.

"All right then," said George. "Next on the agenda – packing."

CHAPTER 12

Kaylie woke up in the middle of the night with a start.

She sat up in bed, the threads of a strange dream still floating through her mind.

She'd been in a rocking chair, holding a baby. She'd looked down at her hands, and they were old and wrinkled. Then she saw the baby's face, and he looked like Justin the daytime director.

It was creepy.

She looked across the small bedroom and the graveyard crew (two young camera girls) sat on the floor playing cards, their cameras mounted on tripods pointed at the bed.

Only a week and a half in, and Kaylie was already sick of this.

She had to keep reminding herself that she was getting paid *very* well to endure this inconvenient intrusion into her life. She did the math and determined she was earning about a hundred and ninety bucks an hour, twenty-four seven.

Tough to beat that.

And that didn't even include the medical care.

She was going to walk away from this a rich woman.

But would she walk away a mother?

The uncertainty gave her a knot in her stomach and brought back the headache that had faded with her sleep.

She pulled back the covers and stood.

The camera people sprung into action, dropping their playing cards and grabbing their gear so they could follow her every move.

Most everything Kaylie did was just boring, everyday stuff; but Justin, who had a lot of experience directing reality shows, explained that you have to shoot everything so you don't miss anything. You never know when something interesting is going to happen, or what kind of footage (even the boring stuff) the editors might want to use as they piece together the next week's episode.

So the cameras followed her to the bathroom, where she got some Tylenol for her head, and peed once again. This twice a night peeing was becoming an unwelcome habit. She imagined it would get much worse as the baby grew and started putting more pressure on her bladder.

Back to bed.

Tomorrow was supposed to be a big day – she was going to meet Molly the Midwife.

Next morning, Kaylie got up, had some breakfast, and straightened up the place a little. Molly the Midwife would be making a house call. Kaylie had read online that home visits were this midwife's trademark, as she was all about comfortable, natural environments and holistic healing.

At nine-thirty (nearly halfway through Justin Mitchell's workday), the doorbell rang. The crew readied their shots and the action began as Kaylie opened the door.

Molly Braithwaite was about forty-five, rotund, with a bun of red hair and a big smile for Kaylie. "Hello, Kaylie! I'm Molly. A pleasure to meet you. How's the mommy-to-be this morning?"

Kaylie shook her hand and stepped aside to let her in. "I'm doing well, thank you. Please come in." The two sat down at opposite ends of the couch. "Can I get you anything?"

"No, I'm fine." She dug into her large bag. "Do you mind if I light up?"

"Uh, what? Um, this is a non-smoking apartment building."

Molly chuckled. "Oh, no, sweetheart." She pulled out her incense and little wooden holder. "I'm talking about a little aromatherapy. To set a nice serene mood."

"Oh! Sure, go ahead."

Molly slid a long, thin, purple colored incense stick out of a little plastic sleeve and placed it in the holder. She lit it with a shiny chrome Zippo, blew it out, and the end glowed red for a moment before it began to emit a thin stream of smoke that soon met Kaylie's nose.

"Mmm, what is that?"

"It's called Mystic Moments. Mostly lavender, with some sandalwood and a gentle touch of cinnamon. It should make you feel dreamy and relaxed. And the baby will love it."

She reached over and gently patted Kaylie on the belly. Kaylie recoiled ever so slightly.

"Oh, I'm sorry, dear. I didn't mean to invade your bubble!"

"Oh, you're fine. It's just – I'm not used to that yet. I mean, I know people like to touch pregnant women's bellies, but, I'm not even showing yet. It just took me aback a little."

"You may not have much of a bulge, but I can sense that little person in there."

"Huh. No sense yet as to the sex?"

Molly pursed her lips and shook her head. "Nope. Not yet. Just a being. A presence. But that's it so far. Medical technology can tell you by about week twelve, but I can tell usually about week eleven."

She said "medical technology" as if it smelled bad.

"I see. So, do you, like, deliver babies and stuff?"

"Oh yes, of course! Ha ha, that's why I'm here."

"But I already have an OB/GYN."

"Right. But I'm here if you so choose. It's up to you. You can go with the cold, harsh, production line of the industrial medical establishment's baby machine; or, if you like what you experience with me and our visits together, you can choose to have your child the way the Universe intended – one hundred percent naturally, in the comfort and warmth of your own home, surrounded by love and joy. It's up to you."

"Natural? You mean, like, with no drugs to kill the pain?"

"Of course, sweetie. But it's not like we don't have methods to deal with the pain. Stuff that's been around for a few centuries longer than the vaunted American Medical Association."

"Oh. Okay, well, I guess we'll have to cross that bridge when we come to it. If we come to it. I mean, they did tell you the premise of this show, didn't they?"

Molly's expression fell. She looked a little scary when she wasn't beaming. "Yes. Personally, I think it's horrible. I believe in the value of every life. The idea of mob rule determining whether this little one lives or dies is abhorrent to the Universe. But I'm here for you, no matter what happens."

"Thanks. I'm not sure how I feel about it, myself. Part of me feels, I dunno, motherly – but sometimes I think that's just the hormones playing tricks on me. Part of me thinks I've just got a clump of cells growing inside of me — the result of a stupid choice – and really just wants to get on with life, kinda hoping the viewers will vote to end the pregnancy. Kinda get me off the hook, ya know? Plus that way, I won't feel responsible for what happens."

"Dear, one thing I do believe in is personal accountability. The Universe is all about cause and effect. Each cause has to be owned by the agent that created the cause, or all would be chaos." She leaned forward and put her hand on Kaylie's. "No matter how this turns out, the ultimate responsibility lies with you."

Kaylie gulped. "Yeah. Huh. Well, thanks for coming over today. I look forward to our next visit."

"You should – you'll be getting a full body massage."

Kaylie smiled at the thought. Guilt trips she could do without, but a trip to massage heaven would be perfect. "Great! See you then."

CHAPTER 13

Jake put his armful of groceries down on his front step and rushed over to help the older man and woman carrying items into the empty apartment next door.

"Here, let me get that," he said, grabbing a box from the woman.

"Oh, thank you," she said. "Thank you very much, Mr. —"

"Granville. Jake Granville. I live next door."

Jake placed the large cardboard box inside and headed out to grab another from the loaded minivan backed up to the edge of the parking garage, as close as possible to the row of apartment doors. He quickly ran in several boxes as the lady watched.

As he took in the last box, the man walked up to shake his hand.

"Well, that's about it," said Jake. "If you need anything, let me know, I'm right next door. I'm pretty handy with a screwdriver   rench. The management here is great, but their maintenance teams can't always come right away – they take care of a lot of properties for the management."

"Well, thanks again," said the man.

"What's your name?" asked Jake.

"George and Ellen. Adams. We'll be here for a while – not permanently – but likely for a few months," said George.

"George and Ellen. Great. Well, take care. Remember, if you need anything, just knock on my door."

As Jake walked back to his door, unlocked it, and picked up his grocery bags, he heard the woman remark, "What a nice man."

He went inside and started to put away the food when his phone rang.

"Jake Granville."

"Dave here. Listen, it's your turn."

"My turn? For what?"

"The CVS test. We were playing with running it week after next, but decided to keep it for this week, to have a strong follow-up to the season premiere show. Ratings were strong, but not strong enough. We need to promo the hell out of this the next few days, make the viewers come back for more."

"But I thought paternity couldn't be established this early?"

"Turns out it can. The UCLA Medical Center has a new twist on the old technique. It's one hundred percent accurate, and can be done as early as week seven. Crazy, huh?"

"Yeah, crazy. All right, when do you need me?"

"*Right away, if you can. I already sent a crew to the hospital, and I have a camera on its way to your place as we speak, to follow you in.*"

"Fine. But I don't like this, Dave. I created this reality show. I had no intention of becoming a part of it."

"*Law of unintended consequences, my friend. Don't worry about it. It'll be fine.*"

"It better be."

"*Just get your butt to the hospital. But wait till Keith arrives with his camera.*"

"Right. I'll talk to you later."

Jake hung up just as a knock came at the door. He opened it, expecting Keith.

It was the new couple from next door.

"Hello!" said Ellen. "We just wanted to thank you again for your help. To tell the truth, the circumstances of our move here are not at all pleasant, and it really made a difference for us to run into such a nice welcome. We'd like to take you out to dinner – if that's okay."

"On us," George added, as if it were necessary to convince Jake and "close the sale."

"Uh, gee, thanks. But actually, right now I have to go to the hospital."

"Hospital?" said Ellen. "Is everything okay?"

"Uh, yeah. I hope so anyway. It's complicated."

At that moment, Keith showed up with his TV camera. "You ready to go, Mr. Granville?"

"Yep – be right there."

"A TV camera?" said George.

"Like I said, it's complicated. Thanks for the offer, sir. Ma'am." Jake stepped out of his door and locked it. "I'll see you around."

"Can I start rolling now, Mr. Granville?"

Jake walked toward the parking garage. "Yeah. We'll take my car."

They hopped in his AC Cobra, Keith filming the whole thing from the apartment, down the road, and to the medical center. The camera followed him inside and to the lab.

"Okay, time to get this over with," Jake mumbled.

CHAPTER 14

Amanda Adams sat alone in her parents' home and stared at the old family pictures framed on the wall of the living room.

She pondered a photo of her and her brother and sister – sometime around when Amanda was in middle school – all sitting side-by-side on the big wooden swing that still hung from one of the great oak trees in the back yard of this old house. Big smiles on their young faces.

Were they ever really that young? Everything seemed so much simpler back then – so innocent.

That was before – everything happened.

Before the secret Amanda kept buried in her heart.

She thought back on those days five years ago – the pain she had gone through – and the lie she continued to tell everyone. She almost believed the lie herself – but all this business with Kaylie brought the past freshly back to life and erased any chance that the lie was true.

What had happened was real.

And now Kaylie was embroiled in something similar.

But not so similar.

Kaylie had gotten herself into this mess by being a careless skank. And now she was capitalizing on it with fame and fortune.

And she won't even have to decide how to deal with it – she can just ride the wave and go with the flow.

And Mom and Dad are there for her no matter what.

It wasn't so easy for Amanda.

The summer before her senior year of college – the *first* time she was a senior – she'd taken a job at a local bar – the Bard's Brew.

She met a guy. Larry seemed nice, so she consented to go out on a date with him.

That date ended in disaster.

Under the pretense of showing her a nice view of the valley, he'd driven her several miles up Dead Indian Memorial Road and parked off the highway in a secluded spot.

And then had his way with her.

She'd tried to fight off the drunken jerk, but he was much bigger and stronger.

But that wasn't all.

A few weeks after that trauma, she was horrified to discover she was pregnant.

She couldn't bear the thought of carrying that vile man's offspring. She was mortified at the thought of anyone finding out what had happened. She immediately went to the student health and wellness center on campus and started asking questions.

She was put in contact with some crisis services people who promised confidentiality.

All she needed was some money.

Kaylie had just been paid for a bit acting job for a production at the Britt Festival. Amanda called her up and Kaylie loaned her the money, no questions asked.

And then it was done.

Amanda returned to the safety of school, never venturing out into the workforce again, and not doing any dating for the next three years.

Her parents and Bruce thought she was just a bookworm.

And Amanda was fine with that.

Kaylie had taken off to L.A. and never did ask her about the money she'd loaned her.

And Amanda was fine with that.

Now everyone was rushing to Kaylie's side, and fighting to make sure there'd be no abortion in this family.

Amanda wasn't so fine with that.

CHAPTER 15

"We're on in twenty," said Dave, coming into Jake's office.

Jake sat at his desk, surfing the web and frowning. "Uh huh."

Normally, Jake would be looking forward to viewing one of his creations, but this was an episode he was dreading. And he wouldn't be watching this one from the comfort of his office. He'd be in the Green Room for most of the show, and then on stage for the "big reveal."

"C'mon, Jake. We gotta get you down to makeup. You can't avoid this."

Jake looked up at Dave with a glare. He closed the lid on his laptop and stood. "Fine, let's go."

They left the office and navigated the corridors of the building, then across the elevated walkway to Studio 18. Jake headed downstairs to the makeup chair while Dave went to the production booth.

This was going to be a long night.

"Hello, Mr. Granville," said the chirpy makeup artist, an effeminate bald fellow who introduced himself as Wayne. "We'll just tuck this cloth in your collar and get a little of this paint on your face so you don't look like a *ghost* on camera."

Jake sat through the ten minute makeup session that was peppered with the makeup artist's gossipy remarks about the "honcho" getting in front of the camera, then hurriedly headed to the Green Room.

He opened the door to find Kaylie sitting on the couch, and two other guys in chairs on the other side of the room.

The short list.

Everyone seemed to be glaring at each other.

Jake gave Kaylie a terse nod, then sat in the one vacant chair to the left of Dude Number Two.

Five minutes to show time.

The assistant floor director, Tracy Smith, entered the room, headset on and clipboard in hand. "Ah, glad to see you made it, Mr. Granville." The sarcasm was unmistakable, and to be expected from this crew, who had mostly only known Jake as "one of the suits" up to this point.

Tracy clipped a wireless mic to Jake's lapel and attached the receiver to his belt at the small of his back. "You know Kaylie. That's Greg Simmons and Kirk Rogers. We're four minutes out. Can you give the booth a mic check?"

"One, two, three," said Jake, monotonously.

"We're good." With that, she disappeared out the door.

Jake looked over at the other two guys. Greg was tall and thin, with a mop of red hair and pale white skin, accented by a tiny soul patch under his thick bottom lip.

He wore a cheap gray suit and black loafers. About twenty-five, he looked like he might be some kind of IT guy or accountant.

The other man, Kirk, was about the same age as Greg, maybe a little older. He was shorter, with tight black corn-row hair, rich dark brown skin, and deep brown eyes. He was clean-shaven and wore a yellow Adidas t-shirt and black cycling pants and high-tops. Judging by his meaty biceps, he worked out.

Kaylie clearly had a wide variety of tastes in men.

Of course, as drunk as she was that one night, she probably saw them all through beer goggles.

Jake looked up at the air monitor and saw the commercials end and the show's graphic intro begin. His stomach started to turn into a pretzel and his feet tingled.

The four of them watched in silence as Troy Tanner appeared center stage and started into his monologue, speaking briefly about what we saw in last week's premiere, and hinting at what would happen tonight.

Jake had seen the show's rundown and knew the Green Room would not appear on camera until the end of the first segment; and then only visually – no audio.

The plan was to tease the viewers through the first half of the show, then introduce the men in the second half, and have the hour culminate in an onstage reveal of the paternity results.

To preserve the "reality" aspect of the show, even Jake had not been apprised of the test results, so he sat there as nervous as everyone else, with no clue how things would turn out fifty-six minutes from now.

As the man behind the scenes, pulling the strings, he hated not being in control. And he hated no longer being *behind* the scenes.

He still couldn't get over the dumb luck of it all –
what were the odds, with hundreds of girls trying out,
that Hal would pick someone Jake had slept with
recently?

Jake rolled his eyes at the thought, chiding himself.
As it was, the odds were pretty good, considering how
he'd been conducting himself. Too bad his recent urges
to settle down and reform himself had not occurred to
him a little earlier in the summer.

Now he was paying the price for his foolishness. And
he had only himself to blame for the fact that he was now
in the hot seat.

Suddenly, his affinity for reality television and
making real people squirm on national TV – the
schadenfreude he had developed while watching and
enjoying his successful entertainment creations – was
morphing into a hatred of the genre and receding behind
a feeling of dread.

Never mind being gawked at by millions – millions
who will now know that he's a "love-'em-and-leave-'em"
kinda guy – but what if the unthinkable were to happen,
and he ended up being the father?

What if tonight was just the beginning of this
nightmare?

As he stewed in the grim possibilities, the minutes
ticked past.

The show aired segments from the past week,
including a vignette about Kaylie's first visit with her
midwife – where *did* Hal find that space case anyway? –
and another backgrounder on Kaylie, with a montage of
old photos of her with her family when she was a child.
Her parents looked oddly familiar.

One final segment that included Kaylie's first visit
with Dr. Cho, and then a commercial break. They aired

that scene last, even though it occurred first chronologically, because it was a perfect segue into the paternity test business.

Tracy the assistant floor director popped back into the Green Room. "Okay, folks, we're live in three minutes." Then she proceeded to inform the group what Jake already knew. "We'll start out the segment with Troy. He'll come back here, with a camera trailing him. You'll have a quick little meet-n-greet, then you'll all follow him out to the stage and take your places on the stools. A quick banter with the audience, and then we'll break some news. After that, Troy will tease next week's episode and we're done. You all ready for this?"

They all nodded, none of them looking ready for anything other than crawling under the nearest rock.

"Good. We're on in two."

Tracy stayed in the Green Room as the seconds counted down.

Jake gulped down a glass of water to quench his desert-dry mouth. He glanced over at Kaylie, who was looking down, but then looked back up at him.

Their eyes met for a moment.

His heart leapt slightly.

She was remarkably attractive.

But it was more than that. What if they – together – were the parents of a child?

"And we're live in five, four, three," said Tracy, standing beside one of the cameras.

The show returned.

Troy spoke a few witty and drama-filled words, then the screen split to reveal the Green Room on one side.

They all looked like scared lab rats.

Troy then bounded off the stage and a camera followed him past a heavy stage curtain, through a dark hallway, past a couple of strategically-placed stagehands and grips, and then into the Green Room.

"All right, folks. Here we are. Kaylie, great to see you again. Greg – how are you? Kirk, thanks for coming. And Jake, my man. Of course, only one of you – is *the man*."

A little laugh from the audience.

A little squirm from the men.

"So, Kaylie, have you had a chance to catch up with your old pals, here?"

"Uh, yeah," Kaylie lied. "It's great to see them again."

"Greg," said Troy, "Tell us a little about yourself."

"Uh, well, I'm a programmer for a small contractor to Intel. I mostly write code for anti-hacker software."

Geek. Knew it.

"And in your spare time?"

"I uh, I like to write apps for my iPhone, design VR wetware, and build robots. Oh, and I love to dance. That's how I met Kaylie."

"Great! And Kirk, a little about you."

"I'm a personal trainer," he said in a rich baritone. "I have a few celebrity clients – probably nobody you've heard of, but they're all working actors. And I like to surf."

"Did you meet Kaylie out on the beach?"

"No. We met at a club. I like to dance, too."

"Well, we've got a regular dancing ensemble here! Okay, and Jake, what about you?"

"Yeah, I like to dance, too."

"Nice. What about your day job?" he asked with a wry squint and slight cock of the head.

"Uh, I work odd hours – not just during the day."

106

"Right. But, come on – you have to admit you have an interesting job."

"Yes. I create reality TV shows for a living. It's great fun. Most of the time."

"Okay! Well, full disclosure everyone – Jake here is kinda one of my bosses here at FBC. That's right. And the crazy thing is – absolutely true story – Jake had *no* idea he'd be sitting here. When he conceived this show – oh, maybe that's a poor choice of words – well, anyway, when he came up with the idea for *Canceled* – it was *after* his encounter with Kaylie. And he had nothing to do with the decision to cast her for this show."

A moment of awkward silence. Jake envisioned Twitter exploding.

"So! Now that we've got the necessary introductions and legal mumbo jumbo out of the way, what say we get down to business, here?"

The crowd cheered.

Troy stood and led the group out to the stage, where they took their seats on the five stools.

"Everyone want to get to the bottom of this mystery?"

Cheering and whoops.

"We have the results. We know the truth. And we will share it with you. We will. Right after this break."

Jake's heart was pounding now.

He was surprised how much anxiety this was giving him.

The six minute commercial break felt like six years, and it also felt like six seconds. He was starting to feel a little dizzy, and realized he hadn't eaten anything since breakfast.

He glanced up to the very back of the auditorium to the little glint of light that flashed off the small bank of tinted windows around the production booth.

He imagined Dave in there, smiling at Jake's plight. He knew that despite Dave's verbal commiseration, he was relishing every moment of Jake's discomfort. Partly because he loved these kinds of shows – and partly because that's just what colleagues did – laugh at each other's suffering.

The floor director counted off the final seconds of the commercial break, and they were live again.

"Welcome back, everyone! Before you on this stage you see three men – all connected to our one woman, Kaylie Adams. And one of them has been determined, using state-of-the-art biotechnology, to be the father of the fetus – or baby, if you prefer – that Kaylie is carrying."

Jake could see the small monitor at the edge of the stage facing Troy. It showed what was on the air. The shot of Troy switched to a close up of Kaylie, then panned slowly across the faces of the three men, ending on Jake.

"So, without further ado," said Troy, "Would our guests please stand and step forward."

Kaylie, Greg, Kirk, and Jake all rose and stood on the little "x" marks near the front of the stage. A tall blonde in a shimmering gold mini-dress and high heels entered the stage and passed in front of them on her way to Troy. All three guys turned their heads to watch her walk past. She handed Troy a white envelope.

He opened it.

He read it.

He stepped to Kaylie and placed an arm gently around her shoulders.

"Kirk and Greg – please step forward."

Jake's muscles relaxed in relief. It was one of those two schmucks.

"Kirk Rogers, you are . . . not the father. You may sit down."

Kirk stumbled away and knocked over a stool, then jumped up in the air like he'd scored a touchdown.

Greg buried his face in his hands.

"America. Kaylie Adams. Greg Simmons. The man who contributed his DNA to Kaylie's developing offspring – the father of this child – is . . . *Mr. Jake Granville.*"

Kaylie's hands flew up to her mouth as her eyebrows shot up, and she went a little weak in the knees. Troy supported her inconspicuously.

Greg and let out a huge sigh of relief, and within seconds looked relaxed and happy. He backed away shaking his head and smiling.

Jake Granville gulped. He looked over at Kaylie. He looked at the camera.

Then his vision narrowed and he fell flat on his back.

Jake's head was pounding.

He lay on the couch in the Green Room, a cold compress over his brow, his head tipped back on the arm rest.

His vision cleared and he saw the clock on the wall.

In the dim light he could see it said ten after ten.

He'd been out for a whole twelve minutes.

Out.

Oh yeah. He had passed out.

That had to be the most embarrassing moment in television history.

Not only was he named as the father, but he fainted in front of millions of people.

"Hey there, Sleeping Beauty," said Dave, who was sitting on a chair in the corner, enveloped by shadow.

"Hey."

"You okay, man? Your head hit the stage pretty hard." He stifled a laugh.

"Yeah, thanks for the compassion. Doing great here."

"Listen buddy – I'm sorry for finding this a little amusing. I know it's a pretty crappy situation for you."

"You think?"

"But man, oh man, are the ratings going to *soar* now! I've got fifteen messages on my phone in the last ten minutes. I haven't listened to them, but I know what they are. Money."

Jake sat up slowly and removed the compress. "Money."

"Money. I can tell you right now, we're going to push the show to two hours. We'll need it to fit in all the ad time. This twist of fate that is probably not the highlight of your day is absolutely going to shoot this show through the roof. It's freaking gold, baby. Gold."

Jake sighed heavily. Then he got up and walked to the door. As he opened it, he turned to Dave and said, "I need a good night's sleep. I'll call you in the morning."

"Just so you know – I'll be sending Carla Erickson over with a crew at six tomorrow morning."

"A crew? A *crew*?"

"Well, yeah. Of course. This show is about you, too, now."

Jake shook his head and shuffled out, leaving the door wide open.

CHAPTER 16

George Adams sat in the tan microfiber armchair with his head in his hands while Ellen paced the room.

"I cannot believe it," he said. "The TV executive who created this abominable show is the father of the child?"

"And he lives next door to us!"

"He seemed like a nice guy. Now I just want to put my hands around his neck and squeeze."

"George. We need to talk. I mean, all of us. We need to get Kaylie and that Jake guy in a room and discuss this thing."

"Yeah. Good luck doing that without the whole world being privy to our conversation next Thursday night." He stood up wearily and walked to the kitchen, opening the white fridge and staring at the sparse contents.

"I'm going to go visit Kaylie."

George looked over at his wife. "You sure that's a good idea? She didn't take the news of us being in town very well."

"She was just surprised, and stressed out by everything – what with those cameras following her everywhere. I'm sure it was just one more thing that caught her off guard and made her freak out a little. But I think she'll be glad for the company."

"Fine. I'm staying here. I think she's still scared of what I might say to her. And frankly, so am I."

Ellen grabbed her purse and gave George a kiss on the cheek. "Try to relax. And if you see our neighbor, try not to strangle, him, okay? After all, our grandchild has his DNA."

George rolled his eyes.

"And quit foraging in that fridge. Just order some pizza or something while I'm gone."

George nodded and closed the fridge.

Ellen took the keys to the minivan and left.

George sat back down, pulled out his phone, and looked up the nearest pizza place. He ordered a large Carnivore King for delivery, and flipped the TV back on.

The late news was on. They were actually running a "news" story about the latest episode of *Canceled*.

Infotainment at its best.

And another way to boost ratings through more exposure.

George flipped the channel, but nothing caught his interest. He couldn't stop thinking about his daughter and this mess.

He started thinking about the kind of people who would put a show like this on the air. He thought about Jake. The "nice" neighbor. He did seem like a fairly upstanding guy. Maybe he had just spent too much time in Hollywood and lost his perspective on what's decent.

Of course, he also had gotten Kaylie pregnant.

George steamed a little, but his wiser instincts soon took over. He took a deep breath and remembered that everyone makes mistakes – some far more serious than others – but the real test of character was how they chose to deal with the consequences.

How would Jake react to this news?

Would he exploit it for all it was worth, or would he strive to do the right thing by Kaylie?

Maybe with the right influences, Jake could step up and be a good man.

Or maybe he was a complete jerk and needed to have his windpipe clamped down on.

For now, George decided he was willing to let the jury stay out.

A few minutes later, there was a knock at the door. Pizza.

George opened it and paid for his meal. Before he closed the door, Jake walked up on his way to his own door.

"Jake!" said George.

Jake looked like a kid caught stealing. He stopped in his tracks.

"Yes?"

"Come here. I want to talk to you."

"Uh, I can't right now, Mr. Adams. It's late, and I'm not feeling so well." He rubbed at the back of his head.

"Do you know who I am?" asked George, holding the pizza box with one hand and pushing back the front door with the other.

"You're George Adams, my new neighbor."

"And my name doesn't ring a bell?"

"No, Sir." Jake walked toward him slowly, looking curious, and tired.

"I know you've already received a bit of a shock tonight – I saw the show, I know – but I have some more news for you. I'm Kaylie's father."

Jake didn't faint this time, but his face blanched, and his angular jaw hung open slightly. "Excuse me?"

"Kaylie Adams – the star of your show. She's my daughter. Ellen and I are her parents."

Jake leaned against the brown wooden support beam that held up the long porch overhang that ran along the front of the building.

"Why don't you come inside for a few minutes," said George, feeling more compassion than he had expected to. "This pizza's getting cold, and I can't eat it all by myself."

Jake, stunned, followed George inside and sat down hard on a wooden dining chair. He remained silent.

This man was clearly a pretty high roller at the network, but right now, he looked so pitiful - like he'd been socked in the gut – George didn't have it in him to come down on him the way he had been fantasizing since the beginning of the show earlier that night.

Now, Jake just seemed like a scared kid.

"You like Carnivore King pizza?"

Jake nodded. "Yes, thank you."

The two ate in silence for a couple of minutes.

George got up and grabbed a couple of beers from the fridge, tossed one to Jake.

They popped them open, and George spoke. "Look, I have to admit, when I saw you on the TV tonight, lined up as one of the possible, er, you know – I was *fuming*. Ask Ellen. I nearly put my fist through a wall."

Jake stopped chewing.

"And when I found out who you are – the show's creator – a bigwig at FBC – well, I was really ticked. And *then*, when you turned out to be the father, my mind quickly formulated ways to kill you and dispose of the body."

Jake gulped the unchewed pizza in his mouth, choked a little, and reached for his beer can.

"But," continued George, "I'm a reasonable man – I believe in trying to take a Christ-like approach to situations. I calmed down some. Took a few deep breaths, listened to my dear wife. And then I saw how this is affecting you."

He stopped to take a stray piece of crusty pepperoni out of the box and pop it in his mouth. "Question is, how *are* you taking it? I need to know where you stand, Jake."

Jake wiped his mouth and sat back. "Well, I'm obviously in a bit of shock, as you can imagine."

"Oh, I don't have to imagine – I saw you pass out and hit that stage." George couldn't help but smile. "Now *that* was good television."

"Thank you," Jake said wryly. "You know, I just haven't had any time to wrap my head around it."

"Well, surely you've had some time – before tonight – to at least ponder the possibility. To think about what would happen if it turned out this way."

"Yes. And, to tell the truth, I've found myself – uh, conflicted. Look – I gotta say I feel a little weird just baring my soul to a stranger." George frowned. Jake continued quickly. "On the other hand, I don't really have anyone else to talk to, and I suppose you do have an interest in this. Plus – if I don't say what's on my mind now, I may not get another chance. I mean, without being on camera. This, I am realizing, is one of my last private moments for a while."

"Then spit it out – what's on your mind?"

Jake took another sip of beer. "Here's the thing, Mr. Adams. I've been wasting my life."

"Sorry?"

"Wasting my life. I mean, I'm a successful network executive, gotta great office, a nice car – a *very* nice car – have you seen it, the Cobra? I have my health, I've made some good investments. But I'm starting to realize something's missing. Mr. Adams, I've spent the better part of the last decade and a half just fooling around. Playing."

"Golf?"

"Yeah, lots of that. But I'm talking about girls. Women, that is. I've been, uh, let's just say I have known a lot of women. But never anything serious – nothing *lasting*."

"So, you're a – a male slut."

Jake rolled his eyes. "That's one way of putting it. 'The envy of my peers' works, too, but I suppose it's farther from the truth. The truth is, I've grown tired of living that lifestyle. And, as you can see, it's gotten me into a fix."

"You? What about my daughter? She's in a bit of a fix, don't you think?"

"Yes. Absolutely. And a pretty unconventional fix, thanks to my brilliant idea for a TV show."

"You sound regretful."

"This isn't how I saw things coming together."

"I bet it isn't. So, what are you going to do about it? What are you going to do to get this show – *canceled*?"

Jake hung his head and shook it, then looked up. "I can't."

"What do you mean, you can't?"

"It's not going to happen."

"But you're a big wheel down there at the network – you just said so yourself. Take charge! Make an executive decision. Be a man!"

"It's not that simple! I'm not the only one with a say in this. There's a lot at stake."

"I'll say there is! The life of my grandchild, for one thing! The dignity of my daughter for another! Not to mention my family's reputation!"

"Mr. Adams, you don't understand. There's hundreds of millions of dollars tied up in this thing. People's jobs – their livelihood. Expectations. From the network – and from America. And my boss, and his boss – there's no way they would ever let this end now."

"Because you don't have the guts to make it happen?"

"Because I don't have the power. A contract is a contract. And there are all *kinds* of contracts here – sponsor contracts not among the least of them. This thing isn't going to go away."

George looked like he'd eaten something sour. "You just don't care enough. You don't care what happens to the child."

"Actually, Mr. Adams – actually – I do. I do care." Jake put his head in his hands. "I – I've realized what's missing in my life."

"A baby?"

"Permanence. Stability. The things that only a family can provide."

"You don't have any family?"

"No. I have an uncle in Michigan – my parents are dead. But I'm talking about having my *own* family. A wife, children. Set-settling down."

"You say that like it's a bad thing."

"It's just very much *not* what I'm about – what I've been about. But I'm ready to change."

"You better be ready, son – because time is not going to stop and wait for you – and neither is this baby."

"If the baby survives the season."

George sighed heavily. "Fine. So you can't stop the show. But you still have a say in things, right?"

"Right. In some things. At least for now. As I become more a part of the drama itself, they may decide to change things – to avoid conflicts of interest, or just to make the show more interesting. It's likely I'll end up as powerless and subject to the whims of the powers that be as – as Kaylie is right now."

"Huh. Well, for now, you *are* the powers that be. And here's what I want. You need to get Ellen and I on next week's show. We need a full segment in which we can state our case – plead to America to vote for life – to vote for life every week and save our grandchild."

"I can get you that platform. We were planning on bringing in the family a little later anyway – I'm sure I can get you on this coming week."

"Good."

"The question is – are you ready for this? It will not be easy. You'll become famous overnight – and you might become the target of both admiration and hatred. This show is certain to cause sharp divisions. Internet forums are already popping up, and a lot of them are very pro-choice and they're not saying kind things about you."

"Ellen and I are ready to do whatever it takes. We can endure being 'unpopular' – we raised three kids! If it means saving a life, we're ready for anything."

"All right then. I'll talk to the right people and make it happen."

CHAPTER 17

The knock at the door startled Kaylie.

She'd been sitting on the couch scrolling through social media, but was starting to doze.

Post after post was talking about her and the show.

Whole blogs had developed – either espousing views for or against abortion, or just tracking the show and speculating.

Yep, she was big news.

And her email inbox was jam-packed with emails from agents – many of them the same ones who wouldn't give her the time of day a few months ago.

She had already hired one, though. After the first episode. Andrea Weinberger — a top name in the business.

Kaylie set the tablet aside and got up to get the door.

At only eight weeks pregnant, Kaylie didn't think she should be so lethargic. Molly the Midwife said it was stress-related – that the show was wearing her down.

That was one thing she was probably right about.

Kaylie opened the door just as the person on the other side knocked again.

"Mom!"

"Hi, Sweetie."

"Come in, please."

Kaylie stepped aside and let her mother in.

Ellen came in and took off her light jacket. As she went to hang it on the back of a dining chair, she spotted one of the two camera people, who had a camera trained on her, and dropped the jacket short of the chair. "Oh! I forgot about these people. I don't know how I did, but I did."

"It's okay, Mom," said Kaylie, picking up the jacket and placing it in the chair. She took her mom by the elbow and led her to the couch. "Just ignore them. They do a good job of uh, blending in. You really will forget about them after a while."

Ellen sat down and eyed the tablet. "Catching up on the latest news?"

"Yeah. It's all about me. Hey Mom, I just wanted to say – I'm sorry I freaked out when you and Dad first showed up. I just wasn't expecting it, and with everything going on –"

"It's fine. Speak no more of it. We're here – we're here for you – and that's what matters."

"How's Dad doing?"

"About the same."

"Still angry at me?"

"Honey, I don't know if he was ever angry at *you*, exactly. Just the situation. More than anything, he was disappointed. But he's coming around. He just needs a little time."

"Is that why he's not here right now?"

"He's just afraid he'll let his emotions get the better of him. But he'll be fine soon, I'm sure."

Kaylie got to her feet. "I'm so sorry, Mom – I'm a terrible host. Can I get you anything?"

Ellen jumped up. "Absolutely not. You sit right down young lady – I'm here to serve *you*. Now, what can I get for you?"

Ellen headed to the kitchen and started fussing around in the cupboards, tidying as she went – despite the fact that Kaylie was trying to keep house better than usual.

"Actually, if you could just light that incense there on the counter, that would be great."

Molly had left a stash of Mystic Moments for Kaylie after her last visit.

Ellen lit it and blew it out, to produce the stream of smoke. "Mmm, that's nice. So, what's next on the agenda for you?"

"Well, I have an agent now – a big player named Andrea Weinberger. She represents fairly big names in Hollywood."

"Anyone I would've heard of?"

"Uh, probably not – unless you're into dystopian urban fantasy romances."

"Oh."

"Anyway – she's got me hooked up to make some appearances on some network shows like *Good Morning America*, *The Tonight Show*, a few other big ones."

"And that's okay with the producers of *Canceled*?"

"Oh yeah, in fact, they encourage it. They want all the exposure they can get, just like any other show or movie. It's entertainment, after all. They do have some caveats – rules I have to follow about what I'm allowed to reveal – but for the most part, I can just go on these

shows and talk. It's great publicity for me as an artist –
you know, if I ever actually get a real acting career
underway."

Ellen just nodded and said, "Hmm."

They sat in silence for a few moments, then Ellen
asked the inevitable question. "So, how do you feel about
tonight's news? I mean, learning that Jake Granville is
the father?"

"Mixed."

"Did you know he's our next door neighbor at the
apartments?"

"Get. *Out!*"

"I'm serious. Dad and I couldn't believe it when we
saw him on the show tonight."

"Wow. That is crazy."

"So, what are your mixed feelings, if you don't mind
my asking?"

"Well, you can either hear about it on Thursday night
when they ask me on-air, or I can just talk to you directly
now. I figure this is best."

"Me too."

Kaylie lifted her leg up under herself and settled back
further into the couch. "Well, of those three guys, Jake is
definitely the cutest." She grinned. "But of course, that's
not what's important. I feel really weird because he's in
charge of the show, and now he's part of it."

"Do you think it was a setup?"

"No. I believe them when they say they didn't know.
I could tell when he first saw me at the studio – he was
just as surprised as me. It's just a weird coincidence. But
that kinda makes me feel weird, too – as if maybe it was
somehow *meant* to be."

"Maybe it was."

"I'm kind of afraid to talk to him, though. I'm embarrassed to say that I really don't know him that well at all – and I have no idea what he's thinking regarding this situation. And I don't know exactly how the show is going to handle it. That's one thing about this show – they tell me not to reveal any secrets when I go on the talk show circuit, but they don't even share their secrets with me. I have no idea what's in store from week to week, or what else they're going to throw at me."

"Then all you can do is take it one week at a time. One day at a time." Ellen rubbed at her eyes. "Are you still – undecided?"

"About?"

"About what *you* want for this baby. Motherhood, adoption, or – or abortion." The last word seemed practically submerged in disgust and abhorrence.

"It's not my choice."

"Yes, but you have to know what *you* want."

"Well, I don't. Not yet."

"And if you decide you can't countenance the idea of killing him or her – then what? Will you stand up and tell America, week after week, to vote for life?"

"I'm not allowed to."

"What do you mean you're not allowed to?"

"It's in the contract. Part of my 'performance scope' – as it's called in the legal document – requires that I refrain from advocating for either choice. They say it's to make the show's voting more fair. Even if I make up my mind, I need to keep it to myself."

"That's ridiculous! How can you *not* talk about that? That's not *reality* TV, it's a gag order. Crazy!"

"It's going to be one of the hardest parts of this, I think."

"Well, the good news is, you have other people who can speak for you. Your father and I are going to get on the show and speak *our* minds. We are going to speak and we're not going to stop speaking until this is over."

Kaylie smiled. "Thanks, Mom."

"So – you want to come over to our apartment? Talk to Jake?"

"Huh, uh, no. Not really, no."

"No point in trying to escape it. You can't run from this. Wouldn't it be better to confront him – or rather, speak with him – with Dad and I there to support you, instead of all alone at the TV studio or something?"

"I guess you're right. Can we wait until after my morning appointment? I'm exhausted tonight."

"Oh, of course. My goodness, I didn't realize it was so late already – nearly midnight. I better be getting back."

"Thanks for coming, Mom. And, tell Dad he's welcome any time. Even if he needs to yell at me a little – to get it off his chest. It's okay. I need you both."

"I'll tell him that."

CHAPTER 18

Kaylie and her ever-present camera crew showed up at the government offices right on time at eight-thirty the next morning.

Kaylie read the names of the departments on the wall next to the elevator and pressed the button for the tenth floor – The Federal Family Planning Commission.

As part of the show, she was required to meet with a social worker from this government agency to get educated and "talk about the options."

She filled out a form then waited for ten minutes.

Finally, a woman appeared and smiled at Kaylie. A smooth-skinned black woman in her early forties, she wore her hair in a tight bun, and a slimming gray checked skirt with suit jacket. "Hello, I'm Vanessa Baldwin. Nice to meet you, Kaylie. Please, come with me."

Kaylie and her little entourage followed Vanessa into a small, featureless office with venetian blinds on inward-facing windows and an oval conference table. Vanessa shut the door and rolled the blinds shut.

"If you're worried about privacy," said Kaylie, "You do realize this is all going to be broadcast to the nation on Thursday."

"Just following protocol," said Vanessa with a plastic smile. "We have a very specific set of rules, regulations and guidelines for maintaining an atmosphere of client privacy."

Oh great, a government droid.

Vanessa sat down opposite Kaylie and in front of a clipboard and a slick brochure of some sort. "So, how far along are you?"

"Uh, about eight weeks. Almost nine, I guess."

"Oh good, not far at all. Just a little clump of cells in there giving you trouble. You do realize how quick and easy it will be to terminate?"

"Uh, no. I don't know much about it, to be honest."

"Well, at your stage, you still have a couple weeks during which you could simply take a pill and make it all go away. It's called mifepristone. Safe, legal, simple."

"I see."

"After that, you can get an in-clinic abortion. There are two kinds. Up to sixteen weeks you can get an aspiration. Later than that you'd need a D and E."

"What exactly's entailed in those procedures?"

"They're basically different versions of the same thing – they vacuum out your uterus and you're good to go. Very straightforward and effective. The D and E is just a little more complex because they have to give you a shot through the abdomen to ensure fetal demise before they remove it. But it's still all over in ten to twenty minutes."

"I – see," said Kaylie, starting to feel a little woozy.

"Are you okay? You look a little pale."

She swallowed. "I'm fine. Go on."

"Now, I'm sure you have lots of questions. Many women in your position do, and many of you share the same questions. This pamphlet here answers a lot of them. One in particular I'd like to address is that of the issue of trauma. Many anti-choice extremists will try to tell you that an abortion will leave you with psychological or emotional distress. Quite the opposite is true. The fact is, you'll feel relieved. Tales of post-traumatic stress disorder are simply false. Making an adult choice to get on with your life will only help you feel better."

"Really?"

"Absolutely. And you don't have to worry about the cost – we're fully taxpayer subsidized here at FFPC."

"Uh, it's in my contract that the show would pay for it."

"Oh. Then no worries. You know, the sooner this is over the better, right? If America does the right thing, and hurries up and votes for the decent, merciful choice, you'll be able to walk away from this with the all the cash and never look back."

"Yeah. You think my career will be unaffected? I mean, lots of career women get abortions, right?"

"Oh, yes. This is not a situation that should slow you down in any way – and there just isn't the stigma that used to be associated with it. About one-point-five million abortions are performed each year in the U.S. It's more common than an emergency appendectomy. Chances are, someone in your own family has had an abortion."

"You don't know my family."

"Well, in any case, after this is all over, I'm sure a beautiful woman like you will have a very promising career."

Kaylie just nodded.

"So, how are you feeling?"

"Well, there's a lot of information here to absorb," said Kaylie, leafing through the pamphlet.

"It can be a difficult choice for some."

"Well, this isn't my choice, anyway. You *have* seen the show, right?"

"Yes, of course. I just – uh – I'm sorry. I suppose I'm on autopilot, just a little bit. Maybe I'm thrown off a little by the uh, you know." She motioned surreptitiously at the cameras.

"You're just doing your job."

"Yeah. Just doing my job. Thing is, I'm supposed to do better than just doing my job. I've counseled hundreds – maybe thousands of girls. But that doesn't mean I shouldn't treat each one like the individual she is. I apologize."

"It's fine. I understand. Now, you know this uh, situation – it could last a while. If they end up voting to end the pregnancy close to the due date – well, tell me about what a late-term abortion is like. Reading through the websites out there regarding the show, I have a feeling it's going to come to that, actually."

"Well, a late-term procedure – that's technically after the twentieth week – will typically be an IDX – that stands for intact dilation and extraction. Anti-choice extremists call that a partial-birth abortion – a hateful scare tactic to try and influence impressionable women and score political points. But it's a relatively straightforward surgery. Basically, the doctor will dilate you, then reach in with forceps to grab the fetus' leg, turn it into a breach position and pull it out feet first as far as the head. Then the fetus' brain is suctioned out – this makes sure it's dead, and also conveniently collapses the skull so it is easier to remove the head."

Kaylie jumped to her feet. "Excuse me."

She burst out of the room, but had no idea where the restrooms were. She scurried as far as the elevator. The doors were open. She rushed in and fell to her knees beside a man in a suit. Just as the doors were closing, the fast-footed male camera operator caught up and jumped through the closing doors just in time to catch her vomiting on camera.

Actually, *on* camera.

Right into the lens.

Well, they wanted "up close and personal" – and they got it.

CHAPTER 19

"Good evening, everyone! Welcome to *Canceled*! This is week three of the show – week nine of the pregnancy – and have we got a show for you!"

Troy Tanner stood in the spotlight center stage. He was wearing a thin shadow of stubble tonight, with black jeans and a silvery sport jacket over a dress shirt.

The crowd roared.

"Tonight, we'll take a look back at the past week in Kaylie's life – including an appointment with a social worker that ended – well, you'll see how it ended. Also, a heart-to-heart with her mother – we'll have the whole conversation. Plus – in their first time on national television, we'll devote a whole segment to the parents of our star. That's right – George and Ellen Adams will join us here on the show – live on stage. All that and more – coming up tonight. And we'll begin – after the break."

The screen in the Green Room went black for a moment while the network went to commercial, then the preview screen from the booth was piped in and Kaylie could see herself sitting on the couch between her mom and dad.

"You ready for this?" she asked, looking from one to the other.

"Ready as you can be, I guess," said George, patting her on the knee.

"I'm just glad we can face this together," said Ellen, "and that we'll have this chance to tell our side of this."

"Back in one minute," said Tracy from beside the main camera, headset on and holding her clipboard.

Kaylie took a deep breath and grabbed each of her parent's hands to give them a squeeze. "It'll be fine."

"And in thirty seconds."

"Thanks," said George. "I love you, honey."

"And in five, four, three."

The on-air screen showed the inside of the Green Room door, and then it opened. Troy walked in. "Welcome back, everyone. I'm just stepping into the Green Room now, where we'll meet the parents."

The camera followed him as he walked up to the Adams' and introduced them to America.

"Ellen Adams – glad to have you here tonight. And Mr. George Adams, thanks for coming. And as always, it's good to see you, Kaylie. We'll jump right in – George, tell us a little about yourself, your background, and so on."

"Well, I'm retired. I was a mortgage broker for a while. Before that I spent some time in electronics – but that was back before all this stuff you have today. I worked on computers the size of this room that could do less – and do it slower – than your cell phone. I also spent a couple of terms in the Oregon State Legislature."

"And what do you do these days – in your retirement?"

"Mostly watch too much TV – including shows like this."

"And Mrs. Adams – Ellen – what about you?"

"Yes, I probably watch too much TV, too."

"Ha ha, no, I meant your background."

"I raised three kids. After that, I did some secretarial type work for the County Planning Commission. Then I did a little part-time work selling my own crafts on eBay."

"Oh really? What kind of crafts?"

"Just little things – sometimes I'd paint china plates, things like that."

"Wonderful. Now, tell us about how you felt when you found out about Kaylie's situation. In fact – let's just play back a quick excerpt of that – since we caught that phone call on camera."

McIntyre rolled the tape – about two minutes of the conversation Kaylie had had with her mother. Then the video dissolved back to the Green Room camera.

"All right. Seeing that bring back some memories?"

"Well, Troy I may be getting old, but it was just a couple of weeks ago."

Audience laughter.

"But seriously – was it devastating? Was it a surprise? What exactly was your reaction – since we didn't have a camera on your end of the phone."

"Well," said Ellen, "to tell the truth, I actually fell over and dropped the phone."

"Were you hurt?"

"A little. Mostly disappointed."

"I mean in the fall."

"No, I was fine. My knees just kinda buckled. Anyway, George needed a little cool-off time before he was ready to talk to Kaylie. But overall – well, we're a family and we stick together and we'll make it through this."

"Okay, well, listen, why don't we take this out on the stage?" said Troy. "We'll do that – right after the break."

During the commercials, the group moved to the stage and sat on the stools. Someone quickly touched up Troy's makeup, and after a couple of minutes they were back on the air.

"Okay everyone. Here we are with Kaylie Adams and her very nice parents, George and Ellen. Let's jump right into the q-and-a segment now – with comments or questions posed from the audience – live! Let's have ladies first – Ellen, you're in the hotseat."

The lights dimmed and a spotlight appeared on Ellen. About a dozen beautiful young women in evening dresses filed onto the stage holding wireless microphones, then made their way out into the audience.

"All right, first question!" said Troy, pointing toward the upper left of the seating area.

"Uh, yeah. Hi, my name is Frank Shaw from Buffalo. My question is, if Kaylie splits some of the prize money with you, what will you spend it on?"

The camera shot returned to a stunned-looking Ellen. "I, um, well, I have never even given that any thought. We're really not here for money – we're here because we want to tell America that it's wrong to take a life for entertainment. We believe –"

"Okay, thank you!" interrupted Troy. "Next question – up front here!"

"Yeah, I'm Kristy Bergen from San Francisco. Have you been trying to pressure your daughter with your beliefs and tell her that she's a bad person for doing this show?"

"Of course not!" said Ellen, just as the camera switched back to her. "We love Kaylie and have always wanted what's best for her. Kaylie has a good head on her shoulders – she's made some mistakes, but who hasn't? The point is, we need to make sure this does not end in tragedy. We –"

"And we have another question up here on the right. Go ahead, please," said Troy.

"My name is Joe Trundle from the Chicago area. I wanna know just what you expected to happen to your daughter, getting her on a show like this? Did you seriously think this would end well for anybody? Or were you just seeing dollar signs?"

"First of all, we didn't even know she was going to do this show. You obviously weren't watching the segment where she informed me this was happening. But thanks for your vote of support!"

Kaylie watched in horror as one after another of the hostile questioners succeeded in making her mother look defensive as she got more and more flustered in the spotlight. Were these people plants? How could everyone be so mean and stupid?

Finally, mercifully, after three more questions brought in via Facebook Live, the segment ended.

After the break, George was next to hit the spotlight.

"Yeah, Mr. Adams. I'm James Chen from Atlanta. Just wondering if you've broken that Jake guy's nose yet – and if not, why not?"

George looked composed – like he'd had the last several minutes to steel himself for the inevitable attacks. "Mr. Granville and I have had a talk. I'm not a violent man – I believe in peaceful solutions and reasonable discourse. I'm sure Jake will do the right thing."

"Question in the back."

"Yes, I'm Shirley Hansen from St. Louis. What do you think should happen on this show?"

"I think America should choose to allow this child to come into the world. Our family is well-equipped to handle this situation without resorting to the injustice of abortion. We –"

"And in the front here, another question."

"Yeah, I'm Jerry Canelli. From Brooklyn. Yo, who are you to try to take away our right to decide? We're Americans, and this show is perfectly legal – the Supreme Court made sure of that back in 1973. Your daughter made her decision a few weeks ago – now it's *our* turn to decide some stuff."

"You think just because you watch TV you have the right to interfere in –"

"Yeah! It's a free frickin' country and I can use the app to vote at the end of the show and I can choose to make sure no more of *your* DNA gets out into the world! That's liberty and justice for all, man!"

"You little –"

"It's time *somebody* made some smart decisions, don'tcha think? Time someone took a stand to prevent little whores like her from overpopulating the planet!"

Kaylie let the slur pass – she was too preoccupied watching the little pinpricks of perspiration around her father's forehead begin to form into droplets of sweat as he struggled to not jump off the stage and beat the living crap out of this loudmouthed jerk.

"You sir, are crossing the line of decency –"

"What do you know about decency? Just look at your loose little girl and tell me about decency! This show is a perfect solution – it takes care of much-needed population control and outs the holier-than-thou hypocrites like you!"

George started to shake visibly. "You – you!"

Then George clutched at his heart and collapsed off the stool, landing on the stage with a loud thud. He convulsed slightly as Ellen and Kaylie ran over to him.

Troy's grin instantly turned into a confused frown as he yelled into the mic, "Someone get medical here, now!"

Paramedics were apparently waiting in the wings, as they jumped up on stage within a few seconds.

As they stabilized George and prepared a gurney, Troy turned to camera one and said, "And we'll have more right after the break!"

The network went to commercial, and Troy bounced over to Kaylie and Ellen who stood watching George get carted out. "This is *great* TV!"

Kaylie turned around in a flash and slapped Troy – hard – on the left cheek, leaving it red. "Great TV? You idiot! That's my dad they're taking away! What kind of jerk are you?"

Kaylie and Ellen then followed the gurney off.

"Uh, Kaylie, you can't leave!" said Troy, rubbing at his cheek. "We need to finish the rest of the show! It's – it's in your contract!"

Kaylie turned around. Then she looked back at her mother. And back again at Troy. She turned back once more to her mom, torn inside. Dad's gurney was disappearing out the side door of the studio.

"Mom, you go. I really have to stay. I – I just don't want to forfeit the contract and lose my prize."

Ellen looked at Kaylie with tears in her eyes, then turned and rushed off to be with her husband. A lone camera person followed closely behind to capture the story for next week's show.

Kaylie returned to the stage, glaring at Troy as she passed him.

A makeup person hurriedly applied a touch-up to cover the growing red hand-shaped welt on Troy's cheek.

"And we're back in ten seconds," said the floor director.

"Welcome back everyone – wow! That was exciting, eh?" said Troy. "Let's get reaction from Kaylie."

He held the mic to Kaylie's face. She grabbed it from him and spoke, her voice even. "Here's my reaction: Jerry Canelli can kiss my pregnant white butt! And I think it's pretty disgusting that you all think that a man having a heart attack is entertainment. This isn't some TV drama – with actors who just get up and walk away after pretending to get hurt. My dad is –" her voice broke and she had to swallow hard, "I love my dad, and now he's in the hospital because of – because you people have nothing better to do than pick on people and be entertained by the difficulties others face. Shame on you!"

"Shame on *you*!" yelled Jerry Canelli in the front row. "Your dad's in the hospital because you're a floozy!"

"All right, that's enough," said Troy. "You had your chance at the microphone, sir. One more outburst and we'll have security escort you out." Troy didn't sound the least bit annoyed – and he had a little gleam in his eye.

"Yeah," said Kaylie with her eyes narrowed, "and that would make *great TV*, wouldn't it, Troy?"

"Okay, well, let's go to our next video segment," said Troy smoothly. "Now we'll take a look at Kaylie's recent visit to the Federal Family Planning Commission, where she met with a social worker who educated her on her options – and where Kaylie had a little surprise for the head of the department as he was about to get out of the elevator. Let's take a look at the tape."

The lights dimmed and a video rolled on the screen behind them. McIntyre took to video directly and shut off the mics onstage.

Kaylie watched as her embarrassing vomit-at-the-feet-of the-bureaucrat incident replayed.

As tears came to her eyes, and she thought about her dad, she wondered how she was ever going to make it through another twenty-eight weeks of this.

In fact, a small part of her hoped America would vote this week to put her out of this misery.

Of course, the voting stage of the show wouldn't begin until next week.

Which meant at least another two weeks of this torture.

CHAPTER 20

"Good to see you, Kaylie," Dr. Cho smiled as she entered the exam room. "How are you feeling?"

"Better in some ways – worse in others," said Kaylie.

The little room was warmly decorated with some harvest colors, and felt much more comfortable than her first visit. That was before she knew how nice Dr. Cho was.

"How's your father?"

"He's stable. They released him yesterday and he's at the apartment resting. They say he's going to be okay. It wasn't a full-fledged heart attack – more of a – what you call it?"

"Angina?"

"Yeah, that's it."

"So you say you're feeling better in some ways."

"Well," said Kaylie, sitting in the wooden-armed chair next to the little desk, "the nausea is mostly gone. I mean, it's not an every morning or an every day thing anymore – but some things will set me off. The headaches come and go. My stress level is pretty high, but I'm trying to do some stuff to offset that." She thought of Molly's incense but decided not to mention it to a "proper" medical professional like Dr. Cho.

"Really? That's great. If you haven't already, you should try some relaxing incense. I love to kick back with a hot bath and some gentle scents wafting, along with a little Mozart."

"Oh. I didn't think regular doctors believed in that alternative healing stuff."

"Oh, please," Cho smiled. "I'm not a stick in the mud. I think some of that hocus pocus is bunk, sure, but who can deny the positive effects of some good incense and a foot rub?"

Kaylie liked her even more now.

"Of course, I wouldn't be a good physician if I didn't also warn you about not making the bath too hot, and the danger of being put into early labor by a foot rub later in your pregnancy."

"Really?"

"You betcha. So, tell me about the other side – the things that are worse for you?"

Kaylie bit her lip and tried not to glance up at the camera. "Well, some of the stuff – you know, the show – it's just weighing on me."

"Are you worried that the viewers will vote for termination?"

"It's not that – I don't even know what I want in that regard. It's just – it's putting a lot of pressure on my family, for one thing. It's all just making me cranky."

"I'm afraid the effects of pressure are going to be par for the course. This is a most unusual and stressful situation. Pregnancy itself can be difficult enough, but when you throw all this into the mix," she didn't try to hide her gesture at the camera, "it just amplifies everything."

Kaylie nodded. "So, what will we do today?"

"Glad you asked. There's a couple of things we'll look at. First, I want you to hop up on the table for a quick look-see."

Kaylie, feeling less self-conscious than previously, dropped her skirt and got on the table.

The doctor probed a little then said all seemed fine.

"I want you to take a look at this," she said once Kaylie was clothed again.

Kaylie stepped to the desk and peered at the doctor's tablet. It showed a web page that included a color 3-D image of a fetus and some information.

"Your baby is now ten weeks old. For the next ten weeks he will be growing very rapidly. Right now, his ears – which are possibly beginning to hear sounds – are moving toward their final position on the sides of his head – which, by the way, is about half the size of his whole body right now."

"You said *he*. When will we know if it is a *he*?"

"We can do an ultrasound pretty soon to be able to determine the sex. Probably in about three more weeks it'll be clear."

"I see. How big is it now?"

"Only about two inches, but by next month we'll be talking eight inches. And speaking of size, I want you to start eating more. You need to be gaining more weight, to provide the nutrients the baby needs."

"I haven't been eating much – partly the nausea, but mostly just the stress."

"Well, I can provide you with a meal plan, or you can just commit to start eating more and make up your own menu."

"Uh, I'll just try to eat more. Thanks."

"Would you like to hear the baby's heartbeat?"

Kaylie didn't see that question coming, and it caught her off guard. "Uh, um – no, no thanks, that's fine. Thanks."

"Hmm. Most women are interested to hear that."

"Well, I'm fine for now, thanks."

"Okay. Now, do you have any other questions or concerns?"

Kaylie thought for a moment. "You said he – or she – can maybe start hearing sounds?"

"Yes."

"Should I start, you know, talking to it?"

"You can if you want. Some say that helps create a better bond with the child. But medically speaking, there's no evidence that it makes much difference."

"Oh. Okay, well." Kaylie stared a moment longer at the image of the fetus on the screen. She thought about her recent wishes for this all to be over. For the vote to go in favor of ending this.

And as she stared at that image of a tiny developing body, she realized there is no easy way out of this.

CHAPTER 21

Jake sat slumped on the couch in his apartment with the shades drawn at midday.

He looked and felt like he had a hangover, but he hadn't touched a drop.

He was just having trouble sleeping, and was avoiding going in to the office. His hair was disheveled, he had three days' growth of beard, and he was wearing sweats and an old UCLA t-shirt.

He kept alternating between wanting to veg out in front of the tube, and wanting to avoid the TV's wall-to-wall coverage of his show.

His phenomenon.

He had checked his work email a few minutes ago and learned that the show was posting a twenty-eight share.

An incredible rating – crushing all the other fall TV shows, with the streaming options garnering tens of millions of views daily.

Canceled was the talk of the town, and the talk of the nation. Breaking the internet, as they say.

But what a bittersweet victory this was turning out to be!

Thankfully, Dave was giving him a break and *not* having the cameras follow him around full time – yet. By next week, Jake's life would likely be on a twenty-four seven wireless video feed to the editing room at the network, just like Kaylie's.

As he sat there he was torn – tempted to tune in and see what the latest hype was, but on the other hand wishing he could just bury his head in his pillow and shut out the world.

"So this is what a mid-life crisis feels like," he muttered to himself.

A knock came at the door, and Jake rose to look through the peep-hole.

It was Ellen.

He opened the door.

"Hey," he said glumly. "How's George?"

"Hey. He's doing better. Still in bed. We were wondering if you would come over. To talk."

"Uh, sure. Okay. Can you give me five minutes, I uh." He gestured weakly at his hair and clothes.

"Just come on over. We're all family here, right?"

That thought struck Jake like a blow in the stomach. He gave a nervous smile. "Uh, yeah. Right. Okay."

He stepped out and closed the door behind him, then followed Ellen to the apartment next door.

They went into the bedroom where George was propped up in bed watching the tube. He switched it off as soon as they came in. Ellen sat on the bed beside him, and Jake took a seat in an overstuffed armchair in the corner.

The room smelled like Ben Gay.

"So, have you talked to Kaylie?" asked George, foregoing the pleasantries.

"Uh, no. No, I haven't seen her."

"Well, you can't run away from this. You need to sit down with her and figure this all out."

Jake put his head in his hands and mumbled, "I know. I just – this whole thing is –"

"Fifty percent your responsibility," finished George.

"Look, I know this is my fault. Or at least, as you say, half my fault. And it's not that I'm afraid to talk to your daughter. I think she's a nice person, it's just –"

"A nice person? You'd better think she's nice. I mean, the two of you – you know. I would hope that's the least you can say for her."

"It's not Kaylie that concerns me. It's those damn cameras. When we talk, it's not going to be a private conversation."

"And that, Jake, is one hundred percent your fault."

"I am aware of that, Sir."

"So what are you going to do about it?"

Jake sighed. "I'm just going to have to face reality – er, bad choice of words – I have to suck it up and accept that my life is no longer private. And I have to accept that more than one of my own choices has led to this result."

"Good. Sounds like you're growing up a little," said George.

Jake was going to protest that he was thirty-five years old, but realized that would make him sound like a teenager. Fact was, for a man in his thirties, he'd been living the last decade or so as if he were a teenager. And he was starting to feel like a change was in order.

"Yes, I think you're right," he said, standing. "I'm going to go visit Kaylie." He started to leave, then stopped. "Oh, hey, where does she live, anyway? I-I don't remember – I was only there once."

Ellen got up and found a scratch pad and jotted down the address. "Here."

Jake took the slip and looked at it.

"And good luck," Ellen added. Then she shrugged and said, "I guess we'll see on Thursday how you did."

CHAPTER 22

Kaylie felt her phone vibrating and managed to wake up from her afternoon nap and answer it before the caller gave up or it went to voice mail.

She'd crashed out on the bed and awoke wet from sweat. She couldn't seem to get her apartment to stay at the right temperature – one minute it was freezing, so she'd crank up the heater – the next minute it was stiflingly hot.

"Hello?"

"*Yes, it's Dave. Dave Kohler. How you doin' Kaylie?*"

"Been better. What's up?"

"*I just wanted to let you know that I've got you scheduled to meet with Dr. Ian – you know, the abortion doctor.*"

Kaylie's heart leapt and she sat up. "What?"

"*Oh hey – no, don't worry – it's just a meet and greet. I want you guys to meet each other, since he's going to play a more prominent role in the show as we go forward. Once the voting segments begin, he'll be there on stage with you and your other costars and stuff. So, how's seven o'clock tonight – down at the studio?"*

"Uh, sure. Fine. I'll be there."

"Great! I'll send a limo. Hey, thanks Kaylie. Feel better, okay?"

"Uh-huh. Bye."

She flopped down on the pillow, her long strands of damp brown hair matted against the side of her face.

The mention of meeting with an abortion doctor had given her an unexpected jolt.

She didn't like it.

She didn't mind the idea of an abortion doctor – what bothered her was her own reaction.

It was as if some kind of weird maternal instinct was kicking in – and she wasn't ready for that. Kaylie wanted her decisions and her feelings to be ruled by her rational mind, not by her raging hormones.

Speaking of the hormones, the mood swings were getting worse and worse lately. Out of control.

She hatred that feeling of helplessness.

She decided her best bet was to nap for a little longer, and was just drifting away into strange dreams when there was a knock at the door.

She dragged herself out of bed and opened the door, forgetting, in her stupor, to look through the peep hole first.

It was Jake.

She nearly fell over backwards.

He stepped in and caught her by the arm to steady her.

"Whoa, hey there – sorry to give you a shock."

Kaylie was embarrassed. She blushed and pushed her disheveled hair back behind her ear and looked down with a little smile. "Oh, no, no problem. My fault. I-I forgot to check the peep hole. You just uh, surprised – I didn't expect to see you."

They stared at each other in awkward silence for a moment or two.

"I look like crap!" said Kaylie, turning away and abandoning Jake at the door. "Come on in – I'll be right there. Make yourself – uh, at home."

While one camera stayed parked in the living room to observe Jake, the other followed Kaylie to the bathroom, where she looked in the mirror and sighed. Then she quickly rinsed her face and ran a brush through her long hair.

What was he doing here? Was this some part of the show's set up – to create an awkward situation for another ratings boost?

Her emotions ran quickly from anger to despair to excitement to frustration to that butterfly feeling you get when you see the one you love.

Riding the wonderful hormonal rollercoaster.

Kaylie finished her brief primp, then took a deep breath and headed out to the living room.

Jake was sitting in the tan vinyl armchair by the window, looking around nervously, trying to avoid eye contact with the cameras.

"So," said Kaylie, fighting hard to put on a smile and seem chipper, despite her roiling emotions, "how are you doing? What brings you by today?"

"I'm well, thank you. I uh, I just thought we should, you know, talk. About stuff. Since – you know."

Kaylie flopped down on the sofa and put her feet up. "Well, you're going to need to be a little more specific, honey. There's so much we could talk about – you know?"

Jake smiled at her flippant words. He brightened a little. "Well, you know, there's that whole *situation* that started a few weeks back – with, if I recall correctly, a cross between tango and a krump."

Kaylie burst out laughing. "Krump? That was *not* krumping, Jake. More like some kind of dysfunctional robot."

Jake chuckled. "Well, I love the eighties – but I do get my moves a little mixed up sometimes."

"Not *all* your moves."

Jake actually blushed. "I have to say my memory is a little fuzzy. Well, anyway – uh, I just thought it would be a good idea to talk about some stuff – about things going forward."

"Not as an executive producer, then, but as – as the father?"

Jake gulped. "Yes. As the father."

"Since that's what you are."

"Yes."

"And what did you want to talk about?"

"I know that because of this massive monument-to-the-law-of-unintended-consequences – that is, my show – the choice of what to do isn't yours. But, I was just wondering what you plan to do in the event that America votes for you to keep it. I mean, will you raise it, or give it up for adoption, or what?"

"I honestly haven't thought that far ahead. It's all I can do to keep up with the week-to-week of this show, with the day-to-day of my life. I really don't know."

Jake said nothing.

"Why," added Kaylie, "what do *you* think I should do?"

Jake exhaled explosively and sat back. "Huh, I dunno." He shook his head. "You ever consider – you know – ah, never mind."

"What?"

"Forget it." He stood. "Look, I gotta go. I'm sorry I busted in on you like this. We'll talk later."

Kaylie sat on the couch and watched as he left in a hurry. She wondered what had him so spooked.

CHAPTER 23

That night, as the six o'clock hour approached, Kaylie jumped in the shower and got ready for her trip to the studio to meet Dr. Ian.

As usual, the cameras followed her every move as she ransacked her closet trying to find the right outfit, changing in and out of four different sets of blouse and pants before settling on a light blue flower print dress. It was still only mid-October in L.A., so the weather was mild. Besides, she was finding that most of her other clothes – which were normally pretty tight-fitting – were getting a little *too* snug in certain areas.

Mostly where she was starting to get a slight tummy bulge.

A bulge like that would've been cause in the past for a recommitment to the gym, but these days she was so sluggish, the thought of working out was very unappealing – despite both Dr. Cho and Molly the Midwife recommending she get regular exercise.

It was the old paradox – you need to exercise to get more energy, but you need more energy to start exercising.

Kaylie put her hair up in a high-mounted ponytail, put on some dangly silver hoop earrings, and applied her makeup, just as the doorbell rang.

It was the driver – a six-foot-six black man with a trim goatee; these days she was escorted from door to car and back to the door again – "for security purposes," Dave had said.

On the way, Kaylie glanced toward the two camera operators sitting opposite her in the limo, and wondered what the studio did with the hours upon hours of video that they didn't use for producing the one-hour show each week. That had to be a lot of very boring footage. Those poor editors must salivate when something actually *happens*, like when Jake came over earlier – or this meeting tonight.

The car arrived at FBC studios and Kaylie was brought inside to the main office complex, where Dave was on hand to meet her.

"There she is!" he said, grinning. "Thanks for coming. Uh, right this way – we'll have you meet Dr. Ian in a special room we have set up off of Studio 18. He's looking forward to meeting our star."

Kaylie was starting to get a little irritated with the way Dave always referred to her as the "star." This did not feel like the kind of "star" she had come to Hollywood to become. She wanted to act, not be gawked at in the bathroom. She wanted to be involved in a great production of a work of fiction – not involved in this bizarre work of populist "fact."

She had to remind herself why she applied to do this show in the first place: exposure. And exposure was something she was getting plenty of. Money, too.

She just resented Dave's use of the word "star" because it sounded as if he was trying to put one over on her – to make her believe she was something she was not.

This show had very little to do with being an acting star, and more to do with being some kind of guinea pig or freak show participant.

But again, as her frustration welled, she calmed herself by remembering that this was just a stepping stone. A temporary situation. And terrific exposure for her face and her name.

Several other reality TV stars had gone on to achieve success and enjoy careers in their various fields. There was no reason why, five years from now, she couldn't be starring – *starring* – in a big motion picture studio's feature film, with wide release. Or at least a strong supporting role in a Netflix or Amazon original.

As long as she comported herself well, didn't make *too* much of a fool of herself, and managed to get the audience to love her – whatever their divergent opinions on abortion may be.

Keeping that in mind, she decided that each of these staged events – meetings with various professionals like Dr. Ian or whoever – were opportunities for her. These events always appeared on the next week's show, so they were a time when she could really try to shine, and endear America to her.

Not to mention perhaps get the attention of talent scouts.

"Here we are," said Dave, as they reached the door. "Look, I'd introduce you, but I would rather not be on camera for this, so just go on in. He's expecting you."

Kaylie recoiled a little inside at Dave's hypocrisy –
"would rather not be on camera." Huh, must be nice.

"Sure," she said, smiling and on her best behavior.
"Thanks."

She entered (followed by the cameras) and found an
Indian man sitting at what looked like a dining table
reading the latest issue of *People* magazine, which
happened to have Kaylie as the cover story.

The room was decked out like a well-lit studio
apartment – a mini set in the midst of the much larger
studio building.

"Ah, hello, hello," he said, grinning and putting down
the magazine. He stood up and shook her hand. "I am Dr.
Ian R. Chaitanyanam-Burke. You can just call me Dr.
Ian."

Kaylie shook his icy cold hand and smiled. "Nice to
meet you, Dr. Ian." She wondered how she'd have
managed to call him by his last name anyway.

"Come, sit with me over here on the couch – we will
talk."

The two sat at opposite ends of a blue suede couch.

"So, you're an abortion doctor," said Kaylie, trying to
sound light and airy.

"Well, I am a surgeon. I do perform abortions, yes. I
suppose you could call me an abortion doctor – I do
perform about three hundred such procedures a year,
yes."

"Whoa! I mean, wow, you are a busy man."

"They do not take that long. I do not perform them
every day, but most weeks I will have several termination
procedures."

"So, you do all kinds? Like, you know, the D and E
and the IDX and all that?"

"It sounds like you have been doing your studying, yes?" Dr. Ian smiled, displaying the little gap in his teeth.

He pushed up his glasses in the middle, using his index finger, and for a moment, Kaylie saw him as a teenager – a geek. Like looking back in time.

How did someone who was once a kid himself go around now ending the lives of hundreds of kids each year?

She shrugged away the thought, recognizing it as the voice of her mother in her own head. The fact was, nobody knew when a person became a person, and as far as the law was concerned, this nice man was simply earning an honest living providing women with the medical services they requested.

"Uh, yes, I had a visit with a social worker at the Federal Family Planning Commission. She provided me with some educational materials."

"Ah, yes, I recall seeing that on the TV. The FFPC does good work – and they send me lots of business, I am pleased to say. So tell me, how do *you* feel about all this, I am very curious, yes."

"All what? The pregnancy? The show?"

"Yes, the show. This must be a truly singular experience."

"You could say that," said Kaylie, struggling not to roll her eyes. "Being pregnant is one thing – add to that the stress of the show – the cameras, the weekly live broadcast – learning on live TV that the father is the show's creator – and not knowing how this is all going to turn out – well. It's a lot."

"Oh, I can only imagine, yes."

"I mean, it's crazy not knowing from week to week whether I'm going to need your – uh, services."

"Well, this is an unusual case for me, too, Kaylie. Under most circumstances, the women who come to me know exactly what they want – or rather, what they *don't* want – and they know exactly when the procedure will take place. This uncertainty, well, I can see how it would be a bit unnerving for you – tell the truth, it throws me off kilter just a bit!" He chuckled.

"Good to see I'm not the only one who finds this whole thing a little nuts," Kaylie smiled.

Then she got serious. "Tell me, Dr. Ian – what's it like? I mean, it's just a medical procedure, right? Why should everyone get so up in arms about something like having your appendix out?"

He shrugged. "I wonder the same thing sometimes. But I do know this – America is filled with very old-fashioned and superstitious people. From televangelist faith healers to exorcisms to voodoo – people believe in a lot of crazy stuff. But every day I deal with tangible things – real things that I can see with my eyes and touch with my hands. And I know a person when I see one. The things I remove from otherwise healthy women on a regular basis are not people – they're unwanted growths that have, in most cases, been allowed to fester too long. It sounds cold hearted, but science doesn't have a heart, Kaylie. Just a very sharp, rational mind."

"Right. Rational."

"And as a physician, I always have my patients' best interests in mind, yes. If someone wants an elective surgery, and it is something that will not harm them, and in my medical judgment it is advisable for whatever reason – I have taken an oath under which I will provide services accordingly – to meet the needs of the patient. So, my actions are both rational – and ethical."

"Makes sense," Kaylie said. She still wasn't completely convinced, but she didn't want to debate it, either. This man had clearly made his mind up long ago, and then erected a carefully constructed wall of logic to defend against any intruders who may try to tinker with his paradigm. She was sure that was necessary for him to remain so even-keeled.

"I'm sorry," he said, looking abashed. "I didn't mean to lecture you. I'm sure that was all you needed."

"No, it's fine. I asked the question. I was interested in knowing your point of view. Thank you."

"You are welcome. And thank you for meeting with me. One more question for you, if you don't mind, yes?"

"Sure."

"What are the father's wishes in this situation?"

That question threw Kaylie. She gulped and shifted a little in her seat.

"I, uh, I don't know. We talked, but didn't really get to that. I honestly hadn't given *his* wishes a second thought. I mean, it's not relevant, is it?"

Dr. Ian crossed his legs and leaned back in the cushions.

"Any relevance it has – is entirely up to you."

CHAPTER 24

With the big ratings jump last week, the show was moved to a new studio – a much bigger auditorium with a balcony level.

Forty-five hundred in the packed audience.

Including George and Ellen, who sat in a special section of the balcony. Jake watched from the booth, while Kaylie waited in the Green Room for the show to start.

Five minutes out, Jake noticed Kaylie in the preview monitor, wiping away tears. He asked to borrow the chyron operator's headset and opened the channel to Tracy the assistant floor director.

"Hey, Tracy. Ask her if she's all right."

Tracy relayed the message, then spoke back through the headset. *"She says she's fine."*

Jake turned to the sound board operator. "Hey, can you open her mic?"

Her mic was opened, and he asked Tracy to ask Kaylie if she was sure.

"*Yeah, I'm just having a little hormonal attack*," said Kaylie on the screen. "*I'm sure I'll be laughing it up with Troy in another five minutes. It's like the weather in Southern Oregon, ya know? If you don't like my mood, wait a couple minutes and it'll change.*"

The mic was closed and the one minute warning given.

Jake sat back on his stool and unconsciously held his breath.

In the Green Room, Kaylie held her breath for the final few seconds of the countdown to air.

The show opened with a new graphic intro. The music was the same orchestrated, dramatic fanfare, but now the screen was filled with a CG animation of a woman's silhouette, with a growing belly and a question mark that grew in the belly to fill the screen.

The open dissolved to the camera one stage view of Troy Tanner. Tonight he was dressed in a sharp black suit with a bright blue shirt and plain gold tie.

"Welcome! This . . . is *Canceled* – week four of the show, and week ten of the pregnancy – and have we got a show for you tonight! But before we get to that, welcome to our new digs!"

He spread his arms wide, and the camera panned in a slow three-sixty, showing the entire theater full of screaming, cheering viewers, and returned to Troy.

"That's right folks, we're now housed in the James Brown Memorial Theater at FBC Studios – and I . . . feel . . . *good!*"

The crowd erupted in another round of cheering and whistling.

"Huuuh! Thank you, thank you. Now – on with tonight's show. We'll watch Kaylie as she meets once more with her OB/GYN, the lovely Dr. Jenn Cho. Also, we'll check out a very special conversation between Kaylie and the father, Jake Granville, at her apartment. Then later, we'll pop in on Kaylie's first meeting with our very own Dr. Ian!"

More cheering.

"And then – tonight is the night, ladies and gentlemen – the very first chance for *your* voice to be heard. At the end of the show tonight, we'll open up the voting app and America will have the first opportunity to give a 'thumbs up' or 'thumbs down' on this pregnancy. Tonight we make history, as, for the first time, we turn one woman's decision into a democratic *event!*"

Once again, the crowd went wild. Troy appeared to be eating it up, beaming from ear to ear. After several seconds, he reined it back in.

"And it all begins . . . after the break."

The camera pulled out and then dissolved to a shot of Kaylie waiting in the Green Room before fading to black for the commercials.

Kaylie let out her breath. She couldn't possibly have been holding it through that whole segment – it just felt like it.

She sat in the Green Room for most of the show, holding her breath through the segments, exhaling for the commercial breaks. At the end of each segment, the camera would show her waiting patiently on the couch, like a lamb awaiting the slaughter.

Finally, the moment she was dreading arrived.

The final segment.

She was brought out on stage and sat on a stool next to Troy.

The much larger crowd took her breath away – she felt overwhelmed and almost broke down in tears again, but managed to hold it together.

She reached down inside to her thespian roots and put on a happy face. Smiled at Troy. Smiled at the crowd.

She knew Mom and Dad were out there somewhere, and that thought gave her a little boost of strength, too.

She wasn't alone.

"And we're back in five, four, three."

The music surged, the little red light on camera one lit up, and Troy lit up like a Christmas tree. "Welcome back for the moment we've all been waiting for!"

Cheers.

"First, let's chat with Kaylie for a few – let's get a sense of how our star feels tonight. Kaylie – how *do* you feel?"

"A little queasy," she said with a sheepish smile.

Pure acting.

Truth was she was scared to death, and for some reason she couldn't put her finger on, she felt a little angry, too.

But tonight, for Troy, for the studio audience in the grand James Brown Memorial Theater – and for America – she was chipper, excited, and "a little queasy."

"I bet those butterflies are doing acrobatics in your belly," said Troy, doing his own acting job, pretending to show compassion. "What else – what do you think is going to happen tonight?"

"I think millions and millions of people are going to open that app and swipe up or down. And I think the first of many weekly decisions will be made. Made for me."

"And how do you think they'll vote? Any predictions?"

"Troy, I predict that Americans will vote their conscience. That they will do what they each, in their hearts, believe is right." Kaylie looked into the camera and smiled sweetly.

"Well, now I don't know what to say," said Troy. "You stole my line!"

Kaylie just shrugged and smiled.

"Well, there you have it folks. And now, if you have downloaded the app, the voting is officially . . . open. Swipe up to vote for Kaylie to continue with the pregnancy, and swipe down if you want her to go see Dr. Ian and take care of business. Again, that's *up* for keep it, and *down* to end it. Simple as that. But make sure you're sure, because the app allows only one vote per week, and no do-overs."

Kaylie maintained her smile, though her face was starting to get tired. Funny how it doesn't get tired when the smile is natural.

"And tune in next Thursday for another week in the life of Kaylie Adams, along with, of course, the results from this historic vote. Goodnight everyone!"

The crowd roared, the credits rolled, and the floor director started directing the team to clean up and shut down for the night, as the crowd filed out, murmuring and swiping madly as they went.

Kaylie's plastic smile disappeared and she made her way off stage, headed to the dressing room where she intended to have a good solid cry – cameras or not.

CHAPTER 25

Bruce Adams published his latest updates to www.savekayliesbaby.com and closed the lid on his laptop. He'd added a link to the FBC voting app with a plea to "do the right thing."

The Portland airport, PDX, was good for getting work done while waiting for a flight – with strong WiFi available almost everywhere and plenty of comfortable seats near the gate area.

He'd managed to get some time off work – despite being pretty new at the job – so he could take a trip down to Medford. Both Amanda and Cynthia had asked him (separately) if he could get away to visit for a little while.

Amanda said she wanted some companionship in their parents' big empty old house on Black Oak Drive; Cynthia wanted dinner, a movie, and some "alone-together time."

Time with sis and a date with Cynthia sounded good to Bruce, so he booked a flight for Friday after work.

The flight was only an hour, but after a long day at work digging into code and managing issues with the executives' ever-changing project requirements, Bruce nodded off on the runway at PDX and didn't stir again until the plane was on the ground in Medford.

Amanda was there to pick him up – he spotted her in the small terminal as he came out of the corridor from the gate.

"Hey there, sis!"

"Hi Bruce. I'm glad you could come – how was the flight?"

"Couldn't tell you – I was unconscious for the entire thing."

His dark green suitcase came out on the conveyer and he grabbed it off, extended the handle, and wheeled it behind them as they left the terminal, crossed the street to the parking lot and got in Amanda's Honda hybrid.

"Have you eaten?"

"I grabbed something at PDX, but I could eat again. Did you wait for me to have dinner?"

"Yeah. I was thinking we could grab some Senor Sam's."

"Absolutely. But let's get it to go – I just want to get home and stretch out on the couch."

And stretch he could – at six-foot-six, Bruce needed *two* couches. The Honda could barely contain his legs.

"That'll work for me."

"So, have you been watching the totals?"

"Yeah. I can't believe how close it is."

Bruce was referring to the app's real-time voting totals from last night's show. The producers had decided to keep the voting transparent as a way to entice more people to get the app and vote, as they watched the tally for each position grow. The voting would be open from the end of the Thursday night show, all day Friday, and through the weekend, with voting closing at noon Pacific Time on Monday. However, to maintain suspense, the real-time ticker would be hidden for the final eighteen hours of voting.

"How does it work, anyway?" asked Amanda.

"They've got a pretty amazing system, actually – from an app developer's point of view. FBC has co-opted the government's e-ballot infrastructure, which allows for anonymous voting but constrains it to one vote per user. Essentially, you have to create a unique ID when you install the app, but an individual can only create one, and it's tied to your phone's IMEI as well as the specific user. Yet the individual's personal information is encrypted so nobody knows which user cast which vote. It's ingenious, actually."

"And a little over my artsy-fartsy head, I'm afraid. I'm glad you understand it, though."

"So – where does it stand now?"

"It was basically a dead heat before I left the house." He pulled out his device and opened the app. "Right now it's fifty-point-three percent for keeping the baby, forty-nine-point seven against. And check this out – you can turn on notifications for instant updates if the vote tips the other way. Cool."

"Not really," said Amanda. "Doesn't it bother you that these votes are going to determine our sister's future? Don't you care that they've made a puppet out of her?"

Bruce sighed and looked out the window at the headlights reflecting off the wet road surface. No rain right now, but recently enough to have built up some long puddles along the sides of the road. "Yes, of course I care. I just find the technology fascinating – and you

171

gotta admit the whole idea of this show is marketing gold."

"Yeah – the brain child of the man who got it on with Kaylie. How crazy is that?"

"They claim it's all a coincidence. What do you think?"

"It must be. Otherwise Kaylie would've said. For it to not be a coincidence, Kaylie would've had to be in on the whole thing from the beginning. From what Mom's said, there's just no way."

Bruce put his phone away. "So Mom believes baby Kaylie, and we're supposed to take her word for it, too?"

"Are you serious? You really think this whole thing is a setup? That Kaylie and this Jake guy conspired to put one over on America? I don't think so."

"I don't know what I believe – but that's just a theory that some guys were batting around at the office this week."

"Well, I've been watching the show closely, and it seems to me that Kaylie is on the up and up, here. Either that, or she's the best freakin' actress in Hollywood – and if *that* were the case, then she wouldn't need this job on reality TV. So, by my logic, she's legit, and it's a big coincidence that Jake's the dad."

"Well, that's pretty good logic. Given the facts we know. But maybe there's a lot more money than the prize in it for Kaylie – under the table, of course – enough to convince her to take part in the biggest fraud ever put over on the American people."

"Our sister is not a sell-out."

Bruce could see that Amanda was getting frustrated and was gripping the wheel harder than necessary. He smiled at her. "Amanda, I'm just screwing with you. You know that, right?"

Amanda's right arm shot out and socked Bruce across the chest. "Jerk."

"It's what big brothers are for!"

"Whatever. I should just take you back to the airport."

"You know what, though? I bet there are people across the country tonight having that same conversation – only seriously. As for me, I do believe what Kaylie has said, and that she's genuinely in over her head. And that's why I'll do whatever is necessary to help make sure our whole family – Mom, Dad, Kaylie, you, me – and the unborn – all come out of this thing intact."

"Well, unintended pregnancy is nothing to joke about, Bruce. So I'd appreciate it if you would quit messing with me."

"This whole thing has you kinda worked up, doesn't it?"

"I've had some – friends – who've been through stuff. Nothing's cut and dry, you know?"

"So, are you saying you're not sure if Kaylie should keep the baby?"

"To be honest, I'm not sure what I think. Abortion, adoption, being a mother – only Kaylie really knows what's right for Kaylie."

Bruce remained silent.

"Just don't tell Mom and Dad that I'm on the fence, all right? I don't need them leaning on me right now – and they don't need the extra stress."

"Sure. I'm just surprised, Amanda. I always figured we were on the same page on this issue. I guess too many years in college turned you into a *progressive*, eh?" He smiled.

"No, jerk. I just – never mind. Can we change the subject?"

They cruised through downtown Medford on Riverside Avenue, seeming to hit every red light, until they finally arrived at Senor Sam's. They ordered two burritos and took them home to their parents' spacious old nineteen-sixty-two rambler, surrounded by tall oaks and pines.

They entered and Amanda flicked on the lights, then went to the kitchen to pull some plates and silverware out.

"Wanna stream the show?" she called from the kitchen.

"Again? I thought you wanted to change the subject."

Amanda came in with the utensils and a couple of cans of Pepsi. "Well, I just like watching the scene where Kaylie's chatting with Jake – I'm trying to figure him out, get a sense of where he's coming from. I guess I do have a sort of morbid fascination."

Bruce sat down in front of the TV and cracked open his soda. "I'm sure that Jake guy is just crapping his pants over this. I would be."

"I know – but what does he expect the outcome to be? What does he want?"

"I imagine a sharp TV exec like him wants the ratings to shoot through the roof. He wants to make a bazillion dollars – he wants to become a phenomenon behind the scenes at FBC. Have guaranteed jobs for life."

"But he's *not* behind the scenes anymore. Now he's part of this thing – sucked into his own wicked creation. A little poetic justice, eh?"

"I guess."

They sat and chewed on their food for a few moments.

"You gonna see Cynthia tonight?"

"Nah. She's working the late shift – not off till eleven thirty. I'll be snoring hard by then. We'll hook up tomorrow."

"Got plans for the weekend?"

"Just hang out, I guess. Update the site. Maybe get in touch with some old friends, like Charlie. If he can, I'd like to play a round of golf with him."

"In October?"

"Absolutely. But I think as soon as I'm done with this burrito, I'm gonna crash. It's been a hell of a week."

"Fine – but don't spend all your time here being *not* here. I asked you to visit so I wouldn't be all alone here."

"Okay, okay. I'll be sure to save some time for you, Sis."

⊙

Bruce awoke to a surprise in the early morning light.

Cynthia was lying next to him.

In his bed, in his old bedroom. The room he grew up in.

She was fully clothed, gently snoring, her bobbed blonde hair falling gently across her face.

"Hey," he whispered.

She opened her eyes groggily.

"Where'd you come from?"

"Channel 12 News," she said dreamily.

Bruce chuckled. "Well, Cynthia Davis, Channel 12 News – what's the scoop, live from the scene of Bruce's childhood bedroom?"

"Woman seduces man, story at eleven."

He smiled. "Seriously, though – how'd you get in?"

"I stopped by after work, your sister – the non-famous one – was still up. We chatted for a while – a long while – and she said I should just crash here tonight. I agreed."

Bruce rolled onto his back and threw an arm up under his head. "Huh. Well – I'm glad you're here. Wanna go to breakfast?"

"Go? Why not have breakfast here?"

"You cooking?"

"You got bacon and eggs?"

"We can go find out."

Bruce sprung out of bed and threw on a pair of sweats from out of his suitcase that sat open on his dresser.

He caught a glance of himself in the mirror. His bare chest, once ripped and toned, was starting to show the subtle signs of a career devoted to staring at a computer screen all day. Sure, he was getting to the gym a couple times a week, but that just wasn't cutting it – not since he was eating larger meals than ever and having a hard time saying no to an extra helping of dessert.

He knew eating was his way of dealing with stress – but knowing it was only half the battle. The other half seemed out of his control, and winning the battle really just didn't seem to be a priority at this point in his life.

He liked food, and he would deal with "moderation" at some other time.

"You make the eggs and bacon," he said, "and I'll whip up some pancakes."

Cynthia rolled her eyes. "You've got a hot TV reporter in your bed, and all you can think about is breakfast? What's the matter with you, boy?"

"Man's gotta eat."

He walked out of the room, heading to the kitchen, knowing Cynthia wouldn't be far behind.

And she wasn't. He'd barely opened the box of Bisquick when she came around the corner. "So," she said, "what do you think?"

"Of what?"

"Of your littlest sister's wild situation."

"Heh. Oh yeah, *that*. Well, it is what it is. She got herself in trouble, and in true Kaylie fashion, went one better and got herself in even *more* trouble. And she's finally getting her dream – her face on national television."

"And how do you feel about the – you know – the whole 'life or death' thing with the fetus?"

"That's the saddest part of the whole thing. Kaylie gets fame and money, Jake Granville and FBC get a runaway winner of a show, America gets entertained – and that poor innocent little baby gets to be made into a sport, to live or die at the whim of mob rule – a.k.a. democracy. Definitely sad."

"I saw your website – it looks great. I haven't had a chance to read it – but the layout is really nice – for a pro-life website."

"Thanks. I know you don't agree with me on this issue, but we're talking about my family here. The website is basically just a way to try to reach out – try to make a difference. I know there are already thousands of websites and blogs devoted to each side of Kaylie's issue – but mine is the real deal – the one and only authentic and official family-owned site. Hopefully having our name on it – and my SEO skills – will make sure it ranks highest on Google searches."

"You really think you can make a difference – sway the vote? We're talking about tens of millions of people."

"Voters are individuals. We only need to worry about influencing one at a time."

"Remind me why you didn't follow your father's footsteps into politics? You'd make a great candidate for – something."

Bruce flipped a pancake and caught it in the pan, smiling. "I love the tech too much. That's all. Just love the tech too much."

Amanda wandered in, rubbing the sleep out of her eyes. "I'll take one of those," she said. She reached into the fridge for some orange juice.

"So what about you, Amanda?" asked Cynthia. "Are you a right-wing zealot like your brother here, or are you a liberated woman of the twenty-first century?"

"No comment, Ms. Davis," Amanda chuckled. "Way too early in the morning to face the big questions."

"Oh, come on," said Cynthia, "enquiring minds want to know."

"Fine," said Amanda. "Just between you, me, Bruce and the pancakes – I think America could do us all a big favor – most of all Kaylie – if they just vote to get this over with."

CHAPTER 26

Cynthia waited until she was in her car before reaching into her pocket, pulling out her phone, and stopping the recording.

She always found undercover reporting assignments to be a rush – but this was the first time she'd had occasion to spy on her own fiancée and his family.

And she'd done a terrific job.

Between the late night candid discussion with Amanda, and the things Bruce had said over breakfast, she would have some nice dirty laundry to air.

Well, the network would.

They had contacted her specifically, and her news director at the station had given her permission to spend the next few weeks – however long was needed – to work directly for FBC and give them whatever scoops they needed.

An assignment like this, if carried off well, could land her a job at the network in L.A.

She felt a little bad about the subterfuge, but when she balanced it against her career aspirations, and considered that this family affair was not exactly private anymore – she found it surprisingly easy to justify her behavior.

Besides – she'd been having second thoughts about Bruce for over a month now – ever since she'd met the new six o'clock news anchor, Brett Leamey. Or, Dreamy Leamey, as the girls around the station called him. She preferred to think of him as Steamy Leamey, and figured a network gig just might get his attention and send some of that hotness her way.

Despite the clear stone on her ring finger, Cynthia had decided to keep her options open – so she only wore the ring around Bruce and his family.

She slipped it off and placed it in her purse, then drove back to the station to begin editing the audio and cut her own script track for upload to the network.

If Bruce's little sister could sleep her way onto national television, Cynthia wasn't above doing a little dirty work, herself.

Boyfriends and fiancées came and went, but a shot at the network spotlight didn't come along every day.

CHAPTER 27

Kaylie showed up at the Santa Monica offices of Dr. Len Hamlin at four o'clock on Wednesday afternoon, her two camera people in tow.

She'd never seen a shrink before, and wasn't really looking forward to this experience. Although she wouldn't mind having someone neutral to talk to about her crazy life, she imagined a stereotypical psychiatrist exchange: her lying on a leather couch, him probing her with "Tell me about your childhood."

She took the elevator up to the third floor and down the hall to a pair of teakwood double doors. She entered and spoke to a receptionist, much like any doctor's office.

"Hi, I'm here to see Dr. Hamlin – I'm Kay –"

"Kaylie Adams! Oh my gosh!" exclaimed the young, short-haired brunette at the desk.

"Uh, yes," said Kaylie, unprepared for this little moment of idol worship.

"I'm sorry," said the girl, striving to curb her enthusiasm, "it's not like we don't get a number of celebrities in here. But I'm just a big fan." She grinned. "Love your attitude, love how you talk to Troy Tanner on the show – and I think you've got an amazing set of cohunes. It takes serious guts to do a show like *Canceled*."

"Well, thanks," said Kaylie. She found herself standing a little taller, and realized this was the first time anybody had had anything good to say about her for being on the show. She had subconsciously assumed the world hated her, and she walked around under a self-imposed cloud of shame. "I appreciate that. So, is the doctor available for my appointment?"

"Oh – sure. Sorry. Uh, can you just fill out this and he'll be ready for you shortly." The girl handed Kaylie a tablet open to a digital intake form, and Kaylie sat down in one of the blue microfiber chairs to fill it out.

She turned it in, the girl reached out and shook her hand with a smile. "By the way, I'm Felicity Jones. Again, it's great to meet you. The doc should be right out."

Kaylie sat down and considered her first fan encounter. Not as she had ever dreamed, but still a good thing.

After a few minutes of staring at the wall, feeling like Felicity was staring at her from the side, a man came out from the private door behind the reception desk. Kaylie had the fleeting thought that she wished all the time she spent waiting could be edited out of her life, the way it would be cut from the video feed for tomorrow night's inevitable vignette.

She assumed the man was the previous patient leaving, until Felicity said, "Here's Len now."

Hamlin didn't look the way she envisioned a shrink would look. No wooly sweater, no glasses, no pipe between his lips – and no hair. Hamlin was only in his late thirties, with head shaved, a shaggy ginger goatee, and a well-toned body under a tight black t-shirt. He wore a small black ring pierced above his left eyebrow. He put out his hand to shake hers, revealing his beefy forearms, covered in sleeves of tattoos. "Hi there! I'm Len Hamlin."

"Hello, doctor, I'm Kaylie."

He waved his hand dismissively. "Call me Len. Come on in."

Kaylie entered what she expected to be a mellow study with books lining the walls and a fireplace in the corner. Instead, it looked like a bachelor den – two pinball machines, a video game console hooked up to a big flat screen TV mounted on the wall, a couple of overstuffed recliners and three cushy couches – and the crowning touch of a shiny, vintage Harley Davidson parked at one end of the room on a small pedestal.

"You like the place?" asked Len, taking a seat in one of the recliners. The camera operators took up positions at each end of the room where they could cross-shoot Kaylie and Len's faces but stay out of the way.

"Uh, yeah. Just not what I expected." She sat in the other recliner.

"And what were you expecting?"

"I dunno – a stuffy little library. A day bed. A desk of some sort. And a clipboard or note pad or something."

"First time seeing a shrink, huh?"

She smiled. "Yes. I guess my expectations were based on what I've seen on bad TV shows."

"Speaking of bad TV shows," said Len. He said no more, but his eyes darted to one of the cameras.

"I know. So, how do you feel about having a private counseling session broadcast to the world?"

Len frowned in mock anger. "Hey, I'm supposed to be the one asking about feelings." Then he chuckled and shrugged. "Eh, it's fine with me. Confidentiality rules exist to protect the patient. In this case, you've waived your right to privacy in this setting, so it's really no skin off my nose. Hell, you've waived your right to privacy in *all* settings, haven't you?"

"Yeah. I can't take a crap without a camera capturing the precious moment for posterity."

"And how do you feel about that?"

"How do you think? It sucks. But, I also know that I have only myself to blame. I signed up for this show."

"Blame. Hmm. Interesting." He pushed the recliner back to raise up his feet. "So, are you finding the pressure of this experience . . . taxing?"

"Oh yeah. It's hard enough to be pregnant. And to not know what you're going to do. But then, to have that choice being decided by others, and to be under constant scrutiny – well, let's just say that it wears on you. My doctor and the midwife have both been unable to put an end to these headaches. I try not to complain, but it's really getting to me."

"Hmm." Len pushed the recliner back another notch, lowering his head and raising his feet. "Would you be interested in a possible way to relieve your headaches?"

"Of course!"

"Ever heard of hypnotherapy?"

"Like, you wanna hypnotize me?"

"Is that a request?"

"Ha – no. I mean, yes, if you think it'll help – I'm game for anything at this point."

"Okay. First, you need to do this."

184

"What?"

"This. Put your feet up. Kick back. Relax."

Kaylie pushed back and the chair took the shape of Len's. "Okay, now what?"

Len stayed where he was and began the process without further explanation. "Ten. Focus on one of the black circles on my ceiling and listen closely to the sound of my voice. Nine. Take three deep breaths, letting them out very slowly through your nose. Eight. Imagine the rest of this room is a white, formless void. Seven. Imagine you are floating an inch above the recliner. Six. Focus on your skin – every pore, every hair follicle, the temperature in the room, the sensation of the air moving. Five. Close your eyes. Four. Take three more deep breaths, counting to five in your mind as you exhale each breath. Three. With your eyes closed, imagine that circle on the ceiling. Two. Imagine yourself inside the circle. One. In your mind, invite me into that circle with you."

Kaylie felt like she was transported to another world, where the world was white like a snowstorm, but peaceful as a summer's afternoon. She was warm and relaxed. In all directions, a thin black line formed an unbroken horizon. And Len stood before her, strong and friendly, comfortable and safe. When he spoke, his voice seemed to echo in her head.

"Kaylie, tell me about your childhood."

Kaylie laughed out loud. "Ha! I knew you were going to ask me that!"

"Are you ready?"

"For what?" she barely moved her lips when she spoke.

"For everything coming your way?"

Her brow creased gently. "I don't think so. I don't know what to expect, so how can I be ready?"

185

"Does anybody know their own future?"

"No."

"Are some people ready, anyway?"

"Yes."

"How can you make yourself ready?"

She shook her head slightly. "I – I don't know."

"How do others ready themselves for the unknown?"

"I guess they – they consider the possibilities, and come up with a plan for dealing with each scenario they can think of."

"Yes. What are the possibilities for you?"

"I – I don't know."

"Don't know? Or don't want to think about them – don't want to face those scenarios?"

"D – don't want to."

"Do you believe that having a plan in place for each of the most likely possibilities will help you have a little more peace?"

"Yes."

"It will. And peace inside will relieve your headaches. Do you want that?"

"Yes."

"What are the possibilities?"

"Um. At any point, the voters could make me go see Dr. Ian and end the pregnancy. Or, the voters could make me carry the baby to term. Or something could happen to the baby at some point – an injury, or a miscarriage."

"Any other possibilities?"

"If I have to have the baby, I could raise it myself, or give it up for adoption."

"Any other possibilities?"

"A crazy viewer could decide to hurt me or my family."

"More?"

"I could marry Jake Granville and settle down and have a family."

"*More?*"

"I could die in childbirth. I could have the abortion and regret it for the rest of my life. I could step out in front of a bus tomorrow. I could run away and hide."

"*Good. I think that covers all the plausible options. "Now, think about each of those, and – just in your own head – think about what you would do – and what you would FEEL – in each of those circumstances. Take a few moments.*"

Kaylie ran through the scenarios in her head, honestly appraising each situation in as much detail as she could stomach, and ran through the whole gamut of emotions regarding each possibility. Finally she said, with tears streaming from the corners of her closed eyes, "They all suck."

"*They do. But they each have redeeming qualities, too. Think about them again, but focus on what might be good about each possibility.*"

Kaylie was silent for a few minutes, and at one point started to fall asleep, but refocused on the exercise. "Okay. So, it's not all bad."

"*Good. Now, I'm going to slowly count from ten to one. While I do that, I want you to take all of the good things – all the positive things about each of those circumstances, and package them up in a little round silver box – no bigger than an egg. Stuff them in, if you have to. All the collective goodness of your many possible futures. Put them in that little box. Ten, nine, eight, seven, six, five . . . *"

Kaylie pictured herself in that white circle, stuffing good stuff into the box. The good stuff was like multi-colored play-dough that resembled the things she thought of, but was malleable and able to be pushed into the tiny box.

"*Four, three, two, one.* Open your eyes, Kaylie."

Kaylie blinked a few times and looked over at Len. He was sitting in the recliner, right where he was before. How long before?

"Was I asleep for long?"

"You were never asleep. But you were under hypnosis for close to twenty minutes. And you did great!"

She sat the chair upright and took a deep breath. Then she smiled. "My headache's gone!"

"You just had some roadblocks in your mind that were impeding your recovery. There's a strange and mysterious relationship between thoughts and the physical world, Kaylie. All we did was loosen things up in there a little." He tapped his temple. "You shouldn't be bothered by the headaches anymore. And if you are, all you'll have to do is look at this, or just hold onto it."

He handed her a shiny chrome-plated box, rounded at the corners, about the size of a small egg.

"Put that on your keychain. Reach into your pocket and rub it between your fingers if you feel a headache coming on. If it gets bad, pull it out and look at it."

"What's in it?"

"Nothing. Everything. Only you really know – you filled it up yourself."

"What are you, the Wizard of Oz?" she smiled.

"Just Len, the shrink to the stars," he grinned. "Now, we have almost a half hour left – you up for a game of pinball?"

CHAPTER 28

"The episode: five. The pregnancy week: eleven. But the most important numbers tonight? You'll have to stick around to the end for the vote tally. Welcome to *Canceled*!"

Troy Tanner wore black slacks over black snakeskin boots, a white shirt and a pale yellow silk vest with a silver bolo. Kaylie figured it was some strange attempt by the costume department to coordinate with tonight's big country musical guests.

Troy grinned widely and spread his arms as if to embrace America, and the screen in the Green Room showed his image dissolve into the CG opening sequence.

Following his announcement of what to expect in tonight's show – a quick checkup with Dr. Cho, a foot massage with Molly, and an eventful and healing visit with Dr. Len Hamlin – he teased the upcoming voting results and tossed to the break.

Kaylie sat through nearly another hour in the Green Room, watching her life played back (in edited form), looking into the camera before each commercial break. The musical guests were great – but it was hard to just relax and enjoy the music. She reached into her pocket and rubbed her little silver box, took a deep breath, and felt a little better.

Finally, she was brought out on stage for the final segment.

She sat in her stool next to Troy.

Then, to her surprise, Jake was brought out, too.

And then Mom and Dad.

They wanted to get the full spectrum of reactions to the news.

The first result.

Technically, it could all end here tonight.

If America decreed it, she would visit Dr. Ian live on next week's show, and then walk away from this nightmare.

Walk away rich.

And be done with this.

Take a break for a while, then talk to her agent and new contacts about some acting jobs.

Maybe that would be best.

Her hand moved unconsciously to her gently bulging belly as the crowd roared.

The stage lights seemed so bright tonight.

"Ladies and gentlemen, please welcome to the stage the *Canceled* family – George, Ellen, and of course, Jake." He turned to the guests. "Thanks for joining us tonight. Glad to see you on your feet again, George. So, are you all ready for this?"

Kaylie recalled Len's words – "are you ready?"

Once more, she reached into her pocket and felt the little box of goodness.

Yes, she was ready.

"In our nationwide poll of viewers, conducted from last Thursday night until just one hour ago, utilizing our secure voting app, we received more than *seventy-seven million* votes."

Big cheer.

"That's right, ladies and gentlemen, seventy-seven million. A very impressive response. Obviously, America cares what happens here tonight. And we'll find out what's going to happen – right after the break."

Kaylie was starting to despise those words – "right after the break." It wasn't just teasing the viewers, it was putting her life on hold to sell cars and computers and whatnot – and it was torturing her.

Just get it over with, already!

She glanced at Mom and Dad, who were standing together, holding hands tightly.

Jake looked frozen in place, his hands clasped behind his back. He wore a nice dark tan suit, his hair was slicked back, and he needed a shave.

Was this what it was going to be like every week? Like a defendant in a capital murder case waiting for the note to be passed from the jury foreperson to the judge?

The show returned, and Troy stepped to Kaylie, put his arm around her. "Here we go. Let's have you step to center stage, for us."

Kaylie let Troy guide her to the mark on the stage. Camera one framed her and Troy, with Mom, Dad, and Jake in the background.

"I hold here the results." Troy held up an envelope.

The crowd cheered. Then they fell silent, and the music played a low drum roll accented by high electronic sounds here and there that barely perceptibly mirrored the show's theme music.

He opened the envelope and read it aloud. "Tonight, Kaylie will . . . *not* terminate the pregnancy. The fetus will remain on the show for at least another week! And of course, Kaylie, too!"

The crowd erupted into a cacophony of cheers, boos, whistles and clapping.

Kaylie's legs felt weak, but did not buckle. She applauded meekly, along with Troy, like all good game show contestants are encouraged to do. She forced a smile, unsure how she really felt in that moment.

She could see in the small stage-facing monitor at the edge of the riser that behind her, Dad exhaled heavily and Mom brought her hand up to her chest with a look of relief.

And Jake seemed to smile. Just a little.

CHAPTER 29

Jake found himself back in his apartment through most of the next week.

Again, the shades were drawn, and he sat on the couch.

He was starting to feel like this little cave, with its dim lighting and quiet ambience, was an escape of sorts – a last refuge from the madness that was his life, which was spinning out of control.

He also felt that this place of resort would soon be just another one of the off-site sets of FBC – another window into the world of one of the characters of *Canceled*.

He could feel the walls closing in, as a prelude to their explosion.

Or implosion.

Soon, Dave would assign a full-time crew to Jake, and his privacy would be at an end. At least for the next several months. And, depending on the level of phenomenon the show achieves, possibly for a lot longer than that. He could wind up with plenty of residual "celebrity" status, appearing on the cover and between the covers of the nation's seediest tabloids for years to come.

And he would deserve that, too.

Poetic justice.

His phone buzzed on the coffee table, the vibration causing it to slide a few inches to the left. Another buzz, and it nearly fell off.

Jake caught it and answered it.

"Jake Granville."

"*Hey Jake. It's me. Kaylie.*"

He sat up straight. "Hey. How you doing?"

"*Well, I want to talk. Face to face.*"

"Where?"

"*I'm next door at my parents' place. I can come right over.*"

"Uh, okay. Sure. See you in a minute."

He hung up and went to the bathroom, checked his look in the mirror. He ran his hands through his thick black hair, then pulled off his t-shirt and threw on a blue polo and ran his hands through his hair again, just as the knock came at the door.

He opened it up.

Kaylie stood there, looking particularly good. Sort of – radiant.

Her hair was pulled back in a pony tail, and she wore a pink blouse that accented her tummy bulge, along with a black skirt that came down just above her knees, and a pair of sandals.

A pair of camera operators standing behind her completed the outfit.

"Hi."

"Hi. Uh, come in." He stepped aside.

"Actually, I vaguely recall – from the night we first met – that you have a really nice car. My dad has admitted to drooling over it a little himself. I was wondering if you would show it to me."

Jake was surprised at this odd turn. "Uh, sure." He reached into his jeans pocket and felt his keys. "Let's go."

They headed out to the parking lot, saying nothing as they went. One camera followed, and one went ahead and shot back at them.

They reached his AC Cobra, which was parked tail-in. Kaylie ran her fingertips along the shining fender. "Dad wasn't kidding – this is sweet."

"Thanks. I actually bought it from my uncle – it's all original. And crazy fast."

"Can I sit in it?"

Jake opened the door for her and she climbed into the low-slung sports car. Then he went around and got in next to her. "This is actually the original radio, too."

"Start her up – I want to hear the engine."

Jake smiled at her unexpected interest in hot cars, and turned the key. It growled a low, rumbling sound as the eight big-bore cylinders chugged to life.

Then Kaylie leaned over and whispered in his ear, "Get us out of here, now."

Jake looked at her, perplexed.

She leaned in again, placing her hand on his cheek, "I said, step on it! Leave the camera goons in the freaking dust!"

Jake glanced at the camera operators, who were standing each side of the vehicle.

He slowly released the emergency brake.

Then he threw it into gear and peeled away with engine roaring, throwing up a cloud of white smoke that enveloped the camera operators, who fought through the fog and tried to run after the sports car.

"Yeee-arghh!" whooped Kaylie as they bounced out of the parking garage, scraping bottom and throwing up some sparks.

Jake couldn't believe they'd just ditched the camera crew. He simultaneously felt heroic and like a self-saboteur.

After all, this was *his* show.

Kaylie turned to him, grinning, her ponytail whipping in the wind. "I feel so liberated!"

Jake smiled. He may have been helping her to breach her contract, but that smile seemed to make it all worth it. "Where to?"

"I don't care – anywhere. How about the beach?"

Jake glanced in his rear-view and said, "Don't look now, but I think they're actually *chasing* us!"

Of course, Kaylie did look. And there it was, the white FBC production van, two cars back, swerving and trying to pass the vehicles blocking its way.

Jake dropped a gear and floored it, weaving in and out of the traffic like an Indy car driver.

"Wow!" said Kaylie, holding the door with one hand and the dash with the other. "You're good!"

"I like speed," Jake said. "I have a '69 Ferrari Dino I keep out at the raceway – run some races during the summer."

He turned a sharp right, then a left, one more right, and then stepped on it, jumping on the 405, where he opened it up to a hundred.

"There's no way that van will catch us now," he yelled over the lashing wind and road noise.

At the I-10 junction, he headed west and then went south to Venice Beach.

For the first week of November in Southern California, it was actually a little cool – overcast, with a breeze. The surf was strong, and plenty of wetsuited boarders were riding the waves at the Breakwater.

They parked and got out to walk along the boardwalk.

Jake inhaled the salty air, glad for the reprieve from his self-imposed house arrest.

Kaylie looked at him and giggled, then said, "Thanks. I can't tell you how much I appreciate this. It's been almost six weeks since I *didn't* have a camera following my every move."

"Well, it's the least I could do, considering the whole thing is my fault."

Kaylie looked at Jake. "You were just doing your job – you create reality TV shows. People sign up to go on them." She laughed. "And then we go crazy and kidnap ourselves just to get away for a few precious minutes of solitude!"

"Well, you're still not alone."

"Believe me, this *feels* alone, compared to having those camera people around all the time. This feels – normal – for a change. Besides, I like your company."

A portly man in a Dodgers baseball cap came out of nowhere and said in a nasally voice, "Hey, aren't you Kaylie and Jake, from *Canceled*?"

Before they could confirm or deny his recognition, he had grabbed his iPhone and started recording video of the pair.

"So much for anonymity," said Jake. He grabbed her hand and started to run. "Come on."

"So much for no cameras!" she said, hurrying along with him.

They trotted back toward the car, and as they arrived, so did the white FBC van.

"What the?" said Jake.

One of the camera operators jumped out, followed closely by the other.

"How did you know where we were?" asked Jake.

"GPS," said the crewman, his face turning from an angry scowl to a smug smirk. "Kaylie's phone."

Enough said.

Between the escape, the chase, their apprehension, and the iPhone guy (who would likely make a killing selling the video to the network) – Jake was sure the show would have plenty of material for a juicy segment in tomorrow's show.

"I'm sorry," he said to Kaylie. "Sorry we couldn't get away for longer."

"It's all right. A few minutes was better than nothing. Thanks for trying."

They got back in the car and drove back to the apartment, this time at legal speeds. The camera van tailed closely behind. The Cobra being a two-seater, the camera guys didn't have much choice but to follow and shoot out their van window.

"Can I ask you a question?" asked Kaylie as they pulled into the parking garage.

"Sure."

"The other day at my apartment – it seemed like you were going to say something. What was it?"

Jake knew exactly what she was talking about.

"I don't know what you're talking about."

"Huh. Okay. It was right before you left in such a hurry."

"I dunno. Sorry, I don't remember."

"Now's your chance, Jake – before the cameras catch back up to us. The van is pulling in now. Tell me."

"It was nothing, really."

"Fine. Well, thanks for the ride," she said tersely, getting out and slamming the car door.

Jake watched her as she strode to her parents' apartment door and entered without looking back at him.

The cameras followed her in.

He exhaled a melancholy sigh, wishing already that he'd gotten over himself and answered her question truthfully.

CHAPTER 30

"Episode six, week 12 of the pregnancy – and one hell of a show for you tonight!"

Troy stood center stage in a pale blue suit, white dress shirt, no tie. Tonight he sported the beginnings of a goatee and his hair was slicked flat. His change from week to week in attire and facial hair made it seem to Jake as if he were trying to find the right look, but couldn't quite hit it – even though he looked good regardless. When the show was over tonight, Jake was going to mention it to Dave and see if they could get a little more visual consistency from their host.

Meanwhile, Jake sat on the couch in the Green Room. Kaylie sat at the other end. The two didn't speak.

The screen switched to a shot of the two of them as Troy said in voiceover, "And we'll also get these two out on stage tonight for a little discussion about these hijinks," the screen changed to show the high-speed chase from the angle of the FBC van. "That's right folks

– we'll hear all about their little run to the beach – and much more – tonight, on a special two-hour episode of *Canceled*."

When the show returned, a series of vignettes brought viewers up to speed on the latest in Kaylie's life, from a follow up visit with Dr. Len Hamlin (where she got to know her fan, Len's assistant, Felicity, a little better), and another appointment with Dr. Cho, in which she learned more about the current development stage of the fetus.

Jake actually found the whole thing fascinating, and could understand why the show was now garnering close to a thirty share – virtually unheard-of in television history.

After an hour of watching the details of Kaylie's life unfold, the second half of the show started, and Jake and Kaylie were brought on stage.

"So, tell us, Kaylie – first off – how are you feeling? I mean, with the pregnancy?"

"Not bad, I guess," said Kaylie, who was wearing a flattering red dress tonight. "I'm a little tired, but the headaches are almost all gone, the nausea has gone away, and I generally have more energy than I did the first few weeks."

"Speaking of having energy – my goodness! – can we roll that tape once more, with the high-speed chase?"

In the booth, McIntyre took his cue and the large screen behind the stage dissolved from a view of the stage to a shot of smoke clearing and Kaylie hollering "Yee-argh!" as sparks flew from the undercarriage of Jake's Cobra.

"I'll say you've got some energy," said Troy, and the crowd laughed. "Let's talk about yesterday, and what happened there. Was that a planned thing, or just some spur-of-the-moment pregnant-girl madness?"

"Honestly, I planned the whole thing," said Kaylie, surprising everyone, including Jake. "I needed some time away from the cameras. I wanted a chance to speak to Jake alone. So, I made it happen."

"And what did you talk about, once you got him alone?"

"Now, what would be the point of telling you? There's a reason I wanted the privacy."

"Well, well. Okay then. Not even a hint?"

"Truth is, we didn't even get a chance to talk. And when we did, we didn't."

"Beg your pardon?"

"Let's just say Jake is a man. Communication doesn't come naturally. Am I right, ladies?"

All the women in the audience let out a collective cheer.

Jake clenched his jaw.

"What do you have to say for yourself, Jake?" asked Troy.

"Not much, obviously," said Jake, throwing a glare at Kaylie. He shrugged. "I was just out for a nice drive. I really don't know what all the fuss is about."

"Well, Jake, I think you do. Your little escapade constituted a breach of Kaylie's contract. That jaunt will have consequences."

"Such as?"

"We'll find out – after the break."

Jake squirmed a little on his stool as the commercials played. Consequences? Why hadn't Dave mentioned any of this?

Before he had time to process anything, they were back on the air.

"Welcome back, folks. We have Kaylie Adams and Jake Granville on the stage with us tonight at the James

Brown Memorial Theater. And Jake, tonight, we have some good news, and some bad news for you. We'll start with the bad news."

Jake gulped.

To his great surprise, Tom Highgate, CEO of the network, walked out on stage wearing a black suit and holding a manila envelope. The old man strutted across the stage toward Jake, a stern look on his face.

He stopped beside Jake and handed him the envelope. Troy handed Tom the mic, and he said, "Jake Granville – you're fired. Those are your severance papers. Since there's clearly a conflict of interest here, and since we can't *undo* what you've done to land yourself here as a participant on the show, our only recourse is to terminate you. After the show, clean out your office."

With that, he handed the mic back to Troy, turned, gave a little wave to the audience, and briskly walked right back off the stage.

Jake was stunned.

He blinked repeatedly, his mouth a little open, the hand holding his walking papers shaking slightly.

Didn't see that one coming.

Wait, this can't be happening. He'd taken years and so much hard work to build up this career.

Can't. Be. Happening.

The crowd was going crazy.

This *is* happening.

And, the more he thought about it, the more he realized it was inevitable.

Should've seen it coming.

Troy spoke into the mic and tried to gain control of the audience reaction. "Folks, folks, thank you, thank you, yes, amazing." He waved his arms in a downward fanning motion, and the crowd quieted down. "Jake

Granville, former VP of New Network Programming for FBC – tell us, how do you feel?"

Jake bit his lip and shook his head slowly, closing his eyes for a moment. Then he opened them and looked at the microphone that was shoved in his face, looked up at Troy's beaming face, and glanced over at Kaylie, who looked shocked and saddened at this turn of events.

Then he took a deep breath and exhaled, and grabbed the mic. "I can see why FBC felt it was appropriate that I leave the network, given the obvious conflict." He looked down and shook his head again. "But the way it was done – I don't think it was all that appropriate." Then he gave a quick, rueful smile. "Wait – I take that back. It was unpleasant. It was callous. It was humiliating. But, in all reality, it was, you could say, entirely appropriate – a little poetic justice for me, I guess."

"And what are you going to do now?" asked Troy.

Jake shrugged. "Look for a job."

"Well, we may just have one for you," said Troy. "After the break, we'll break the *good* news to you. Stick around."

They went to commercial, and Kaylie leaned toward Jake and said, with true sadness in her eyes, "I'm so sorry, Jake."

"*You're* sorry? Thanks, but this is all my doing. All my undoing. It's all – it's all right. Don't worry about it. I'm not going to be out on the street any time soon – I've done all right for myself."

"Huh – my folks wouldn't let that happen anyway – they like you so damn much they'd probably take you in."

Jake smiled. "Heh. Well, it won't come to that. But thanks."

"And we're back in five, four, three," said the floor director.

"Okay, Jake," said Troy, jumping right in. "Now for the good news. It's time to reveal the results of last week's voting. But we're introducing a new feature. This is the end of the first trimester – that's right folks, we are one third of the way there – and we'll also do this at the end of the second trimester, if we make it that far. It's called the trump card show. What that means, Jake, is we will reveal the vote results, and you will have your own vote – worth two hundred million votes. That is, your vote, Jake, can trump them all. If you decided for an alternate decision, you may use that trump card to reverse the call. But *only tonight*."

The crowd went crazy, with shouts and cheers and a strong contingent of booing.

"And for the end of the second trimester, the trump card will go to Kaylie. So, Jake, are you ready to have the most powerful vote in the land?"

Jake nodded.

"Ladies and gentlemen," said Troy, the lights dimming and the drum roll music playing, "during this past week, you voted. One hundred and thirty *million* votes." Cheering, then hush. "And the result was remarkably close. To show just how close, we have to go out to *four* decimal places. The result: forty nine point nine nine nine eight – said 'stay the course' – and fifty point zero zero zero two said go see Dr. Ian and end this thing!"

The crowd went nuts.

"Now, Jake. Jake. Here's your chance to reassert some of the authority that was just stripped away from you on live national television. You have the power – this week only – right now – to change that vote, or to let it stand. What are you going to do? Will you use your trump card?"

Jake felt his heart beating hard. He could feel the sweat starting to moisten his brow. He looked at the floor, then over at Kaylie. Her face was a mix of emotions that gave him no clue as to what she might want him to do.

He gulped hard and breathed deep. "Troy, I'm pulling the trump card. I vote she keeps it."

The crowd leapt to its feet, a virtual riot. Screaming, whistling, cheering, booing and jeers.

Troy let it go on for nearly thirty seconds before regaining control. "Folks, folks. Don't worry. This is just the way we play this game. If you're feeling disenfranchised, vote again this week, and next week, and the week after that. There's always another chance to make your voice heard. And folks, we promise, there's only the one more trump card."

The crowd was still loud, but they sat back down and began to settle in as Troy wrapped things up.

"So again, pull out your phone, login to the app…because we're opening this week's voting right now. Here's your chance to change – or not change – a life. Or two, or three lives – it all depends on how you look at it. That's our show tonight, folks. More big surprises next week. Thanks for watching. Good night."

The lights came up in the theater and everyone filed out boisterously, cell phones in hand, swiping away.

Troy bounced off to his dressing room, and Kaylie put a compassionate hand on Jake's shoulder as she walked past to leave.

Jake knew she cared about his job loss, but still couldn't tell if she was glad or mad that he had trumped the vote.

What they needed was another trip to the beach.

And next time, he wouldn't be afraid to share his true feelings.

After all, he had nothing to lose now.

◈

Jake opened the door to his FBC office and flicked on the light.

Two cameras were waiting for him, shooting him as he came in and sighed heavily.

And Dave Kohler was sitting on the couch.

"Hey, Jake. I'm real sorry about the, uh, the whole getting canned thing."

"Right." Jake moved to his desk and started shifting things around, procrastinating the task of packing up.

"But we have an offer for you. Look in the envelope."

Jake opened the walking papers Tom Highgate had handed him and flipped through the packet.

A contract.

Some decent money if he agreed to be under camera surveillance twenty-four seven, just like Kaylie.

An offer to become a full-time cast member of the show. Bound by contract to live in the fish bowl.

"Huh. That's a tempting offer."

"Look man, you're going to be in the national spotlight for the next few months either way. Why not score a cool two-hundred grand while you're at it? After all – you *are* unemployed."

"I assume they'll bleep out the contract terms you just revealed when they air this footage?"

"Of course – I approve everything that hits the air, and I assure you most of this conversation will be left on the cutting room floor. Contract confidentiality does still exist, even in reality TV. The lawyers wouldn't have it any other way. Surely you noticed that we bleeped out Kaylie's pay rate back in episode one, when she was spilling the beans to her mom."

Jake considered for a moment, then said, "Fine. But I want two-fifty, and I want one hour a week with no cameras – on me *or* Kaylie."

"Yes to the money, no to the free hour."

"Had to try."

"Can't blame you. So, you in?"

"I'll probably regret this," he said, signing the contract with his silver Cross pen.

Dave smiled slyly. "Yeah, probably."

CHAPTER 31

George returned to the apartment from the grocery store to find Ellen on the phone. He started putting the groceries away in the small kitchen, stowing some Oreos in a cupboard, fruits on the counter, and milk in the fridge.

"Yes, okay," said Ellen. "Well, give us a call when you get in – we'll pick you up. You can stay here – we have a couple of couches."

George put the last of the items in the freezer and grabbed a beer, cracked it open.

"Oh, really? A limo from the airport to the L.A. Live Ritz-Carlton? Well, that beats our minivan and our shabby little apartment . . . yeah, you're right, the suites probably *are* bigger than this apartment. Okay, then, just let us know when you're settled in and we'll have dinner, if it's not too late. Okay. Okay, bye – love you – bye."

"What's going on?" asked George, lowering himself into the puffy recliner in the living room and working the lever to raise his feet.

"That was Amanda. FBC is flying her and Bruce in for this week's show. They're bringing them in tonight."

"Tonight? But Thursday is three days away. That oughtta add up at the Ritz."

"Like the number one TV show in America has cash flow issues."

"Good point. I guess if that's how they want to spend their money. Have they been told what they're expected to *do* on the show?"

"Nope. You know how this show is – they're all about mystery and surprises."

"Which means it's probably bad news."

"Probably. But, it's also another chance for our family to get our message out."

"Right – like last time when they wouldn't let us get a word in edgewise and they heckled me into a convulsing, steaming pile of old man. I'm not so confident the show is ever going to really give us a chance to state our case."

Ellen leaned a hand on the counter and pinched the bridge of her nose with the other. "Well, all we can do is try."

George let out a deep beer belch. "Yup. Just keep trying. It'll only take one time, just one week's vote, to make this thing end in tragedy."

Bruce grabbed his sister's two huge blue suitcases off the carousel in the United Airlines arrivals area, then spotted his own luggage and squeezed between two other men to snatch the green canvas duffel before it passed.

It still had his name stenciled on it from his three year stint in the U.S. Army.

Of course, that was all over six years ago.

Three years as a grunt getting top-notch training in technology, four years at the U of O's computer sciences school, and two years trying to find an IT job in a down economy. Getting hired in Portland was a major blessing, and it was likely his veteran status helped him beat the odds in the tough job market.

He was lucky his bosses were big fans of the show and willing to give him a little extra time off for this trip.

"Look!" said Amanda. "There's a limo driver holding a sign with our name on it! That is so . . . cool."

The two approached the driver, who said, "You Bruce and Amanda?"

"Yep," said Bruce.

The driver promptly grabbed both of Amanda's rolling suitcases *and* threw Bruce's duffle over his shoulder, and said, "I'm Frank. Follow me this way, please."

He led the way, weaving in and out of the crowd, taking them outside into the cool air where a seemingly endless row of limousines lined the curb. He walked up to a long double-stretch white Lincoln and popped the trunk remotely.

In went the luggage, then he opened the rear door. Amanda had dressed for the occasion, wearing a cream-colored skirt suit with tall black heels. She stepped into the car and sunk into the leather back bench, followed by Bruce.

Bruce sniffed the leather that permeated the air, pleased to be in a car where he could actually stretch his extensive legs, especially after the cramped flight.

He could swear they were making those airplane seats smaller and smaller.

But this . . . this was nice.

The car pulled away and crawled through the bumper-to-bumper traffic out of the airport and onto a freeway. Bruce saw a sign that read "Century Freeway" and hoped that didn't refer to the length of the commute in this crazy rush hour traffic.

He had thought Portland was bad, but really, this made Portland look like Medford.

Then they made a turn at an interchange and were on the four-oh-five. This one was a parking lot.

"I'm calling Mom, telling her we can forget about dinner tonight," said Bruce.

Bruce made the call then stared out the window at the commuters. How could people live like this every day?

"Do you think they'll be filming us the next couple days?" asked Amanda.

"I think you can count on it. It was in the fine print of that legal stuff they emailed us and had us sign."

"You read that stuff?"

"You signed something without reading it first? What is the matter with you, 'Manda?"

She shrugged.

"You do realize that's how Kaylie got into this whole mess in the first place, don't you?"

"Oh? I thought it was because she was living like a drunken ho."

"I'm talking about the show."

"Yeah. Well, I assumed it was just your standard stuff like those stupid software license agreements that nobody ever reads before clicking 'I accept' and installing."

"I read 'em."

"You would – you're a software geek."

"No, I'm smart. Never – never sign your name to something unless you understand what you are agreeing to. That's common sense, Sis."

"So what did this fine print say?"

"It said we'll get flown down here, driven around in a limo, put up at a hotel, and brought on the show for the live November 13th edition of *Canceled*. It said they'll pay our expenses for up to three days, and we'll also get paid a convenience fee of five thousand dollars for our time."

"Five grand? I had no idea! We're getting paid to be treated like movie stars? Nice!"

"Then, in the fine print, it said that we may or may not be photographed, videotaped, audiotaped, and our likenesses used for FBC's sole purposes and profit with no further remuneration to us. It said we will have no right to any of the raw or edited material produced – they'll own it all, forever – and that we will hold them harmless for anything that may happen as a result of our being involved in the show."

"Ick. What does that all mean?"

"How many decades have you been in college now?"

"Only one. And a bit. But I'm not studying freaking contract law – I'm learning about ancient history."

"It means that when we do the show, they can do whatever they want with the video and stuff that we're in, and they own it and they can make all the profit they want off it and we can't try to get a cut – other than the five grand they're paying up front – and we can never sue them for any reason."

"Like I said – ick. So, why did you sign it?"

"Because it's pretty much the standard, boilerplate legal junk like those software license agreements."

"But you said – "

"But I *read* it. So I knew what I was signing. Get it?"

"Yeah."

"Besides, I could use the five grand, and I figured this actually might be kinda fun. It's a pity Cynthia couldn't come along – she had to work."

"Fun, yeah. I'm sure it will be. It'll also be scary as hell. We have to get up on that stage in front of millions of people and tell them to please let Kaylie's baby live. That's daunting."

"Eh. It won't be millions of people – I mean, yeah, they'll be watching, but the James Brown Memorial Theater only holds like five thousand people."

"And when, exactly was the last time you addressed five thousand people face to face, Mr. I.T. Man, who sits alone in a cubicle and communicates mostly by email?"

"Good point. But, the thing is, we need to do this. We need to support Kaylie, and we need to help save that baby."

"I agree. And I regret what I said about Kaylie – the whole 'drunken ho' thing. I'm just kinda frustrated with her. But I love her. And I know we all make mistakes."

"Good, 'cause I'm sure all she needs right now is her family coming down on her with a bunch of moralizing. Actually, I'm surprised just how well Mom and Dad – especially Dad – have been taking this. They always surprise me because they're always so particular and anal about the little things, but then when big stuff happens, they become so . . . cool."

"Maybe we'll understand one day, when we're parents ourselves."

"Maybe. But it almost makes me want to mess up big-time just so they'll leave me alone about the small stuff and come stand by my side."

"Careful what you wish for, Bro."

CHAPTER 32

Kaylie had a busy day ahead.

Tomorrow was another show, but today she had back-to-back appointments with Molly the Midwife, Dr. Cho, Vanessa Baldwin at FFPC, Dr. Ian, and Dr. Hamlin.

Then she had dinner with her family, and was hoping to talk to Jake as well tonight.

A *very* busy day.

She got herself ready for the day, barely even noticing the cameras anymore.

Justin Mitchell, the director of photography for the early mornings, wasn't even showing up many mornings – he'd set the crew on autopilot.

Today, however, with so many locations and a lot of logistics to manage, he arrived with the relief crew when the graveyard shift shuffled out.

"Mornin' love," he said with a grin and a hand clap. "Ready for a nice big day of shooting?"

"Sure," said Kaylie. "Can we start by shooting your bosses?"

"Ha! You are a cheeky one, aren't you? Um, got any coffee?"

Turned out she did – the night camera crew had been keeping her cupboards stocked with it for weeks now, just to help stay awake through all those uneventful hours of darkness.

Kaylie finished getting ready, putting on more makeup than she normally would for a handful of doctor's appointments – but she'd come to realize, watching the playback of the vignettes during the show episodes, that she looked a lot better on camera with a little extra paint.

Molly arrived and they chatted for a while. Molly revealed that she is now certain the baby is a boy. Kaylie nodded and smiled (convinced by now that Molly was a bit of a kook, but always glad for her amazing reflexology foot rubs that were designed to relax her without putting her into early labor).

Molly also supplied her with a new batch of incense and some 'meditation' music by some new-age guy named Aeoliah. Once Molly's appointment was over, Kaylie munched on some Cocoa Puffs (she couldn't get enough of those sweet, crunchy balls of crack cocaine lately), then checked the time.

Kaylie finished getting ready by throwing on a pale green cashmere sweater – November in L.A. was still mild compared to her cooler, wetter Oregon roots; but she was getting acclimatized and to her, fifty-five felt a little chilly.

At least until an hour from now when the internal thermostat in her pregnant body decided to go haywire, as it did most days.

She slipped on a pair of sponsor-supplied New Balance sneakers (nice shoes were hurting her feet these days) and was on her way.

With all the excitement and hype over the show, she was getting recognized all the time (and sometimes harassed), so FBC had now arranged for her to be chauffeured everywhere. She stepped into the limo and they were off to Dr. Cho's.

"Hi Kaylie," said Cho. "You're looking well."

"Thanks, Jenn. How have you been doing?"

"Not bad, not bad at all. I've actually been getting a lot more women signing up for me to be their doctor. Apparently the show is good exposure."

"Glad somebody is getting something good out of all this."

"And you're not? I mean, you get me," said Cho, smiling.

"True. This whole thing is actually a big mix of good and bad, I guess."

Cho checked Kaylie out on the table, providing the standard exam, which Kaylie was getting used to. Then she spread a little gel on Kaylie's belly and began an ultrasound.

"Ooh, that's cold," said Kaylie.

"Oops, sorry – I usually warm it up a little."

She placed the probe on Kaylie's belly.

"Looking good," she said, staring at the shifting image on the screen mounted up on the wall. "Everything is right where it should be."

Kaylie squinted at the screen, astounded at the depth and clarity of the three-dimensional form before her.

"So, do you want to know?" asked Cho.

"Know what?"

"Boy or girl?"

"Oh. You can tell?"

"Yeah. I can make a solid assessment at this point."

"Okay."

Cho rubbed the probe across the belly further, angling the view direction with expertise, until the image was a clear frontal. "There. Oh, yeah. Yep – definitely a little boy. You see that – right there?"

Kaylie could see what Cho was pointing at, and there was no way she could've mistaken that protruding male genitalia.

"I see it."

"I would say there is virtually no way that is *not* a boy. Very clear. Very, very clear." She looked at Kaylie and grinned.

For a moment, Kaylie felt a little more respect for Molly the Midwife. Then it occurred to her that Molly had a fifty-fifty chance of being right, and suddenly her prediction didn't seem so awesome.

Cho switched off the machine and wiped Kaylie's belly down. Kaylie sat up and pulled her top back down.

"So, you gonna tell Jake?"

"That it's a boy?"

"Yes. Normally the father is present for these kinds of things. You should at least tell him before these people," she motioned at the cameras, "put it on the air."

"I guess you're right. I'll try to have a talk with him tonight."

"Changing the subject, have you been taking your prenatal vitamins?" asked Cho.

"Yeah. But I really haven't been eating that well. Sorry."

"Don't say sorry to *me*. Just start eating better. You'll be glad you did – and so will *he*." She gestured at her belly. "Right now, he is still growing very quickly, and

222

needs those nutrients. Did you know that his eyelids have now fused shut to protect his eyes as they develop, and that he can actually put his tiny thumb in his mouth – though he can't really suck yet – that ability is yet to develop."

"It – I mean, he – can suck his thumb?"

"Amazing, isn't it?"

Kaylie was surprised. She had been refusing to think of this thing inside her as a person – as a little baby who could cry and suck his thumb and think and walk and talk and grow up. Not knowing if she wanted it, and knowing it could be terminated any time, she preferred to think of it as just a blob. Something that made her tired and hungry and emotional – like a sickness. Something in there that was sort of alive, but not really real.

"I'm starting to get a headache."

"Have you still been having a lot of trouble with that?"

"No. My shrink actually helped me get rid of them. Good thing I'm seeing him today. Maybe he can help again."

"Well, if you need anything more, uh, medical to deal with that – you know where to find me. Well, that's it – we're done for today."

"Thanks, Jenn. I'll see you, what, next month?"

"Yep. See you then."

Kaylie threw her sweater back on, grabbed her purse and was followed out by the cameras.

Next stop: the Federal Family Planning Commission.

Vanessa Baldwin was already waiting for her when Kaylie arrived.

"Hello, Kaylie," she said warmly. "How are you?"

"I'm well, thanks. You?"

They sat down at the plain gray table in the plain gray room. Only a telephone on the table and a generic landscape painting on the wall.

"I'm fine. I'm a little worried about you, though," said Vanessa.

"Oh?"

"Yes. I'm just concerned that you're – getting some conflicting messages that may cause you unnecessary stress."

"Go on."

"It's important that you remember that your condition is nothing more than an inconvenience – not a life-changing event. Soon enough, the vote will turn up in your favor and you'll be able to go in for one of the simple procedures we talked about last time, and move on with your life."

"Is it really that simple to you?"

"Of course. I counsel hundreds of women every –"

"He can suck his thumb!"

"*It* is just a collection of cells – a parasite."

"That's not – I just don't know. Let me ask you this. At what point *does* it become a human being? When does the fetus become a little baby boy?"

"That's easy. When it's born."

"So, one second it's not a person – the next it is?"

Vanessa considered. "Well, you have to draw a line somewhere. That's the most logical place, and it's where California law does, so yes."

"So, what about babies that are born prematurely? Are they not a person until they reach their normal due date?"

"No, it's not about the date, it's about – look, this is really a philosophical question – perhaps for some people a religious one. Ultimately, it comes down to what is best for you – what *you* want. If you are not planning on being a mother, that thing inside of you is just tissue, and you have every right to choose for yourself to get rid of it. It's *your* body. Your choice."

"Normally."

"Normally, yes. Of course, in this case, it's someone else's choice. *Everyone* else's. But either way, it's nothing you need to let yourself get worked up about. Please, Kaylie, don't stress over this. The anti-choice extremists try so hard to make this so sentimental and emotionally charged – but it's just a tactic to try to push their superstitious religious views on everyone in the country. Don't listen to them."

Kaylie thought of her parents, about how passionate they were about these things. They did seem a little overboard sometimes.

Vanessa continued. "I'm sure that sometime soon America will vote to let you off the hook, and you can get the procedure done and be good to go. I can't imagine the viewers would be so cold and cruel as to punish you with a child – to make you carry and deliver it. That would just be wrong."

"Well, thanks. I'll try not to worry about it. I must be going now – I have a very busy schedule today. Thanks again."

Kaylie left, feeling less nauseous than last time, though somehow a little sick inside anyway.

Not in her stomach, but in her heart.

She still didn't know what she wanted, didn't know how she wanted the vote to turn out. She still had her doubts about the nature of life – what was and what wasn't a baby. She knew how she'd been brought up, what her parents and siblings believed. But she'd never really made her own mind up about it all. Never really cared to "take a stand" on the issue one way or the other. Never understood what all the controversy was about.

She knew most people had a very strong opinion about it, one way or the other, but she was never the political type – unlike Dad – and never figured she would be in this situation herself.

Who ever did?

As she headed to see Dr. Ian at his office, she doubted he would provide her with any more answers.

The friendly Indian welcomed her in like an old friend visiting his home. "Kaylie! I am so glad to see you, yes?"

"Yes, it is good to see you, too," Kaylie said. In a sense it was – he was such a jovial and kind fellow. On the other hand, something about him made her uneasy somewhere in the back of her mind.

Dr. Ian led her to a private consultation room that was decorated in earth tones and featured two soft armchairs with a small round table between them. They took their seats and Kaylie tried her best to keep a positive look on her face while the camera people found positions in the corners of the room.

"Our appointment today," said Dr. Ian, "is just to make sure you don't have any specific technical questions about what will probably be happening sometime soon. As you know, we could be taking care of you in as little as two weeks, depending of course on how things go with the vote, yes."

"Well, I – I don't really have any questions about the procedure. Overall, I understand it to be fairly painless – maybe some discomfort, cramping, and so on – but I just was wondering more – on a philosophical level – when do *you* believe that life begins?"

"Why, at conception, of course."

"What? But, but –"

"Life, yes. Humanity? Personhood? Ah, now that is a different question. The fetus is alive – there is no denying that simple medical truth. But at what point does that creature become a person? I ask you – at what point did *you* become a person? When were you self-aware? At what point had you accrued memories you could access later? When did your life have *meaning*?"

Kaylie thought for a moment. "That depends."

"On what?"

"On whose perspective. I don't recall a lot about things in my life before about age four. But I was still a person. Any doctor in the world would try to save a sick toddler's life. But my life had meaning to my parents from the moment they found out my mother was pregnant with me. I know that."

"So, there is a matter of subjectivity, yes?"

"Are you saying there is no answer? That it just depends on what you believe?"

"I can tell you that no patient who has ever come to me for a termination of pregnancy has ever wanted that life inside her to become a person. No woman who has ever had an abortion has killed a baby. It is that simple."

"Maybe not as far as she was concerned, but what about what other people think? We can't just define our own reality."

"Can't we? Don't we all live in a construct of reality that is of our own making? It is only when that construct becomes radically out of line with the general consensus that people's realities become a social liability – what we call insane, or in some cases simply aberrant behavior that is named on a spectrum from quirky to sociopathic. But we all live in our own little worlds, yes."

"And what about when those worlds intersect? What about if the mother wants an abortion and the father doesn't? Is it a baby or not?"

"I am reminded of the old thought experiment called Shrodinger's Cat. Long story short, the answer is *both* are true. But the only answer that really matters is that of what the woman believes, for it is her body, and thus her reality that defines what transpires within her uterus and within the walls of my practice."

"I see." Kaylie felt as confused as ever. "Well, thanks – anyway. I have to go – lots more on today's agenda. Good bye, Dr. Ian."

Kaylie left in a hurry, her head spinning.

Maybe Dr. Hamlin – Len – would be able to help her make sense of it all.

She arrived at his offices and was met by a smiling Felicity Jones.

"Hi Kaylie! How are you doing?"

"It's been a pretty crazy day – but I'm glad to be here."

"And we're glad you're here. You just light up the room."

"Really? I kinda thought I had a dark cloud hanging over my head wherever I went."

"Oh no. You are special. Just the couple of times we've talked, I've been able to tell that there is so much more to you than this stupid show."

"Stupid? I thought you were a big fan."

"The more I get to know and like you, the less I like the show – what it's doing to you, and to your family. But of course, I can't resist watching each week." She laughed sheepishly.

"Well, thanks. You know, maybe when all this is over, we could hang out sometime."

"Why wait?"

Kaylie thumbed toward the cameras. "You really want these guys hanging out *with* us?"

"Good point. But if you change your mind, I'll brave the videographers. Just say the word."

"I will. Is Len ready for me?"

"Sure – hold on."

She gave a quick phone call back to Len, who appeared shortly at the doorway leading to the back.

"Kaylie, please come back."

She went back to his office-slash-games room and wandered over to the pinball machines. "Can I play?"

"Of course. Just push the start button – it's loaded with unlimited credits."

"Doesn't that take the fun out of earning a replay?"

"Nah. Hearing that cracking sound when you get a high enough score for a replay still feels good – gives you that feeling of reward."

She pushed the button, then pulled the plunger and released to shoot a ball into play. "Huh, I'm feeling a little like a pinball inside lately. Can't decide what to think or which way to go. And the headaches are back."

Len stepped up to the machine beside her and started a game of his own. He chatted while he played. "We can try hypnosis again, but you already have your token – the silver box – and if that's not working anymore, we should probably just talk it out."

He wiggled his hips and bent over while slapping the flippers. Clearly a pinball wizard in his own time.

"I'm just having some trouble with some of the ethical issues, now."

"Wrestling with the big questions, eh? What is life, what is death – all that stuff?"

"You could say that. My parents have always – very vocally – believed that a person's life begins at conception. They say that's when the *soul* enters the body. And they always taught us kids that, too."

"And you're doubting what your parents taught you?"

Kaylie slapped both flippers at the same time as the ball rushed straight down between them with a *clunk*. "Well, I still believe in the soul. I just don't know when a fetus becomes a baby – when this thing inside of me magically transforms from a lump of developing organs into a human being – a person with rights. A child, with a right to live."

Len hit his ball up a ramp that activated the multi-ball feature in his game, and started slapping the flippers frantically as his score jumped up in huge chunks, accompanied by a chorus of electronic sounds. "Ah – the timing is everything, isn't it? I mean, if left alone, you know that at some point, that 'thing inside of you' is going to become a walking, talking, learning, loving individual – one with many traits in common with yourself, I might add. But you also know that every day across the country – and across the world – women end their pregnancies with no problem at all. How, you wonder, can they kill a child? Of course, the answer is, it's not a child – at least not as far as they were concerned. Question is, are they right? And if they are, how could your parents have been so wrong all this time?"

"Yeah, I guess that sums up my dilemma."

"Well, think about this – the first position you uttered, as you tried to reason this out, was that of your parents – the first position to which you'd been exposed. Now, you could've just as easily started with the opposing view – the one you've been exposed to more recently."

"So, you think I defaulted to my upbringing because that's what I believe deep down? And I've just become confused by all these other voices in the world today?"

"I'm not saying that at all. That's your own analysis. I'm just guiding you – getting you to think not just about the issue, but the way your own mind works when you think about the issue. It's up to you to figure out why you think as you do. Did you default to your parents' position because it's comfortable – the most familiar? Or for some deeper reason? Are there other important issues with which you irreconcilably disagree with your parents? Are you a clone of them, or do you think for yourself most of the time?"

Kaylie sprung a new ball and watched it bounce vigorously off the power bumpers below the scoreboard at the top of the table.

"I think I'm pretty independent in most things. I still believe in God, like my folks do, but I don't go to church or live a very Christian lifestyle. And I'm not an activist – I've never bothered to vote, and don't really care for politics – whereas they are very active in their conservative political causes. We have wholeheartedly disagreed about the direction I chose – to leave home and come to L.A. instead of going to college. I wanted to follow my dream, and they just didn't understand that. So, I don't think I follow them just to follow them, no."

"So, you feel that your beliefs are partly a product of some indoctrination by your parents, and a lot of finding your own way?"

"I'd say so."

"So," said Len, as his machine let out a big mechanical cracking noise from somewhere inside, indicating he'd earned a replay, and causing a tiny smile to flicker across his lips, "going back to the issue of when life begins – what does your gut tell you – independent of your parents, your friends, the media, the government, Vanessa Baldwin, Dr. Ian, Dr. Cho, Molly the Midwife, Jake Granville, or me?"

Kaylie watched helplessly as the ball bounced up and down on the edge of the side rail. A little more to the left, and it would roll down the edge and disappear. Game over. A little to the right, and it would slide down the chute to her left flipper.

Without thinking, she nudged the table with the butt of her palm, and the ball found its way into the flipper chute.

She slapped the flipper and it shot up into a retaining gadget that held it for a moment before shooting it up a ramp. "I think – I believe – I'm not sure. I don't know when it happened, but at some point, this thing I'm carrying became a person."

"And how does that make you feel?"

Kaylie's machine let out a "replay crack" and the scoreboard lit up. She smiled, but then quickly frowned. "Worse than ever."

"Why's that?"

"Because I still don't know if I want it to be born. What kind of person does that make me?"

That evening, shortly after returning from Dr. Hamlin's office, Kaylie put on a baby blue maternity blouse her mother had given her last week, slipped on a plain denim skirt and a pair of flat-soled shoes that Molly had recommended.

Then she took the limo to the Galaxy Apartments in Brentwood, the two camera operators right there with her as always.

She knocked on the door and was greeted by her brother.

"Hey, Sis! Welcome to the Adams family home-away-from-home!" He gave her a big squeeze.

"Hi, Broots," said Kaylie, calling him by the name she'd called him when she was too little to say his name properly. She looked him up and down and smiled. "It's good to see you. Have you lost some weight?"

"Heck no – I've packed on about twenty more pounds since you last saw me."

"Well, you're carrying it better. Must be 'engaged life' – being an official *fiancée* makes you stand a little taller."

Bruce grinned and led Kaylie in.

Amanda, sitting curled up on the recliner, spotted Kaylie and gave her a lukewarm wave. "Hey there, movie star. How you feeling?"

"I'm fine," said Kaylie. This was about the twentieth time she'd been asked that today – the hundredth time this week – and it was getting old. But she couldn't blame the asker of the question – after all, it was the first time for her. "Hanging in there. You?"

"Same ol' same ol.' Still plugging away at my education."

"Yeah, she's now a super-super-duper-senior," quipped Bruce.

"You shush, Bruce," said Amanda. "I'm working hard – and I think I may now be only six years away from my doctorate."

"Uh, isn't that about how long it usually takes in the first place?" asked Kaylie.

"Well, if you want to go about it the boring way," said Amanda. "I prefer to take the scenic route."

Just then, Mom walked in from the kitchen, holding a hot dish with pot holders. "Kaylie! You're just in time – the food is almost ready."

A few minutes later, they all sat down at the cramped little dining table, which Mom had decked out nicely with a burgundy table cloth, china plates and water glasses, along with salt, pepper, butter, and all the other necessities for a great meal.

Dad came out of the bathroom and joined them. "Well, it may not be as lavish as some of our family meals back home, but I think your mother has done a splendid job with what she has to work with here in this little apartment."

Murmurs of agreement all around.

Dad then offered up a brief but heartfelt word of prayer over the meal, and they dug in.

"How are you feeling, Dad?" asked Kaylie, a preemptive attempt to turn the attention to someone else.

"Never better. I'll be damned if I'll let some little bout of angina keep me down for long," he said, dishing a big spoonful of peas onto his plate. "Seriously – I feel good as new. And ready to give 'em hell next time I'm on that blasted stage."

So much for keeping the subject of Kaylie and the show off the table.

"Speaking of that," said Bruce, his mouth full of pork chop and gravy, "when are Mom and Dad scheduled to go back on – anyone know?"

Kaylie buttered a roll. "Nope. They like to keep everything a big secret. Not much is revealed in advance – and only then what is absolutely necessary – like you and Amanda. They had to let that cat out of the bag because they had to get you down here to set it all up. But other than that – each week is always something new – some big shocking reveal or another."

"Sounds like a real pain in the butt," said Amanda. "That would drive me nuts. I like always knowing what's ahead – for instance, I know that at noon next Tuesday I will be in my Chuuk Cultural Art Studies class. We'll be studying Chapter 14 – Kosrae influence on stone carvings. That kind of stability and structure gives me peace."

"Gives me a case of the yawns," said Bruce. "How can you study that stuff?"

"Some of us like to broaden our horizons, to enlarge our minds."

"Yeah, your head's getting pretty big."

"Enough, you two," said Dad, not harshly. "Please pass the butter."

"So, how was your doctor's appointment today?" asked Mom.

"Which one? I saw four different people with doctorates today – plus one who's great at yoga."

"Your OB/GYN. Everything okay with the baby?"

Kaylie swallowed and nearly choked over her mother's choice of words.

Baby.

As if there was no doubt what this thing inside her was.

"The fetus is fine," she answered.

"Fetus?" said Dad.

"Yeah, that's what it's called, last time I checked," said Kaylie.

"Maybe to the medical establishment, and to pro-abortion types, but around here we know what people have known for millennia – you're carrying a baby."

"Yes, well. Anyway – it's fine."

"Any word yet on the gender?" asked Mom.

"It's a boy."

"What? Why didn't you tell us right away?" said Mom smiling, as the others murmured in surprise.

"Yeah, why hold back the news?" asked Dad.

"Kind of slipped my mind, I guess."

"Slipped your mind?"

"It's been a long day. Sorry." Then she faked a celebratory voice and expression and said, "Yay, Kaylie's having a boy! Let's all say hooray! That is – if it lives beyond the November sweeps."

The smiles at the table vanished.

"Sorry," she said. "Forgive me if I'm not that excited. I still don't even know what I want." She suddenly broke into tears. "All I know is I have a really bad headache, and my mood swings are really bad right now. Excuse me."

She pushed her chair back and hurried off to the bathroom. One camera followed her, while one stayed behind to keep shooting the dinner scene.

Inside the small bathroom, she grabbed some toilet paper and wiped her eyes, blew her nose, then straightened her hair in the mirror.

Deep breath.

She returned to the table after a few minutes. "I'm sorry."

Mom reached out and patted her wrist. "You're fine. I'm sorry, too. I know you are under an immense amount of pressure right now. Let's just talk about something else and enjoy the evening together, all right? After all, it's been how many years since we were all together for dinner?"

"Like six," said Kaylie.

"Okay. So, let's just eat and then watch a movie on TV or something, okay?"

"Okay. Thanks."

After dinner, after the movie, and after a much more relaxed conversation on the couches in the living room, Kaylie and her siblings said their goodbyes.

The image of two limousines waiting outside for them was surreal.

What a strange life!

Here they were, in Los Angeles, stepping into limos after having a family gathering at a strange little apartment.

An apartment that was right next door to her baby's father's apartment.

Jake.

Before stepping into her limo, she decided she ought to knock on his door.

No answer. But a light was on inside.

He opened it after about a minute.

"Oh, hi," he said. "Come on in. It'll be a little crowded though."

Kaylie stepped inside. "Crowded?"

"Yeah. Have you met my two new shadows?"

"They've assigned a crew to you too, now?" Kaylie asked, surprised.

"You betcha. Twenty-four seven. Now I'm just like you."

"Well," said Kaylie, cupping her hands over her bulging abdomen, "not *just* like me."

"Right."

Jake fluffed a pillow on the couch and gestured for Kaylie to sit down. She obliged, and he sat down opposite her in an armchair.

"So, do you think we'll ever have another shot at a private conversation, just you and me?" asked Kaylie.

Jake looked around at the four cameras pointing at them from all sides. "Well, our chances of that just went way, way down."

"Well, if you ever feel like spilling the beans, and aren't afraid to share it with my two friends, your two friends, and a couple hundred million Americans, you know where to find me."

Kaylie, dog tired from an exhausting day, stood up slowly and stretched. She knew that if she sat much longer, she wouldn't want to get up and leave.

"Yes, I do," said Jake.

"Well, I'll see you around."

CHAPTER 33

Troy Tanner opened the episode from within the Green Room, which also hosted Kaylie and her siblings, along with Jake Granville.

"Here we are folks – episode seven, thirteen weeks into the pregnancy. Tonight we have with us some special guests: Bruce Adams and Amanda Adams – Kaylie's older brother and sister."

Troy then walked through the door and along the dark passageway to the stage, followed by a hand held camera as he walked and talked over his shoulder. "We'll bring them out on stage – here – this evening. And we'll have a special in-depth report from another special guest. Of course, we'll have a recap of Kaylie's week, and we'll have the results of the past week's voting. And – depending on those results – we'll find out what the future holds for Kaylie. All that and more – tonight, on *Canceled*!"

The show's CG intro then rolled, with the dramatic music, and Troy then gave his usual tease-and-toss to break. It seemed this show was getting more and more packed with commercials.

For Kaylie, this was good news on two fronts: less time squirming in front of the camera and having her life dissected, and more money for the show. And success for the show meant success for her – as that meant more viewers, a bigger phenomenon, and greater exposure for her name and face. It was a bit of a paradox – less time on camera equal to better exposure – but that was the way she saw it. As long as people were tuning in, she wouldn't mind if she was only in the hot seat for a few minutes each week.

The show returned and they started with the edited video highlights of her week, including her day-to-day struggles and her appointments with all the specialists – and also her family dinner.

The family get-together made for a perfect transition into the Bruce-and-Amanda segment. They were led out on stage during a commercial break.

Kaylie watched from the Green Room. They looked like deer in the headlights when they got out in front of those stage lights and nearly five-thousand people in the audience.

"Welcome back, everyone," said Troy, who wore faded jeans, an open white dress shirt and a navy blue blazer tonight. He sat on a stool alongside Bruce and Amanda, who were also perched on the stools center stage. "Ladies first – Amanda, tell us a little about yourself."

"Uh, hi. I'm Amanda – Amanda Adams. I live in Ashland, Oregon. I attend Southern Oregon University."

"A student. What's your major?"

"I've had several. I'm kind of a lifer there," she smiled. "Right now I'm knee-deep in Ancient Micronesian Women's Studies."

"Sounds fascinating. And Bruce, what do you do?"

"I'm a web developer – computer geek, I guess."

"Where do you live?"

"I'm in Portland now – I work for a company called Imaginate. Hi guys!" He gave a tepid wave.

"Great, great. And I understand you're dating a reporter? Tell us about that."

"Actually, we're engaged," said Bruce, blushing a little. "Cynthia Davis is her name – she works at Channel 12 in Medford."

"You guys set a date yet?"

"No, but I think we will soon. Things are going great. Hi, honey!" Bruce waved at the camera.

"Okay" said Troy. "Now, tell me, what do you think of this whole thing – it must seem pretty wild to you – I mean, one minute you're up in Oregon just, uh, being Oregonians, and then suddenly your little sister is pregnant and the star of the biggest show on television. What's your reaction to this? Amanda?"

"Um, well, obviously it was a surprise. But when it comes down to it, life happens, and when you're a family you're there for each other. You step up and help out in any way you can."

"And Bruce – what do you think of your little sister's situation?"

"I stand by her. And I think America needs to stand by this family – go to savekayliesbaby.com and read the content there, then do the right thing. We need to –"

"Thanks, Bruce," Troy interrupted. It seemed to Kaylie like the producers were determined to prevent anyone from advocating. "We'll be back right after the break with a surprise report. Stick around."

Kaylie was brought out of the Green Room to sit beside her siblings on stage for the next to last segment of the show.

"We're back," said Troy. "And without further ado, we'd like to introduce our special guest. Here to present her special in-depth undercover report on Bruce and Amanda – to tell us the things they're not willing to tell us on stage here tonight – is our Oregon news correspondent, Cynthia Davis!"

The crowd gasped and cheered as Cynthia took the stage in sharp red mini-dress with heels. Her blonde hair was combed into curves each side of her face, framing her beautiful features and giving her the perfect "anchor" look.

Bruce's eyes bugged out and he actually jumped a little in his seat. Amanda and Kaylie's eyes narrowed and their jaws dropped. Kaylie looked over at Bruce and he seemed to be blinking back tears – either of rage or pain of betrayal.

"Thanks, Troy," Cynthia said, taking a seat on the empty stool next to Troy that had been brought out during the break. "Thanks for having me here tonight."

"Glad to have you," said Troy, leering a little. "Let's jump right into your exclusive story."

"Well, Troy, I had the benefit of an inside track to the Adams family, as I've been involved with Bruce for some time now."

"Romantically?"

"Yes. So, I paid Bruce and Amanda a visit – or two – and we discussed Kaylie and her situation. Here's what I learned."

Tape rolled and the large screen at the back of the stage displayed the report.

It was horrid.

Cynthia had recorded a number of private conversations with Bruce and Amanda, and carefully edited together all the highlights, interspersed with some voice over tracks describing the family's history with some visuals of the family home and family portraits.

The expose included some very frank conversations – some of which was not very complimentary of Kaylie. Kaylie felt the tears run down her cheeks. She looked at her siblings, and they were both wiping away tears, but their faces were furious, not sad.

Bruce looked ready to kill Cynthia.

The segment ended with a direct quote from Amanda, stating that she was in favor of a quick vote for termination. Then the video dissolved back to the camera one stage shot.

"Wow," said Troy. "Some very compelling material there, Cynthia. Anything to add?"

"Yes," she said. "I just wanted to say that I hope Bruce and Amanda – and the whole family – understand that I was just doing my job. And I've actually done everyone a favor by sharing all this out in the open, instead of living with secrets. I hope this brings the family closer."

"Thoughts?" asked Troy, opening it up to the siblings.

Bruce couldn't manage much more than a low growl as he seethed and stared at Cynthia with cold eyes.

Amanda said, directly to Kaylie, "Kaylie, you understand that I didn't mean everything I said – you know how these things work – they take so much out of context and edit it together to make it look worse than it really is. You know I support you and love you, right?"

Kaylie just nodded.

Bruce turned to her. "Kaylie, Amanda's right. We were a little upset in some of those – stolen moments. We were still trying to get our heads around it all, and said things we regret. We've talked since then – you know we're on your side, right?"

Kaylie nodded, then spoke. "I know. I know this was one very dirty piece of so-called reporting. Playing us against each other for entertainment value. Very low."

"Yeah," said Bruce, turning to Cynthia. "Low. And you," he said, pointing an iron-fisted finger at his fiancée, "will return the engagement ring – now."

Cynthia pulled off the ring and tossed it to Bruce. "Here ya go, honey. And thanks."

"For what?" asked Bruce, catching the ring.

"For this great opportunity," Cynthia smirked. "This is worth far more than diamonds."

"Well, there you have it, folks. The family sticks together, and we have a break-up, right here, live on stage! Next, we'll reveal the results of last week's vote. We'll be right back."

As soon as the red light blinked out on camera one, Cynthia hopped off the stool and made a quick escape from the stage.

Bruce clutched the ring in his hand so hard there was an imprint in his palm when he opened his hand up to slip the ring into his pocket.

Kaylie felt so awful for him. She didn't really care so much about the things in the video – they'd get past that easily enough – they always did. But Bruce had been betrayed – used.

And all because of her.

"Well," said Bruce, "I guess it's better to find out now that she's a self-centered witch than after we were married. So, thanks, Kayles." He smiled ruefully. "See? Things always work out."

Kaylie got off her stool and hugged Bruce. "Thanks, big brother. You always know how to see the bright side and to put things in perspective."

"Places please," said the floor director. "We're back in five, four, three."

Kaylie got back on her stool just in time for the show to return.

"And now," said Troy, "after that exciting segment, it's time for the most exciting part of all – the vote results."

A woman in a peach-colored evening gown brought Troy a white envelope.

He opened it.

"After a staggering one hundred and seventy-five million votes – that's right, one hundred and seventy-five *million*! – the results are . . . razor-close."

The crowd murmured.

"By a difference of zero-point-zero-zero-zero-zero-three percent . . . Kaylie Adams . . . will continue to carry the fetus."

The audience broke into an unharmonious chorus of jeers and cheers.

"And so," called out Troy over the din, "and so, the voting will continue as well! The app is reset as of right now – until one hour before our next show. The pregnancy continues…and so does *Canceled*! Good night everyone!"

Kaylie felt herself exhale as the lights dimmed and the crowd evacuated.

Consciously, she was undecided; but at some level, she thought, she must have wanted to stay pregnant for at least another week, because at some level, she felt relief at the voting results.

She looked over at her brother and sister, who looked clearly relieved – either at the vote result, or that the show was finally over – or probably both.

And although she was the one in this mess, at the center of the predicament – she was surprised to find herself feeling sorry for them.

They hadn't asked for this – but here they were in the middle of the fight anyway – and now Bruce had suffered a casualty.

She vowed to someday make it up to them – to her whole family.

Somehow.

CHAPTER 34

Bruce and Amanda returned to Oregon on an early flight the next morning.

Kaylie didn't even have a chance to speak with them after the show. She'd wanted to take Amanda aside and ask her if she had really meant what she said on video – about hoping the show would end in a quick abortion – to see if it was something taken out of context, or if she really felt that way.

But before Kaylie could find Amanda, she got waylaid by Dave Kohler, who wanted to "touch bases" with her and see how she was feeling.

Kaylie hadn't put much stock in his sudden show of compassion. He had a nice streak, but it was only a narrow streak floating in the middle of wide swath of corporate media grease. Kaylie had come to distrust anybody who was capable of putting people through this kind of misery, all for the almighty entertainment dollar.

The only FBC executive she had an inkling of faith in was Jake – and that was only because he was a *former* FBC executive. And, there was something about him – something less greasy than Dave, and more – substantial. He seemed to be a man who was at least struggling with some of the issues surrounding *Canceled* – not the least of which was his very direct role as the DNA-contributor half-responsible for the whole thing.

Oh – and he was *hot*.

And he had a very, very nice car.

That may seem kind of "high school," but this was, after all, an AC Cobra.

Kaylie would've very much liked to have gotten him out in that car again – perhaps to the beach – or somewhere else – and find out just what it was that made him tick.

And what it was he had wanted to tell her before.

But that wasn't going to happen now – not with a full-time crew watching him as well.

She was suddenly reminded of Winston Smith from the Orwell classic, *1984*. He had no hope of ever having a truly private moment, let alone a moment of privacy with Julia, the girl he'd fallen in love with.

The thought actually gave Kaylie some comfort, as she realized she had it better than Winston – and that her sentence would come to an end eventually, and she could return to normal life.

The week flew by – her time kept busy by appointments with Molly, Dr. Cho, and another visit to Len to talk about the latest round of headaches.

These new headaches – or was it just one long headache – focused on the back of her head and her neck. Len told her it was a different phenomenon than her previous headaches. Those had been the result of Kaylie blocking thoughts she didn't want to face. These were because she was experiencing what Len called "cognitive dissonance" – when your outward behaviors are out of alignment with your innermost values and core beliefs.

Kaylie had said she had a tough time buying that, since she didn't even know what her core beliefs were. Len said that some part of her mind obviously did know – even if she wasn't yet fully aware of it herself.

All this ducking and hiding and dancing around herself in her own mind was tiresome – and a little freaky, when it came right down to it. One of the things Kaylie had always believed was that she was an honest person – with others, and with herself. To think that she was playing games with her own head just seemed ridiculous. Yet, she trusted Len's skill and judgment as a psychiatric professional. So far, he'd not led her astray.

But for now, she decided she was more comfortable living with the headache than looking inside deep enough to come to the solid conclusions about her beliefs that would relieve her of the brain pain.

Because she feared that what she'd find in the depths of her soul would make her a thousand times more miserable than she was now.

CHAPTER 35

The silence of the Burbank night was split by the powerful blast at three-thirteen in the morning on the Thursday before Thanksgiving.

The deep, roaring boom sent out a shockwave that ripped through office windows and set off car alarms for blocks.

A fireball climbed high into the sky like a roiling mushroom of orange-red and yellow flames, the glowing sky reflected off the slick wet streets.

A blaze engulfed what was left of the west entrance of the James Brown Memorial Theater, the timbers cracking and popping, the electrical cables sparking and melting, and the glass shards liquifying in the intense heat.

Pungent black fumes reminiscent of the odor of a war zone wafted through the streets and back alleys.

Within ninety seconds, sirens could be heard approaching the FBC studios main gate.

And the TV news live trucks were not far behind.

CHAPTER 36

Jake sat on the couch watching the news.

George and Ellen's couch.

"I can't believe this crap," said Jake. "Who would blow up the freaking studio?"

George shook his head. "According to the news, everyone is blaming each other. The pro-abortion people are blaming the pro-lifers, and the pro-lifers claim it was the work of the pro-abortion people."

"For once, nobody is blaming Middle East terrorists," said Ellen, trying to insert a little humor. "But it is definitely an act of terrorism."

She placed a tray of orange juice and muffins on the coffee table in front of the couch.

It was a little early for breakfast, but the day had started before the crack of dawn, when Dave Kohler had called Jake with the news. Dave had sounded breathless and scared – not his normal calm, easy-going self.

When Jake had hung up, he'd thrown on a robe and shuffled next door, knocking and waking the Adams'. They'd flipped on the TV to watch the live reports, and Ellen had called Kaylie. Kaylie was on her way over now.

"Did your former boss mention what they're going to do?" asked George. "How they're going to handle tonight's show, with the studio in shambles?"

"No. But even if the stage and auditorium are usable – which I doubt they are – it's now a crime scene, and there's no way they'll let us anywhere near it. They need the evidence in place for their investigation."

"Do you think they'll just cancel the episode?" asked Ellen.

"Doubt it. The network can be stubborn. They know that if they cancel, it'll give the bombers what they want. Besides, that would cost FBC millions in ad revenue. No, they'll figure something else out – they'll get a new venue."

A knock on the door, and Ellen opened it to Kaylie, who was dressed in gray sweats and a loose pink t-shirt under a light jacket which she immediately removed. She wore no makeup, and her hair was in a ponytail. She still looked good.

Her two camera people followed her in and joined the two that were shooting Jake from a corner of the room. They whispered to each other, then split up and got four different angles on the family.

"Hey," Kaylie said, sitting on the couch right next to Jake. "Any word yet on who did it?"

"No," said Jake. "Nobody's taken responsibility yet – but plenty of people are pointing fingers." He took a bite out of one of the muffins and spoke with his mouth full. "Who knows what statement they were trying to make?

But one thing it is going to do – regardless of their intentions – is bring the show even more publicity. It's on all the network news stations now, and I'm sure it will be throughout the day – plus follow up stories on the investigation. This firebomb has ignited a fire*storm*." He took a sip of orange juice. "Ellen, these muffins are delicious."

"Thanks," said Ellen. "Not my best – but the best I can do here in this little kitchen."

"Did Dave say anything about tonight? What they're going to do?" asked Kaylie.

"I was just telling your parents," said Jake, "that there's no way they'll cancel the show. They'll come up with a contingency – in fact, I'm sure they're all sitting around a table right now doing just that. Normally, I'd be at that table. Now I'm just an unemployed bum mooching muffins." He took another big bite and said, almost indiscernibly through the food, "Really good muffins."

Ellen smirked.

"If you were there at that meeting – what would you suggest?" asked Kaylie.

Jake shrugged. "I'd probably have my assistants scouting for new locations – something we could use for a week or two – maybe three, if needed."

"Other theaters in the area?" asked George.

"Or maybe something entirely different – some innovative solution," said Jake. "Perhaps a live shot from the beach – weather permitting. I just don't know."

"So, no chance of them canceling the show, eh?" asked Kaylie.

"I seriously doubt it," said Jake. "There's just too much money in it. FBC will go forward one way or another – bomb or no bomb."

Jake's phone buzzed in his pocket. He pulled it out and looked at it. "Excuse me, I have to take this."

He stepped outside the apartment's front door, followed by the cameras. "What's up, Dave?"

Dave Kohler, on the other end of the line, sounded markedly more calm now than he had when he'd called earlier. *"Hey, Jake. Listen, we've been having meetings here all morning. I just wanted to let you know that the studio will be beefing up security – for you, Kaylie, and her parents as well. There's no telling what these crazies may try to do next. Better to be safe than sorry, right?"*

"So, what does that mean, exactly?"

"Round the clock bodyguards for all of you. A little extra surveillance. Nothing too intrusive."

"Compared to what? We've already got a pair of cameras in our faces at all times."

Dave chuckled. *"That's true, that's true. So, it probably won't be all that bad. Like I said, better safe than sorry."*

"Fine. I'll tell the others. Any decision yet on where tonight's gonna happen?"

"Yeah. We're going to see how many seats we can fill in the Coliseum."

"You are pulling my freaking leg."

"Yes, yes I am. We did bat around the idea of doing the season finale in the Coliseum, but for tonight, we're just going to downsize, actually, and return to where we started, at Studio 18. The network would rather keep things smaller and more controllable right now, anyway."

Jake was surprised that they would use a smaller venue, but understood their need to keep a handle on things for now. "Okay. Well, I guess I'll talk to you later."

Jake hung up and went inside, where he related all the latest from Dave to the family.

That night was a fairly mundane show, with more highlights from Kaylie's week, the new perspective of "Jake footage" for a vignette on him, and the inevitable exploitation of the bombing event, complete with security-cam slow-mo replays and interviews with people who'd heard the blast.

The vote was, as always, ridiculously close – once again in favor of keeping the baby. New voting was commenced, and the show came to a close.

Following the show, Jake, Kaylie, and the Adams' went their own ways, each accompanied by a security detail.

Jake laid his head down on his pillow that night, wondering why he had ever thought a show like this could end up any other way – from shock, to mass popularity, to heated contention and controversy – to bombs and security details.

He shook his head, wishing he could turn back the hands of time.

CHAPTER 37

For the first time in more than twenty-five years, the Adams family held Thanksgiving dinner away from their home in Medford.

Bruce and Amanda flew down, and Ellen put together a huge spread in that little apartment in Brentwood.

As the last dish – a bowl of candied yams – was brought to the table, everyone sat down.

"Well," said George, "this is a most peculiar circumstance for Thanksgiving dinner. But what really matters is that we're all together. I'll offer a prayer."

George gave thanks for food, family, and good health. Then everyone dug into the delicious turkey, mashed potatoes and gravy, rolls, creamed corn, and other accoutrements. After a few minutes of shoveling in the food, George stood and said, "I'll be right back."

He stepped out the front door and walked a few yards to the next door, and knocked. Jake answered. "Oh, hello."

"Hi Jake. Listen, I don't know if you've got any family in the area, but uh, we're having Thanksgiving dinner next door, and you're welcome to join us."

"Oh," said Jake, surprised. "Well, thanks. I was just hanging out here by myself. Look, I don't want to barge in on you and your family. Thanks, though."

"Jake, I insist. Thanksgiving is a very special time. It's all about family. I have a Christian obligation to make sure someone I know is not sitting alone today – when we have so much to share. Ellen always makes way too much food." He smiled. "We need your help, Jake."

Jake hesitated a moment, then smiled back. "All right. Come inside a sec. I should at least change out of these sweats."

George stepped inside while Jake went to his room and threw on some jeans and a black polo.

"Okay."

They stepped out, with his two camera operators, and entered the Adams apartment. Everyone stopped eating and talking for a moment when they saw him.

"Jake – and uh, his shadows – will be joining us for dinner," said George, sitting back down in his chair at the head of the table. "Jake, there's a chair in the bedroom – go ahead and grab it."

While Jake went to get the chair, Kaylie and Bruce shifted to make room for him.

"Thank you for having me," said Jake as he returned with the chair. "And thanks for letting me sit right in front of the mashed potatoes."

Everyone laughed softly and Jake served himself up a good-sized dollop of mash, along with a little of everything else.

"Normally we'd eat a little later," said George, "but it looks like FBC wants to see how many people will tune in on Thanksgiving – so Kaylie will have to be at the studio by seven."

"Yeah," said Jake. "They have me coming in tonight, too. Not sure what they have up their sleeve this time."

"I'm sure this nice private family dinner will be broadcast," said George. "It amazes me, really, what people find entertaining. Don't they have their own family dinners to keep them entertained?"

"Well," said Jake, "one thing I learned early on, when I first got into the business, was that the American viewing public has a never-ending, insatiable appetite for what amounts to voyeurism. Something in the collective psyche that makes people unable to tear themselves away from watching other people live their lives. Like – like eavesdropping. Who can resist a little 'unintentional' eavesdropping?"

"Must be a generational thing – back in my day, privacy was valued. Eavesdropping was considered rude and socially unacceptable." George cut into some dark meat with a knife and fork. "Don't you think it's ironic that the Supreme Court case that made this whole ridiculous reality show possible – *Roe v Wade* – was a decision based in a so-called right to privacy?"

Jake bit into a roll. "It's an irony that, previously, I found as delicious as these hot buttery rolls."

"You no longer feel that way."

"No. Now, I see that I was misguided, foolish, ambitious. I didn't stop to think about the real implications for real people."

"So you regret creating this show?"

"Absolutely. And not just because I've become one of its victims – or rather, one of its prime subjects. I see what it's doing to your family – to Kaylie – and I wish I'd never come up with this scheme."

"Not to mention you'd still have a job," added Kaylie.

"Yeah, well there is that. But truly, I just saw dollar signs. I never stopped to think about what this would do to people. I shudder to think – someone could've been hurt in that bombing incident."

"Someone could still get hurt," said George. "There are quite a few weeks left in this show. Lots of opportunities for crackpots to try to damage something or hurt someone."

Jake sipped at his glass of water. "I know. It's a big mess, and it's all my fault."

"We don't need any of that," said George. "We know you feel responsible. What we need to know is what you're going to *do* about it. How are you going to put an end to this madness?"

Jake put his knife and fork down on his plate and shook his head. "I don't know, George. I just don't know."

"Speaking of putting an end to it," said George, "just what did you mean, Amanda, when you said you hoped America would quickly vote to get it over with? Surely you weren't advocating for abortion? I mean, how did they edit that to make it sound so bad?"

Amanda gulped, then shrugged. "I dunno. It seems they can put words in your mouth with the editing they do. I don't even remember the conversation they pulled that quote from."

"Hmph," said George. "Those rotten people. They'll do anything to make us look bad."

"Yeah," said Amanda. "I wouldn't believe anything you see on TV."

CHAPTER 38

Episode 9, Thanksgiving with the Adams family, went off without a hitch, once again at the old Studio 18 location. As usual, the vote came down to a few thousand ballots out of millions.

Once again, they voted for the pregnancy to continue.

Jake theorized that perhaps people just wanted to see more – they didn't want the show to end – so they were just voting to make it continue, without that much regard for the life of the fetus one way or the other.

Meanwhile, Jake sat in his apartment and watched the ongoing news coverage of the show – it was indeed a national debate that was rocking the population. He couldn't help but feel a twinge of pride at having created something that *everyone* was talking about, but it was a bittersweet victory, at best.

He'd taken the opportunity to appear on a few daytime talk shows to discuss his role in his own creation, talk about the development of the idea, and the surreal coincidence of being the father and thus one of the costars of the show.

He figured he would take the speaking fees and exposure now, because he had no idea if he would have any career left at all when this was all said and done.

And he *really* didn't want to have to go do a real job.

He was just drifting off after watching the late news, his feet up on the coffee table and his head back on a pillow on the couch, when there was a knock at the door.

He arose and opened it. "Dave? I didn't expect to see *you* here."

"Can I come in?"

"Sure." Jake stepped aside and Dave entered.

"Uh, Keith, Jim – I'm gonna have you turn those off and step out, please. I need to have a truly private conversation with Jake. Give us ten. Thanks."

"You're the boss, boss," said Keith as he and the other camera operator shut down and left.

"What's this all about?" asked Jake. "Can I get you a drink?"

"Scotch."

"Sorry – I'm not storing any liquor. Trying to quit. You want a Pepsi?"

"Fine, whatever." Dave flopped down on the couch while Jake retrieved the soda.

"You look like crap, man," said Jake.

"Yeah."

"What's the problem?"

"The problem? Ha! Oh, man." He cracked open the can and took a sip. "You know, it was great at first. Every news outlet in L.A. was on the scene. And the hours of coverage after-the-fact. It was the perfect publicity stunt – no victims except the damn insurance company. Then I heard."

"What are you talking about?"

"Jake, there were two homeless people – a father and his teenage daughter – in an alley outside the James Brown. They were killed in the explosion. It took the investigators till today to figure it out. It hasn't even hit the news yet."

Jake's face turned ashen. "What did you just say about a publicity stunt?"

"Dude – it was me." He looked down. "I hired someone to set off the bomb."

"Whoa, hold on now – are you – are you saying that *you* are responsible? It wasn't fanatics on either side of the debate? *You* set the bomb?"

"That's what I'm saying." There was actually a tear in the corner of Dave's eye.

"Holy crap. Holy. Crap."

"I know! I didn't want anyone to get hurt! At first, it seemed perfect – a clean job with nobody injured and no serious damage beyond the theater itself and a few nearby windows broken. But then they found the – the ch-charred bodies." Dave started to break down, hanging his head low and letting out little silent sobs.

"Dave – I can't believe you're telling me this."

"I had to get it off my chest. I couldn't tell my wife – it would break her heart. But I've known you for a long time, Jake. You're in the business – you've got a strong stomach. I knew you would be able to handle it."

"Well, wh-what are you gonna do?"

"I don't know. If I come forward, I'll face murder charges on top of the fraud and whatever the charge is for blowing stuff up. It's such a mess."

"I think it would be manslaughter, not murder."

"Whatever. My life is over."

"Actually, those two people's lives are over. But your career certainly ended the moment you made the stupid, crazy decision to bomb the theater. What were you thinking?"

"The ratings were leveling off – I had to do something to push them over the top."

"They were already over the top! You got greedy."

"No – you don't understand the pressure I'm under, Jake. Highgate and the other execs are breathing down my neck night and day." Dave hung his head. "It seemed like a great idea at the time," he mumbled.

"Well, I know *that* feeling," said Jake.

They sat in silence for a few minutes.

"You need to turn yourself in," said Jake.

"Do I? What if I don't? What difference will it make if nobody knows? Why does anybody have to find out? After all, it was an accident."

"What are you talking about? Of course you have to take responsibility! Those two people had family somewhere – and they deserve to know the truth. And the investigation will be a waste of resources if it's allowed to go on in futility. Plus, they may just figure it out – and you'll be in a better position for a plea if you turn yourself in, rather than waiting to get caught."

"No! No. Maybe if – maybe we can just let it ride – lay low. This doesn't have to destroy everything. I think we should just see how it all plays out."

Jake sat forward. "Are you crazy? Has the knowledge that you've killed people in the pursuit of entertainment and ratings driven you out of your freaking mind? There's no letting it ride, Dave! This has to be resolved."

"What – are you gonna turn me in?"

"If I have to."

"Really? You'd betray my confidence? I came to you because you're the only person I trust."

"And you've put me in a very bad position. Did you really think I could just sit on this? Heck, Dave, my conscience is already racked enough by this whole damn show. I never should've pitched it in the first place. In a way, I'm also responsible for these deaths."

Dave sat and frowned, staring right through Jake.

Jake had never seen Dave look this way – so desperate, so broken. "So, the bomb thing was your idea? Nobody else at the network knows about it?"

"I acted alone. If this gets out, I won't have the protection of the FBC legal team. They'll hang me out to dry. And Jake – the show will go on. Crucifying me won't put a stop to it. In fact, the additional controversy will only be welcomed in the long run. Sure, it'll briefly reflect poorly on FBC, but they'd soon spin it as the act of one crazy man. They'd wash their hands of me, and the show will live on, bigger than ever."

Jake knew Dave was right. The show had become a hungry monster that fed on any and all attention it could get. No publicity was bad publicity, and *Canceled* had gained a life and a momentum all its own, like a rolling tsunami.

A man-made natural disaster that fed the nation's appetite for destruction.

Destruction of decency, destruction of privacy – and now the literal destruction of lives.

Things had gotten completely out of hand. But hanging Dave out to dry didn't seem like a productive way to derail this rollercoaster. All it would do is wreck Dave's life – and the life of his family.

Besides, Dave was Jake's only ally at FBC.

For now, maybe all Jake could do was sit on this information.

And let it eat at him, the way everything else was eating at him these days.

"All right, Dave," he said. "I won't say anything. For now."

Dave looked relieved. "Thank you."

"So, what *did* you want me to do? Why did you come to me with this?"

"I – I guess I just needed to talk to someone. To share this burden with someone I could trust. To talk it out."

"Well, thanks for implicating me."

"Sorry about that. I realize that I'm asking a lot of you – by asking you to stay quiet."

Jake shrugged. "What the hell – I don't have much left to lose anymore anyway."

Dave rubbed his face with both palms, then stood up and went to the door. "Well, I better bring the crew back in."

"Hey – about that," said Jake. "I'd like one thing in return for my silence."

"Yeah?"

"Yeah. I want time. Off-camera time. Relief from the twenty-four seven coverage."

Dave considered for a moment. "I guess can arrange that. Within reason."

"I just want a couple of hours, here and there, where I can speak privately with Kaylie."

"All right. I'll make it happen. But you need to be careful – people will notice if there are important blocks of time missing."

"People? What people?"

"Our chief editor, Gil Samuels, for one. He doesn't miss a thing – he'll notice if there are discrepancies in the time code on the feeds."

"Yeah, but he works for *you*. Won't he come to you if he thinks there's a problem?"

"Maybe. He and I don't often see eye to eye. And he's in good standing with Tom Highgate – he's friends with his daughter."

Jake rolled his eyes. "A lot of guys are 'friends' with Tom Highgate's daughter."

"Oh? Little nympho, eh?"

"Let's just day she has issues."

"Well, in any case, we'll just have to make sure we don't overuse this privilege. Okay?"

"Sure. When I want an hour off, I'll call you, and you can call off your dogs."

"Fair enough." Dave opened the door to leave, and send the cameras back in. "And Jake – thanks. Thanks for listening, and for being a friend."

CHAPTER 39

Kaylie rolled over in bed, unable to sleep.

She wasn't that big yet, but The Bulge was definitely a presence – and starting to make its own demands with regard to such things as sleeping position.

She'd already accepted that The Bulge was now in total control of all the eating decisions – what, when, and what *not*. That battle had been lost weeks ago.

But she'd be damned if she was going to relinquish her right to lie down however she pleased at bed time.

She turned again.

Sighed.

Tossed once more and punched at the pillow.

Maybe she *was* damned.

The lonely, silent graveyard crew sat in a corner playing cards under the dim aura of a night light, their cameras mounted on skinny tripods, aimed at the bed.

Kaylie wondered what transgressions those two had committed to wind up on this lousy assignment. Guess you had to pay your dues in any business.

And she was certainly paying hers.

And she did have her transgressions.

Exhausted and frustrated, she sighed again, just wishing for a little comfort, a little sleep.

Her phone, sitting on her nightstand, lit up. In the hopes of getting some rest, she'd set it to silent, no vibrate. She reached out to it and tipped the screen to see the display.

One new text.

She tapped the screen and read the text.

Your camera crew will be called away shortly. Meet me behind your apartment building. Jake.

Kaylie's heart suddenly started pounding. She was about to sit up when one of the camera people received a text. She watched as he stepped into another room for a moment, and she could hear him talking to someone on his cell. Then he returned and told his partner that Dave Kohler had called and ordered them to leave the shoot for an hour. They shut down the cameras and took them with them. They didn't bother to speak to her, assuming she was asleep.

As soon as they were gone, she shot up in bed and pushed her hair away from her face.

She swung her feet over the bed and stood, then quickly moved to the bathroom and flipped on the light, temporarily blinding herself.

She had no idea what this was about, but it beat lying there trying unsuccessfully to sleep.

And the feeling of those cameras being gone was – *fabulous.*

She just hoped this wasn't some FBC trick to make her *think* she was free, but really under covert surveillance. She wasn't sure if that was paranoid thinking, or just the thoughts of someone who was growing wise to the network's games.

Either way, she wanted to enjoy this while she could.

She quickly primped and slipped into some sweats (she didn't have time to figure out what else might fit – her size changing daily).

She fluffed her long hair, which was getting fuller and longer as the pregnancy progressed. A speedy makeup session in the mirror and she grabbed her purse and ran out, locking the door behind her. She took the back stairs, instead of the elevator (again, those paranoid thoughts plaguing her), then slipped out the rear door.

There in the alley, looking like a knight in shining armor, was Jake in his shining Cobra.

He smiled at her, and she couldn't help but grin back as she climbed in.

They rumbled out of the alley, onto the street, and before long were on the open road.

"What – what's this all about?" she finally said. "How did you swing this?"

Jake breathed deeply and exhaled. "Let's just say I pulled some strings – I still have a little uh, power, at the network."

"But they canned you."

"I'm still friends with Dave Kohler."

"Oh."

"So, we have an hour alone?"

"Yeah. Well, forty-seven more minutes."

Kaylie smiled and laughed out loud. "Yes! I could kiss you!"

Jake smiled, then tipped his head back and laughed. It was the first time Kaylie could remember seeing him really laugh. It looked good on him. "So, where do you want to go?" he asked.

"Twenty-three minutes in *any* direction would suit me fine! As fast as she'll carry us!"

Jake glanced over at Kaylie, then surprised her by reaching over and sliding the lap section of her seatbelt down snugly *under* The Bulge. He gave her a little nod, and she felt an odd little thrill at the touch of his hand.

Then he laid that hand on the shifter and stepped on it.

They flew up the highway, the Christmas-decorated homes each side of the road a blur of colored lights.

"Let's see how far we can get in twenty-three minutes," he said, accelerating to eighty-five. "You don't mind a little speed, do you?"

"Are you kidding? When I moved down here from Medford I made the trip in under eight hours – with a lunch break. Drive-through, of course."

"Not bad. What is that, about five, six hundred miles?"

"Almost seven hundred."

"What were you driving?"

"A '98 Corolla."

"Wow. That *is* impressive. What brought you down here, anyway?"

"This."

"Late night drives in fast cars?"

"No. Fame. And fortune." She smiled. "I wanted to be a movie star."

"Careful what you wish for, eh?"

"Yeah, you could say that." She shook her head slowly, half-smiling. "What kind of wild hair did you get when you came up with this crazy show, anyway?"

Jake smiled. "You know, when you've been doing this for a while, and you're expected to come up with hot new stuff for every fall season – you brainstorm – there's a lot of pressure –"

"– And you go insane from the pressure?"

"Ha ha! No, you are just pushed to come up with stuff that will shock people – stuff that is beyond the beyond – stuff that has never been done before – stuff that will get high-dollar sponsors on board and pull in the ratings. Sometimes you just forget to – to think about it long enough to realize that there can be a human cost. That people could get hurt." He slowed down and pulled off the highway, stopping outside a convenience store. "You forget that people could get killed."

"Killed? Oh, you mean the fetus. Yeah – there is that, isn't there?"

"Do you still think of it as just a fetus? I mean, that's how I thought of it when I dreamed up the show – but, lately, maybe it's just because I'm the father."

"You're getting attached? Don't tell me that, Jake."

"I think I'm getting attached to more than just the baby. It's – it's the whole idea of fatherhood, of family. And I'm getting attached to your family," he chuckled, "my neighbors. And I'm getting attached to you."

"To me?"

"A little."

"A little?"

"Yeah. I like you."

"Well, I like you, Jake. You're not a typical network executive slimeball."

"Oh? So, what kind of network executive slimeball am I?"

"An unemployed one." She laughed at his offended expression and pushed his shoulder, then laughed harder. "I'm kidding, I'm kidding. You're not a slimeball. You seem like a surprisingly decent guy."

"Surprisingly?"

"Yeah. Surprising that the network executive who thought up such a trashy show is not a slimeball. And – surprising that a guy I picked out at a club and had a fling with is not a slimeball. I must've been off my game that night."

Jake grinned. "Thank you. I think. But let's not rewrite history – fact of the matter is that *I* picked *you*."

Kaylie smiled back at him. "Uh huh. How much time do we have left?"

Jake looked at his watch. "About twenty minutes. He opened his door and gestured toward the store. "This place carries my favorite – Old Rock Root Beer – in the bottle. Hard to find. You want anything?"

Kaylie closed her eyes for a moment. "I have been craving a pink Sloshie for weeks, but I'm kind of afraid to go out in public these days."

"I'll bring you back a large."

He closed the door and entered the store, leaving the engine running.

Kaylie looked over at the dashboard – the tachometer showed it idling smoothly at about 1100 RPM, and the speedometer went all the way to 180 MPH. She looked down at the rosewood gearstick knob.

She *so* wanted to drive this car.

So, she got out, went around the back, and climbed into the driver's side.

Jake wouldn't be able to refuse her this simple pleasure, would he?

She looked in the rearview mirror, and adjusted it for her own, smaller stature. An '88 Civic with peeling silver paint parked behind her across the parking lot, and a bearded man got out. He walked past the Cobra and eyeballed her on his way into the store.

Must be jealous of her ride.

She would be too. It was the nicest car she'd ever had the good fortune to –

BANG!

BANG! BANG!

Kaylie jumped in her seat when the three gunshots rang out like muffled firecrackers.

Her heart pounded hard in her chest as she tried to catch her breath.

The bearded man ran out of the store clutching something, and jumped in his Civic.

Without even thinking, Kaylie threw the Cobra in reverse, and barreled backwards across the lot twenty feet with spinning tires throwing up smoke. She slammed "t-bone" into the driver door of the Civic, pinning and knocking out the robber.

Still on an adrenaline high, she jumped out, taking a half second to glance at the man. He may have been dead for all she knew. Or cared.

She ran inside the store.

A woman was lying slumped over the counter face-down, a pool of blood under her.

As Kaylie stopped running, her feet slipped and she nearly fell over.

She looked down.

She had slipped in a slick of blood. Her eyes followed the trail around the corner of the bakery aisle.

And she saw Jake.

He was lying on the floor on his back, covered in blood, clutching at his belly.

She fell to her knees by his side and cradled his head. "Jake!"

"Did he – did he get away? I tried to – I tried to stop –"

His eyes rolled back in his head and he went limp.

"Jake!" Kaylie screamed.

CHAPTER 40

"Somebody's head is going to roll!" bellowed Tom Highgate.

Tom, Dave, and a number of other FBC executives sat around the large mahogany conference table in the dead of night.

"How is it," Tom continued, standing up and slapping the table for emphasis, "that we miss the biggest thing to happen on this show since its inception – the biggest thing that could happen on *any* reality TV show? Where were the freaking *cameras*?"

Dave looked down and said nothing. He was really in a bind, here. If he took responsibility, he'd surely be fired. And if they asked him to explain himself, he'd have to think of something – he could never tell the whole truth about why he'd made arrangements for Jake and Kaylie to get some alone time.

But then, it wouldn't take long before the truth came out that Dave had authorized – in fact, ordered – the standing down of the cameras for one hour.

Which meant it was time to start thinking up excuses.

It was bad enough that his friend had had a bullet put in his stomach and was in emergency surgery at this moment. Now he was going to be unemployed right along with Jake – taken off the most successful television show in history and likely to never work in Hollywood again.

He was starting to think this show was cursed.

"Tom," said Dave, knowing it was better to own up to it now, than to have a brief investigation reveal his complicity, "it was me. I authorized the break in the shooting schedule."

"The break in the shooting schedule? What are you talking about?" Tom's eyes were wide and the veins in his neck and temples were standing out in purple, squiggly lines. "There are no *breaks* in reality TV! You don't just call off the cameras! What were you thinking?"

"I, uh – I made a mistake. I took a risk, and it went horribly wrong. I thought that it could enhance the show if we gave Jake and Kaylie a little alone time to develop their relationship – I figured it would make for a better show if we could show them growing closer. That wasn't going to happen under our ever-watchful eye. I had to create an environment in which we could get some chemistry going, spice up the show. I'm sorry. It was a mistake."

Tom stared at Dave. He breathed big heaving breaths, still riled up from his rant. Then he sat back down and laced his fingers. "Damn right it was a mistake. A very costly one. Why didn't you run such a departure from protocol by anybody else?"

Excited that Tom was buying it, Dave was emboldened. "Because it's my damn show. With all due respect, Tom, since when do I run show decisions past anyone else?"

Tom rubbed at his face and sighed. "Since our blasted stars started getting *shot*! *Off-camera*!"

Dave rolled his eyes in mock indignation.

Tom continued. "Starting right now – you're on suspension, Dave. Without pay." He turned to his assistant. "Sophie, get Wyatt Sloane on the horn. I'm bringing him in as the new showrunner – for now – until we get a handle on all this crap."

"Sloane? Aw, come on!" Dave protested. "Don't hand over the reins to that guy, Tom."

"Why not? Afraid he'll do a better job?"

"I'm afraid he'll do what he did with America's Got Weirdos. That show started out classy and bringing in serious revenue. Then Sloane got a hold of it and turned it into a circus – and the ratings tanked."

"Well, he's experienced, and he's all we've got right now. Go home and take a break, Dave. Now."

Dave glared at Tom as he left, shutting the door behind him with a slam. When he got out in the hallway, he dropped the puffed up façade and breathed a sigh of relief.

For now, he would keep his job – and nobody would know he had cut a deal with Jake for the off-camera time.

And nobody would know why.

CHAPTER 41

"I can't believe they're not pre-empting the episode tonight!" Kaylie complained to Felicity as she waited to see Len.

"Really? Seems to me it's not that unbelievable," said Felicity. "This is going to be a prime ratings grabber for them. I know that's harsh, but you know it's true. One of their stars gunned down? That's money in the bank for those creeps. No way they'd pass up an opportunity like that."

Kaylie sighed. "I – I just can't believe Jake was shot. He was just – just trying to help!"

"No good deed goes unpunished," said Felicity.

Len popped his head out of the door leading to his office. "Ready."

"Thanks for listening," said Kaylie. "Hi, Len."

"Hey Kaylie. Come on in."

Len stepped up to the pool table and lined up a shot – two ball in the corner pocket – as Kaylie sat down in one of the recliners, laid her head back, closed her eyes, and draped a soft lavender-filled silk pouch across her eyes.

"Talk to me about last night," said Len, as the pool balls clacked together gently.

"Len," Kaylie started, but her voice broke and she had to collect herself. "It was horrible. The blood."

Len dropped another ball in the side pocket. "How's Jake?"

Kaylie took a couple of deep breaths. "I came straight here from the hospital. I was there all night. Mom and Dad came, too. He's out of surgery and recovering in ICU. They say he'll live. They won't say much else."

"Does he have any family?"

"No. His parents are both dead. He just has an uncle back east somewhere."

"Hmm. What happened, anyway?"

"Well, we were just out for a drive – we had a chance to get away from the cameras for one hour. So, we stopped at a little market, and he went in, and then – I heard the shots. Then this guy runs out and jumps in a car."

"I heard something about the armed robber getting caught."

"Yeah – that was me. I ran into him with Jake's car."

"Wow. That was brave."

"No – not really. I was just on autopilot. Anyway, then I ran into the store and saw the cashier – she was dead. Then I saw the blood, and found Jake lying there. He looked awful. He could barely breathe. It was just awful."

"Before we move on – tell me about the robber. How do you feel about what you did to him?"

Kaylie shrugged. "I dunno – I mean, he's in no worse shape than Jake. I really don't feel anything about what I did. I made sure he didn't get away, so I feel good about that. I wish I hadn't had to crunch him with the car, but I don't feel bad about it. He's a murderer and he's put Jake in the hospital. I don't really care that I ran him over."

"I see," said Len. "So, you called the cops?"

"Well, I pulled out my cell and dialed 9-1-1 – my hands were so shaky I could barely hit the numbers. I wasn't even sure exactly where we were, but the operator was great – she figured it out and stayed on the line until the police and EMTs arrived. When they got there, I was cradling Jake's head and watching him breathe shallow breaths. They ushered me out of the way and began working on him."

"And then?" asked Len.

"The EMTs took Jake away, and the cops asked me questions. One of them recognized me from TV – which was – weird. I told them what happened, then eventually they let me go to the hospital. Jake was in surgery for a *long* time. Then he was in post-op and they let me see him but he was unconscious. That's really all I know."

"Are you angry?"

"Of course I am! Some idiot trying to steal some Christmas money or drug money or whatever just blew a hole in a friend of mine – not to mention killing the cashier and traumatizing me! Yeah, I'm mad! I'm also angry that the stupid FBC people are still going on the air tonight – that I have to be there and cry on stage and boost their stupid ratings, exploiting this whole tragedy for their gain. And it bothers me that you're so calm!"

Len put up his cue stick in a rack on the wall and came and sat down in the adjacent recliner, kicking his feet up. "Hey, I'm also very troubled by all this. But I'm here to be a soft place for you – a calm, serene repository for your feelings. It wouldn't do much good for me to be all upset, would it?"

Kaylie pouted. "No. Sorry – I'm just angrier than I realized, and probably directing it at the wrong people. Just venting in all directions like a stupid volcano."

"Well, I think you're fine. You've been holding back some anger for a while now anyway – so this is as good a time as any for a little release."

"I have? I've been holding back anger?"

"Sure. Everybody does. And you've had some very good reasons to be angry."

"Like?"

"You tell me."

Kaylie took another deep breath and pulled the lavender sack off her eyes, then sat up slowly.

"Well, I guess I've been mad at myself for getting into this whole situation. I was a little mad at my folks – at first – for just being my folks and trying to lecture me. I was mad at Jake for creating the show, and mad at FBC for the way I've been treated."

"But?"

"But what?"

"You had a tone in your voice that made me think you were about to say 'but'."

Kaylie bit her lip.

"Well, I realize that a lot of that anger is misdirected. My parents were just saying what they said because they love me and care about me. I recognize that now. And Jake was just doing his job. And the network has actually treated me very well, considering. I may not love all the contract terms, but they have certainly held up their end and are compensating me well. So, I really can't complain," she smiled, "but I do anyway."

"Of course you do. We all do. Life is a matter of balancing all the pros and cons. And it's natural to want to complain against the cons. But if you look long-term, the cons don't matter – only the pros. Those are the things you end up carrying with you – as long as you lay aside the anger. Otherwise, you end up carrying the cons – and they can get damn heavy."

Kaylie smiled a little bit. "Yeah, heavy. Thanks, Len. You always help me get centered and remember what's important."

"So, you ready – I mean, emotionally prepared – for tonight's show?"

"Am I ever?"

CHAPTER 42

Jake turned his head and saw a welcome sight: Kaylie sitting beside his bed.

Earlier that morning, he'd woken up for the first time since the shooting. His doctor had explained to him everything that had happened, including a prognosis that he preferred not to think about. All he'd wanted to do at that point was slip back into unconsciousness – the waking reality too much to process.

He'd slept all day, and now he was hungry. He stared at Kaylie for a few moments. She was looking away and hadn't noticed he was awake yet.

She looked fantastic.

Also a little blurry – must be the heavy pain meds.

"Hey," he mustered hoarsely.

She turned and smiled down at him. "Hey, yourself."

"I can't believe you crashed my freaking car," he whispered.

"I, uh, I –"

Jake's grin stopped Kaylie' stuttering, and she smiled back. "Sorry. I guess I might have got a little armed-robber guts on your bumper. I'll try to be more careful next time I'm hunting down people who shoot my friends."

Jake lifted his hand and patted hers. "Thanks. I mean, thanks for taking care of me – for being here."

"All I did was call 9-1-1. And stayed awake all night while you were in surgery. No big deal."

"What's with the bright lights?" he asked, glancing to the other side of the room.

"Oh, you're going to love this," she said. "FBC has some deep pockets and a lot of influence – apparently they've managed to talk the hospital into letting them shoot some of tonight's show right here – in your room."

That explained why she was all dolled up. "Ah. I see. Right here in my freaking hospital room, with me in all my drugged up glory. Nice. I suppose I have Dave to thank for this honor."

"Actually, for some reason, Dave is unavailable. I don't think he's running the show anymore – they put some other guy in charge – Wyatt Earp or something. No – Sloane. Wyatt Sloane."

Jake rolled his eyes. "Great. That creep's been gunning for Dave's job for as long as I can remember."

"Whatever. One greasy studio executive's the same as the next, I say." She winked at him.

"Well, this one is as greasy as they come. He's the kind of guy who can take a nice, tame family show like *Canceled* and turn it into a tawdry three-ring circus. For starters, there's this." He gestured toward the lights, then shook his head.

"Don't worry, Jake, I've got your back. If any of those camera guys try to get a rear-shot of your hospital gown, I'll throw up a diversion."

"Oh yeah? Like what?"

"I dunno, I'll pull up my shirt and show them The Bulge."

"Nice."

Troy Tanner walked into the room without so much as a knock on the door. "Hey there, Jake-o, how's it hangin' my man?"

Jake just lifted his chin a little to acknowledge Troy.

"That bad, eh? Well, I guess you did manage to catch a thirty-eight slug with your gut. Well, anyway, just wanted you to know we're only a few minutes out. Sloane has me opening in the hospital's chapel – it's the only place we could cram in a small studio audience – and we'll cut to a shot of you here for the break one tease. Second segment, we'll be in here for a little chat. Catchya in a few."

With that, he disappeared, the odor of his cologne left lingering for a few moments.

"See what I mean?" said Jake. "Sloane is one class act, turning the hospital's chapel into a theater."

"Sounds like he's resourceful." Kaylie looked at Jake, and when his face displayed revulsion, she burst into a laugh. "And a completely disrespectful butt-nugget," she said. "I'm just messing with you, Jake. Believe me, I am not looking forward to having someone like Sloane running things. But, I've decided I have to just keep a sense of humor about things that are completely out of my control."

Kaylie flipped on the TV with a remote. It was mounted high on a wall bracket near the door. FBC was in the extended commercial break prior to the show.

Moments later, a small crew comprised of a camera operator, boom mic operator, and floor director entered, wearing headsets. Their faces were all business. They didn't even seem to see Jake and Kaylie as anything other than furniture – just subjects that needed to be captured on camera.

"And we're on in five, four, three."

On the screen, the opening sequence played, then dissolved to a shot of Troy in the hospital chapel. He was actually standing at the pulpit, like some kind of televangelist. His normal, jubilant voice and approach were markedly subdued.

"Welcome to *Canceled*, folks. We're broadcasting live from UCLA Medical Center tonight, where one of our stars, Jake Granville, lies in recovery following a dramatic – and nearly deadly – incident."

The screen dissolved to some older footage of Jake's car on the road, and a brief, masterfully-edited segment that described the whole shooting incident. Shots of the bloody floor at the convenience store, police cars and yellow crime scene tape, and exteriors of the hospital with an ambulance racing in with sirens blaring. All carefully crafted to give the illusion that the cameras had been present for the whole thing.

Jake thought only one ingredient was missing: a little title at the bottom of the screen to indicate that it was a dramatization.

But, of course, there was no such title.

The screen returned to Troy.

"Tonight, we'll talk to Jake and Kaylie and hear all about what happened. And, of course, we'll have your vote results. That's all coming up – after the break."

"Standby," said the floor director in Jake's room. She pointed at Jake, and a red light lit up on the camera as the going-to-break video showed Jake and Kaylie in the recovery room.

"And, clear," said the floor director as the TV showed the start of a commercial.

When the show returned, Troy introduced the remainder of the show, which ran like a typical episode, with vignettes highlighting Kaylie's week, and also some portions of Jake's week before the shooting occurred (though his sit-around-the-house routine provided little in the way of entertainment). Jake insisted he was not a performing monkey, and under no obligation to do anything interesting – of course, that all changed when they went for their disastrous little drive.

Throughout the episode, Troy played the "tease" game, keeping the audience hanging for the big Jake interview.

On the next to last break of the show, Troy did his cliffhanger bit, then within a minute of the commercials starting he appeared in Jake's recovery room, a little out of breath from the run from the chapel. "Okay guys, you ready?"

Kaylie and Jake just nodded glumly.

A minute later: "Welcome back, America," said Troy. "We're here with Jake and Kaylie. Let's get right to it. Kaylie, tell us what happened last night."

"Well, we just went out for a short drive – to get away a little and chat. We stopped at a little store so Jake could grab us some drinks, and I saw a guy walk in after Jake went in. Then I heard the shots – no, wait, then I got out and got back in in the driver seat – I wanted to drive Jake's car, and figured he'd let me if I was already in the driver's seat."

She looked over at Jake, who actually smiled a little.

"Then I heard the shots – three shots – and the guy came running out. He jumped in his car, and I – I wasn't even thinking – I just threw the car into reverse and slammed him. Then I got out and ran into the store and found the cashier dead and Jake shot."

"Did it occur to you that maybe the guy running out of the store was just an innocent bystander, trying to get away from the shooting?"

"Uh, no – like I said, I wasn't thinking, I was just acting on instinct and adrenaline.   It all happened so fast –" Kaylie looked down and brought her hand up to her face as she started to cry.

The camera lingered for a few moments on a tight shot of the weeping Kaylie.

"And Jake, tell us about your experience," said Troy, moving it along.

The camera panned quickly to Jake, and the boom mic operator swung the microphone to hover over his head.

"First, let me just preface this with a disclaimer – I am on some very heavy pain medication right now, so I may not be completely coherent."

Troy chuckled, "No problem. Just tell us what you can remember."

"Well, like Kaylie said, we were out for a quick drive, and stopped for something to drink. I went in and grabbed a six-pack of my favorite root beer from the cold case, and was on my way to get a pink Sloshie for Kaylie – when this guy at the counter says, 'Give it to me, *now*!' and then like a second later fires off a round."

Jake seemed to be staring right through Troy as he recalled the incident.

"The cashier flew back and bounced off the cigarette case then came forward and slumped over the counter.

The shooter turned around and saw me, saw that I had seen him, and fired wildly at me – twice – the first one missed, and I lunged toward him to try to take him down, but the second shot didn't miss. I don't remember much after that – the next thing I knew, I was waking up here this morning, listening to the doctor tell me what I'd missed."

"Wow. And what had you missed – what did the doctor tell you?"

"He said I was in surgery for nine hours. They removed a thirty-eight slug from my spine. It had entered through my lower intestine area and struck bone at the top of the L-2 vertebra, shattering it and lodging against my spinal cord. They were able to remove the bullet, but they, uh – he said that it's not likely that I'll ever be able to feel anything below my waist ever again." A pause. "I'm paralyzed from the waist down."

"Oh no!" cried Kaylie, her hands covering her mouth in shock.

"Aw, Jake, we are very, very sorry to hear that," said Troy, sounding uncharacteristically sincere. "Kaylie, this is obviously the first you've heard of this. Tell us what you're thinking and feeling right now."

Jake could see Kaylie clenching her fists.

"How do I – how do I *feel*?" She wiped away a tear. "I feel awful! I can't believe that Jake will never – will never walk again! This whole thing is completely out of control. This show just needs to end!"

"Well, Kaylie, the good news is – there's a provision for that. All we need is a majority of voters to opt for you to visit Dr. Ian – and then it will, indeed, all be over. And that can, potentially, happen at any point. Even tonight. In fact, we'll have results of this past week's voting, coming up."

The show went to commercial.

The end-of show vote results were a re-run of last week – a hair-splitting margin in favor of "the show must go on."

Troy made a quick exit, along with the camera crew, and Jake and Kaylie had a precious five minutes alone together during a shift change before she was required to leave with her graveyard shift camera crew.

"Hey," he said. "Don't worry about me. I'll be fine."

Kaylie wiped away more tears. "But – I can't help but feel responsible, somehow."

Jake shook his head and weakly squeezed her hand. "Don't be silly. This is absolutely not your fault. It's just something that – happened. And I'll make it through. You just need to worry about yourself – get some rest, take care of yourself. Everything will be fine."

The door opened and Kaylie's nighttime camera person – a young girl in a black FBC hoodie – came in, camera already rolling.

Kaylie sniffed and wiped her face again. "I'll see you soon." She reached out and touched Jake's face. "I'm so sorry."

Jake watched her walk out the door. The room was left silent, except for the hum of the computers and medical equipment.

He gulped hard, barely managing to hold back the tears.

Instead, he transformed his trembling pain into a simmering rage, and stared up at the ceiling, cursing the fate that had led to this destruction of his future.

Feeling desperate and trapped, he gritted his teeth and pounded his fist onto the recline-control panel of his bed.

CHAPTER 43

The next three weeks Kaylie visited Jake in the hospital nearly every day.

The show episodes remained pretty bland (despite efforts to sensationalize Jake's recovery process), and excitement for *Canceled* waned as it fell into a rhythm and became lost among all the noise of the Christmas season.

The ratings, although still phenomenal, dipped a little as the temperatures in sunny Southern California dropped and the days grew shorter.

Jake was released to home care just two days before Christmas. He was confined to a wheelchair and assigned a round-the-clock nursing staff. Jenna in the morning, Francine on swing shift, and Marcus at night.

He also spent a lot of hours back at the hospital in physical therapy. Although he was beginning to feel some slight sensations in his legs from time to time, his doctor was not optimistic that Jake would ever regain his mobility.

On Christmas Eve, George Adams invited Jake to come next door the following day for a Christmas Day family meal, and left a small gift-wrapped package with Jake.

Jake opened it later that night – it was a book – *Daddies for Dummies – A Practical and Comprehensive Guide to Fatherhood in the 21st Century – From Conception to College.*

Jake smiled at it and flipped through it.

He wasn't sure if it was a thoughtful gift, a manipulative ploy, or a veiled insult.

Then he noticed that the first blank page was inscribed.

Dear Jake – We hope you enjoy this how-to book. Of course, no book can really prepare you for what's ahead, but we hope that having this on your shelf will remind you that we are always here for you, and glad that you are a part of our family. Sincerely, George and Ellen Adams

That answered his question. It was a genuine, thoughtful present. Of course, he immediately chastised himself for thinking anything different – George and Ellen had shown themselves from the start to be good-hearted and decent people.

Jake thought about the book, about fatherhood, about the kindness of others.

This time, he couldn't hold back his emotions.

He hung his head and quietly wept.

Christmas morning, George came around at about eleven, and wheeled Jake next door.

Compared to his quiet, nearly empty apartment – just him, Jenna the nurse, and one camera person – this place was loud and packed.

There were George and Ellen, Bruce, Amanda and her new boyfriend Scott, and Kaylie; plus Kaylie's two camera people, Justin Mitchell the daytime director, and now Jake, Jenna and his camera person.

Twelve people in all.

Jake thought back to his own Christmases growing up. When he was very young, there was Mom and Dad. But they were killed in a commuter train wreck when he was only six, and then he lived with Uncle Ronnie and Aunt Bev. Then Bev got sick, and then she was gone, and it was just Ronnie and Jake at Christmas time. By contrast, this seemed like a huge family gathering, even if half of them weren't even family.

The only thing missing, it seemed, were children.

But maybe one day, this same scene would play out differently – they'd all be up in Oregon (which Jake envisioned as a land of trees, rivers, and loggers), with no camera people, and there would be a little one – or more – running around laughing and screaming and enjoying the day. Making everybody smile at the innocence and delight.

Jake shook his head and snapped out of his silly fantasy.

Thanks to his show, there would likely be no child at all, and this family that was welcoming him so warmly would never be a part of his life.

A life in which he was now confined to a chair.

He once again shook himself from his thoughts, realizing that his swaying mood must be, at least in part, due to the drugs in his system.

He was still on meds for the pain – though he hoped to be able to quickly wean himself off. He hated being dependent on a drug to feel okay.

He was determined to do more than merely exist without pain – he wanted to actually get better. He was pushing himself hard in the physical therapy sessions – his therapist said "too hard." Lurking somewhere in his subconscious was the hopeless dream of one day being able to run and play with his son or daughter. To give piggyback rides.

These thoughts and feelings, and the pain and the drugs – were all combining to make him very reflective and emotional lately.

He decided it would be best to just stop thinking for a few hours and try to enjoy himself. Or at least to give the impression that he was having a good time.

After all, it was Christmas.

And Ellen was cooking.

CHAPTER 44

It was only six o'clock in the evening on Christmas Day, but Kaylie was exhausted. She really wanted to go home and curl up in bed, despite having napped through most of the family's traditional viewing of *It's a Wonderful Life*.

But there was one thing she still wanted to do tonight.

She spotted Amanda sitting quietly in the corner, and decided now was as good a time as any to get to the bottom of something that had been troubling her.

She got Amanda's attention and gestured for her to follow her to the empty kitchen. A lone light above the sink bathed the room in a dim glow.

Kaylie got right to the point.

"Amanda, I want you to be straight with me. I've been thinking about what you said on tape – in Cynthia's report – about wishing America would vote for an abortion."

Amanda shot a quick glance at the camera that had followed them into the kitchen. "I already told you they took me out of context."

"No they didn't. Your statement was pretty plain and clear. Now, I really don't care if you believe in abortion or not. I don't even know what *I* believe. I just want to know what you really think. Despite how it looks – with all the professionals they've assigned to me, and having Mom and Dad here – I'm really alone in this. I can't talk about this with Mom and Dad because they are so dead-set on their point of view. It sounds like maybe you're not as gung-ho as them, and I just wanted to talk with you about it."

Amanda turned toward the counter and shuffled some plates around, pretending to clean up. "I'd really rather not talk about it."

"Why?"

Amanda turned back, with tears welling in her eyes. "It's personal, okay?"

Kaylie frowned. "Just tell me. Please." Tears started to come into her eyes. "I don't want to feel so alone in this anymore. I still don't know what I want, and nobody understands. Just talk to me. Please."

Amanda bit her lip and looked down. She seemed to be at war with herself inside. Then she seemed to make a decision, and her face took on a look of resolve. She looked over at the camera, and leaned in to whisper in Kaylie's ear.

"You remember that money you loaned me – right before you left home?"

"Yeah," Kaylie whispered back.

"It was because I – I needed it." Amanda breathed heavily, her voice a hot movement of air against Kaylie's neck. "I was in trouble. I used it to – to get an abortion."

"What? You got an abortion?"

As Kaylie spoke those words aloud, George walked in.

And dropped his empty hot chocolate mug on the floor.

"Did I just hear what I thought I heard?" he asked slowly, shock on his face.

A moment later, Ellen was at his side to find out what was going on.

"Yes," said Amanda. "You heard right. There. My big secret is out."

She sunk to the floor and sat with her back to the cupboards.

"I don't understand," said Ellen.

"What's to understand?" said Amanda, tears streaming down her face as she glanced toward the camera that had caught the whole thing. "Five years ago I was raped, I got pregnant, and I got an abortion. End of story."

Ellen's legs buckled and George caught her with one arm, quickly pulling out a wooden dining chair with the other and guiding his wife into it.

Kaylie crouched down and engulfed Amanda in her arms as Amanda began to sob uncontrollably.

Bruce came in and said, "Hey, what's going on?"

He quickly ascertained there was something very serious happening, and started whispering with his dad. Then he looked over at the crumpled Amanda being hugged by Kaylie.

"I can't believe it," he said.

A moment later, Jake rolled in.

He stared at the scene, unable to figure out what was occurring. "Is Amanda all right?" he asked. "Is she hurt?"

"Jake. You'd better leave. I'm sorry," said George. "This is a family matter."

"Are you sure?" said Jake. "You know this is all going to be shown on TV anyway."

George glared at Jake, then softened a little, sighing heavily. "I guess you're right." He turned to his family. "Come on, let's all go sit down in the living room."

They all followed, Kaylie clutching Amanda, who was still sniffling.

The family all sat down on the couches and recliners in the living room, a heavy feeling in the air.

Kaylie stayed close to her sister, and Jake wheeled himself up close to Kaylie at the end of the couch.

"I think," said George, "that given the lack of privacy, this is something we can talk about later – if you want to, Amanda."

Amanda just nodded and wiped away her tears.

The family sat there quietly for a while, each contemplating the news that had just been broken.

After a few minutes, George broke the silence. "There's another serious matter I wanted to talk to you all about."

"Like what?" asked Bruce. "More serious than Amanda getting – attacked?"

"No. Nothing that serious. Just wanted to let you all know what's been going on the last several days around here."

"And what's been going on?" asked Bruce.

"Well, we were getting used to the usual harassment – you know, the phone calls, the emails, the letters, the flame wars on social media, the looks we'd get at the grocery store," said George. He nodded to Ellen, who picked up where he left off.

"But then things started getting scary – a little out of control," said Ellen, "when they started making more concrete threats last week."

"Threats?" said Kaylie.

"What?" said Bruce.

"What are you talking about?" asked Amanda, her voice still a little shaky from crying.

"Well," said George, "we've tried to protect our privacy as best we can, but I guess some sicko followed the FBC camera van to Jake's place a few weeks ago, and then came back again later and knocked on our door. Some weirdo in a Kansas City Chiefs baseball cap. He looked at me all strange and quoted scripture, then cussed me up and down and breathed out some threats and warnings about 'wrath' and 'vengeance' and said he knows where our other children live – which I doubt – he was just a whack-job. But it shook me up a little, and made me wonder about our safety."

"Why didn't you say anything before?" asked Kaylie.

"We didn't want to give you anything else to worry about – what with Jake still in the hospital and everything," said Ellen.

"Did you at least call the police?" asked Bruce.

"No, no," said George. "Like I said, he was just some freak – and that was the first time anybody had come to where we live. The rest were all just long-distance stalker nuts."

"You say that was just the *first*, as if you expect others," said Jake.

"Already had another," said George. "Someone tossed a bucket of what looked like blood – probably from some slaughtered animal – on our van three nights ago. I heard something, and went outside and saw a very pregnant woman hop into a car driven by someone else, and they peeled out of here. I jumped in the van immediately – not to chase them, just to get to a car wash."

"Eww, that is so sick," said Kaylie, her face looking like she'd just sucked on a lemon.

"That's it," said Jake, looking around at this ravaged family. "I'm going to get my lawyer involved."

"You mean, to try to put a stop to it? To end the show?" asked Bruce.

"Yeah – to end the show," said Jake.

"You – you think it's possible?" asked Kaylie.

"I'm beginning to think anything is possible. At least, I have to try. My attorney, Lawrence Klein, is pretty amazing, and knows FBC contracts inside and out. I'm going to contact him tomorrow. He may be able to at least file an injunction, get the show to take a hiatus while we fight it out in court. If it goes in our favor, maybe we'll just have to appear on the show one more time for a cancellation finale or something." He looked directly at one of his camera people. "You get that, Tom Highgate? That's right FBC, we're coming for you."

Kaylie was stunned. "Wow. Why would you try to kill your own show?"

"It's not my show anymore. And it was a mistake to begin with. And I'm not just saying that because of this," he gestured at his wheelchair, "I'm saying it because I know that I just went too far with this one. It's wrong – and I'm ashamed that I didn't see that sooner – that I didn't realize before I pitched it that the show could be a nightmare. All I could see were dollar signs and promotions and fame and fortune." He shook his head, his eyes misty. "I'm sorry. To all of you."

"If you're able to get this stopped, we'll owe you big time," said George.

"Yeah, well, Merry Christmas. But you won't owe me a thing – this is all my doing to begin with. I'm just trying to start undoing the things I've done."

Kaylie looked down at The Bulge. He can't undo *this*. "Well, thanks," she said. "I'm glad you're willing to get *Canceled* canceled. But – what'll happen to me? I mean, the prize money – I won't get anything – everything I've been through will have been for nothing."

"Kaylie, that's the least of our concerns," said George. "I know you want the money – who wouldn't? – but if there's any way to ensure the safety of the baby, we have to do it. I think it's a no-brainer."

"But Dad, I'm still not even sure what I want!"

"I think you know," said Ellen. "I think you know that even if you don't want a family right now, you know deep down that killing the baby is wrong. This isn't like what happened to Amanda. You know that if you want to walk away from this as if nothing happened, that adoption is the only option."

"And that's an option that this show – or rather its viewers – could take away," said Bruce. "This show does not allow for the choice of adoption. It's winner-take-all, loser die."

Kaylie shifted in her seat. "I feel like you're all ganging up on me – I don't like this."

Jake looked perplexed. "I assumed that you – well, I just thought maybe you'd be glad to have the show over. I mean, if the show is over, you can still choose abortion if you want, right?"

The rest of the family frowned at him.

Amanda squirmed and looked down.

"Yes," said Kaylie, "but if it has to be that way, then there's two problems. One, I don't get the money. Two, I don't get to blame the abortion decision on the show."

She looked down. "There, I said it. I hate the show, but it has been – useful – for me, because it has allowed me to place responsibility for the decision on America, instead of on me." She started to cry. "Amanda – you're so much stronger than me! I – I just don't think I could take having to make this decision by myself! The show has been a crutch for me. I didn't even really want to face that until now."

Kaylie realized this was part of what Len Hamlin had been trying to get her to face in their sessions. That she was a selfish, childish woman with no courage. Well, he wouldn't have put it that way, but Kaylie was starting to see it that way, and she started to cry even harder.

Amanda put her arm around her sister. "I know this is different from my situation. And I sometimes wonder if I made the right choice. But I do know we'll get through this. Together."

"The first thing to do is work on getting this thing stopped," said George. "Jake, is there anything we can do to help? Will your lawyer need to talk to us, get statements?"

Jake adjusted his wheelchair, moving it forward a couple of inches. "I don't think so. Lawrence will just move straight to filing papers for an injunction against the network, then, maybe later, he'll probably want to interview each of you to gather depositions and evidence that will help the case. But the first move is to just throw up a way to obstruct FBC from airing another episode."

Kaylie felt a mixture of relief and regret. Not having to do the show anymore would be like being released from prison. But she'd also lose all that money.

As if reading her mind, Jake said, "And Kaylie, don't worry about the money – I'll make sure you get what you signed on for."

"How?"

"Just don't worry about it. I have means. It's the least I can do."

"You have that kind of money, and you're living in an apartment?"

"What do I need with a big house on the hill? I've just been saving up."

"For what?"

"I guess I figured my life would change one day." He looked down at his legs. "I guess it did, huh?"

"Yeah. Well, you'll need to keep your money to pay for – you know – therapy and stuff."

"I'll decide what I do with my finances. And this isn't a conversation we need to have right now. Let's just take this a step at a time."

Kaylie looked at him as he sat confined in his wheelchair. Yeah, a step at a time.

She sighed heavily, her hand on The Bulge. "Fine. And – thanks."

CHAPTER 45

Kaylie was now twenty-five weeks – six months – pregnant.

Jake's call to his attorney had been a success – at first.

An injunction was filed, and FBC was required to stop airing new episodes of the show, and – to Kaylie's delight – stop filming and producing new episodes – until the matter was resolved in court.

For the past five weeks, the network ran re-runs of the show – airing the "best" episodes – the premiere, the reveal of the father, Kaylie yakking at the feet of the head of the FFPC, George's on-stage collapse, the Cynthia betrayal – all the highest-rated stuff. And of course, they ran the "beach escape" segment and the post-shooting material once more.

They also kept momentum by running two lotteries on the app, contingent on the show resuming: one for studio audience seating, and one for a chance to be live in the room for either the birth or the termination – an idea that sickened Kaylie to the core – as if her privacy hadn't been violated enough, she'd have a stranger gawking at her in her most vulnerable moment.

Throughout this time – all of January, and the first part of February – voting was also suspended, giving The Bulge a "bye" each of those weeks.

And The Bulge was growing fast – Kaylie was thinking of renaming it The Mountain.

Of course, with the show in limbo for the legal battle, Kaylie did not have access to any of the cast – Dr. Cho, Len, or Molly. And the entertainment world was hungry for news of America's most famous pregnant woman, with paparazzi around every corner – so she spent the cool January weeks mostly in her apartment, her parent's apartment, and at Jake's place.

She was there today.

A tabloid sat on the coffee table with a blurry shot of Kaylie leaving her apartment, wearing dark sunglasses and a scarf wrapped around her head – a stereotypical *National Enquirer* shot.

The headline read *Is Canceled Canceled?*

The official FBC line was that they were airing the re-runs because of budget issues, but everyone knew that was a cover – this show was the biggest revenue source the network had seen in years.

There was plenty of speculation about a possible lawsuit, but everything was kept hush-hush – FBC had managed to get a gag order rolled in as a compromise for the injunction.

Kaylie picked up the tabloid and leafed through it, mildly amused at the "journalism" between the covers.

A year ago she never would've imagined she'd be sharing an issue of the *Enquirer* with the president's alien love-child, the re-animated brain of Michael Jackson, and Mary Jo Kopechne's zombie.

And beating them all out for the cover.

"Oh, sorry about that," said Jake, rolling himself out of the kitchen to the living room where Kaylie sat. He pointed at the tabloid. "Jenna left that rag here this morning after her shift. I wouldn't normally keep that stuff on hand."

"Oh? You mean you have absolutely no interest in finding out who is the mother of the president's alien baby?" Kaylie laughed. "Or how they brought the King of Pop's brain back to life?"

"Huh, no," Jake smiled, shaking his head. "Really, I don't want to know. I guess I just don't have enough of an enquiring mind."

"Okay. Well, then, I won't tell you. But you may be interested to know that, according to the crack reporters at the *Enquirer*, you're suing FBC for conspiring to shoot you to boost ratings."

"Was that 'crack reporters,' or 'reporters on crack'?"

They laughed.

It was good to be able to keep a sense of humor through all this.

Jake moved his chair to a spot near the couch where the coffee table had been moved away a little to make room for him to maneuver. Then he started the process of lifting himself to the couch.

Francine walked in from the spare room (where she spent most of her shift, to stay out of Jake's way – at his request), and started to assist him in his transfer from wheelchair to couch.

"No, no – I don't want the help. Thank you."

Francine backed away. "You sure, Mr. Granville?"

"I'm sure. I can do this, Francine. Just go away, please."

Francine walked out, shaking her head just a little.

Jake continued his struggle, wincing a little at the strain as he placed one hand on the arm of the wheelchair and the other on the couch, braced himself, and used his upper body to do all the work of getting over to the sofa.

Kaylie watched his forearm muscles and biceps flex, listened to him breathing. Like Francine the nurse, she also felt compelled to help, but understood that Jake wanted to exert his independence and do this himself.

So she held herself back and stared at him.

Suddenly, his grip on the couch slipped and he tumbled toward Kaylie, winding up with his head in her lap, his arms flailing, and his legs draped off the edge of the couch cushion, one foot still on the wheelchair's foot plate.

Kaylie caught him, cradling his head and neck in one hand, with her other arm across his muscular chest. He immediately laughed, and she did, too.

"Graceful, eh?"

"Well, that's one way to get cozy," she said.

"Ah, you see right through me," Jake said, still smiling.

He started to right himself, but Kaylie applied gentle pressure with the arm that was on his chest, holding him back. "No – stay there."

Jake smiled and closed his eyes with a sigh. "Well, it *is* pretty comfortable. You don't mind?"

"Not at all. In fact –"

"Whoa – did you feel that?"

"Yes!" Kaylie beamed.

"That little guy just kicked me in the back of the head! Or maybe it was an elbow. I dunno – but it was a trip!"

Kaylie laughed. "Yeah it was. I've felt him move a few times, but not quite like that." She looked down at

Jake and realized she had started to unconsciously run her fingers gently through his hair.

She didn't stop.

"You ever give it any thought?" asked Jake, scooting his head toward her knees and looking up at her.

"What?"

"You know. The what-ifs. Like, what if – what if you end up having the baby – and what if you want his father to be around, and what if –"

Without thinking, without warning, and without regard for consequences, Kaylie suddenly leaned down and kissed Jake square on the lips, putting an end to his meandering sentence.

A long, upside-down lingering kiss.

It made her heart leap and pound.

He raised his hand to caress her cheek as they continued to kiss.

Then she sat back up and caught her breath, which had been taken away by the passion.

She brushed her brown strands back out of her face and looked down at Jake, who had a dreamy look on his face that made her giggle.

"What?" he asked with a mock defensive tone.

"You. You look like one of those cartoon characters that smells a pie baking and floats along on the scent. You look like you just – uh, like you enjoyed yourself very much."

"I won't deny that I did. You seem pretty well-pleased with yourself, too."

"Do I? Well, I suppose I am."

"Good. Any regrets?"

"That it wasn't caught on tape."

They both cracked up at that.

"No, seriously," said Jake.

"That it didn't happen sooner. And last longer."

"Really? Well, I don't have a time machine, but we could probably do something about the second issue."

Kaylie shook her head. "Not tonight." She motioned with a flick of her head to the spare room. "Too much company."

"Good point. Besides, I think I'd rather not repeat our past mistakes."

Kaylie's heart sank, and she frowned. "What do you mean? It's not like you can get me pregnant again right now. Or do you consider me a mistake in general?"

"Oh – hey, that sounded bad. No, I mean that I don't just want another passion-fueled one-night fling. I'm ready to take it slow and do things right this time. I'm sorry – that was poor wording on my part."

Kaylie breathed again. "Oh. Well, yeah, in that case, yes, you're right. I'm fine with taking things slower. Of course, pretty much any speed would be slower than the way we handled things the first time around."

"Yeah, I'll say. That whole thing made my Cobra look slow! Hey, speaking of, it comes back from the shop tomorrow. Maybe we could sneak out – you could take me for a ride." He grinned up at her. "I know you still want to drive her – but no crashing this time."

She smiled back. "It's true, I do want to drive her. And I'm getting tired of feeling like a prisoner. The cameras aren't on, but I'm still trapped – you know, by the paparazzi and all. I say we take off in the Cobra tomorrow – early – and drive like the wind. They'll never catch us!"

"That's the spirit! Get here before dawn. I'll pack some food, and tell Jenna to take the morning off."

"Sounds like a date."

"Yes, I believe it is."

CHAPTER 46

The next morning, Jake arose early at a little before five and got himself into his wheelchair with not much difficulty, but significant pain.

He popped a pill – just one this morning, instead of the usual three – hoping to dull the pain but not his senses.

Marcus, the night nurse, was asleep in the spare room, but woke up when he heard Jake fumbling around in the kitchen.

"Hungry?" asked the big bald black man in blue scrubs as he rounded the corner and spied Jake staring into the fridge.

"No. But I could use your help. I need you to reach up in the top of that cupboard there and grab down the paper plates."

"But you're not hungry."

"Nope. Just prepping. Oh, and I also need you to see if I have any extra paper napkins in the hall cupboard. Thanks."

Marcus stepped around to the corner and opened the cupboard, and said in his deep baritone, "You got plans today?"

"Yeah – in fact, I'm giving you the rest of your shift off, and having Jenna take her shift off, too."

Marcus returned with napkins and a grin. "Hot date?"

"Actually, yes. I get my car back today, and –"

"Whoa there, cowboy. You can't be driving."

"Not planning on it, dude. My date is going to be doing the chauffeuring. Kaylie's wanted to drive the Cobra for a while now, ever since she got a taste of how quick it is in reverse."

"Ah, Kaylie. I see. Well, the show may be off the air, but at least I still get the inside scoop!" He chuckled with his low, raspy laugh. "Oh, don't worry, man, my lips are sealed. Well, I might tell my wife, but that's it."

"Fair enough. Hey, you feel like helping me make some sandwiches?"

The two men prepared the food and packed it into a large Tupperware box – the closest thing Jake had to a picnic basket. Marcus dug out a couple of old blankets and placed them on top of the box by the front door, and moments later, Kaylie knocked meekly at the door.

Marcus opened it and said, "Ah, there she is now. And not a moment too soon – the sun is beginning to come up."

Jake and Kaylie smiled at each other through the open door, and Marcus grabbed a jacket for Jake, then helped him into the car. He then folded the wheelchair up and placed it in the tiny trunk. He had to press down hard to get it to close.

"Hey, don't bust that latch," said Jake, "I just had the rear-end fixed."

"Don't worry. It's closed, and you're good to go," said Marcus. "Have fun."

Jake watched as Kaylie strapped in, adjusted the mirrors, and turned the key. The seven-liter V8 engine roared to life, deeply chugging and growling like a lion. She placed her hand on the gear stick, smiled at Jake like a school girl, and pulled away.

The car jerked a little at first as she got used to the clutch and the terrific power under the hood, but the ride quickly smoothed out as she took the car through the relatively quiet pre-dawn city streets and out onto the highway.

"Where to?" asked Kaylie, picking up speed.

"I was thinking we could hit this nice little park just south of Pismo Beach."

"Pismo? What's that, about a hundred and seventy miles?"

"Yeah – if you step on it, we should get there before eight. We could catch breakfast at a little café I know, and save the picnic for lunch."

"Before eight, huh? So, you really don't mind if I *drive* her hard?"

"It's what she was built for."

Kaylie put her foot down. She brought it up to top gear and cruised out of the city limits on Highway 101 ahead of any rush hour traffic.

Jake soaked up the beautiful morning, glad to be out of the apartment, and actually enjoying being a passenger. He looked around at the area as if seeing it for the first time.

They reached Ventura in forty minutes and the highway curved northward as they began to follow the coastline. The ocean smelled refreshing as the sky continued to get brighter overhead.

He looked over at Kaylie, who seemed to be wearing a little smile. "So, is it everything you'd hoped it would be?"

"And more. I have to admit, the Cobra was always one of my favorite 'dream cars' when I was a teenager. That and the Lotus Esprit."

"You had good taste. I had a Lotus once – not an Esprit. It was a little green Elan. Fun car."

"What happened to it?"

"I sold it. Needed the money to buy the Ferrari."

"Any regrets?"

"No way. I've had many a good race in that Ferrari." Jake looked down at his useless legs. "I guess my racing days are over. Might as well sell that car now."

Kaylie was silent for a minute. "How's the rehab coming?"

"Eh. Not great. Well, the doc and the therapist say I'm doing phenomenally. But it's not enough – not enough for me. I have some feeling in my legs – sometimes anyway. Which is way more than they ever expected or hoped for. But I still hope for more."

"You think you'll recover? Walk again?"

"I know I will. It's just a matter of time. I don't really care what the doctors say – this is not a part of my life that is negotiable. I won't give up."

"Good. I won't either."

After a while, they pulled into Pismo Beach and Jake directed Kaylie to the little café on a side street east of the highway.

They enjoyed a traditional breakfast of pancakes, eggs, bacon and juice. Kaylie chased hers with a tall chocolate milk to satisfy that Cocoa-Puff craving she still dealt with daily.

They were glad to have been able to eat and get out without anyone recognizing them – except maybe that waitress, who seemed to smirk every time she approached the table, but didn't verbally identify them.

They headed down to the beach park immediately south of the Park at Dinosaur Caves – a little cove that afforded them some privacy on that weekday morning in February.

Kaylie popped the trunk, laid out the blankets, and assisted Jake in getting from the car to the spot where they planned to sit and chat the morning away, staring at the incoming waves.

"Okay," she said, looking him in the eyes, "now here we are. Alone. Together. No cameras, no people, just you, me and the sea. And you can't get up and run away – I've got you trapped. So it's time to fess up and tell me what it is you've been meaning to tell me for – well, months now. Go ahead, I'm all ears."

Jake looked at her. She was truly beautiful – more so every day. He knew he had nothing to lose, so he spoke his mind. And his heart. "Kaylie, I – I don't know how this is going to turn out – nobody does, I guess. But I do know this – that I am seriously having, uh, feelings – feelings for you."

"Seriously having feelings for me? Wow, is that the best you can do, Mr. TV Executive?" She smiled to let him know she was kidding, but she also wasn't going to let him off the hook.

"Uh, yeah. I think I'm falling in love with you."

"That's more like it," she smiled again. "Go on."

"Yes, there is more." He took a deep breath and exhaled. "I'm also falling in love with him."

"Who?"

Jake pointed at her belly. "Him. I'm becoming very enamored with the idea of being a father – of having a family. Of *us* being a family."

Kaylie blushed and turned away momentarily, then turned right back, the coastal wind flipping her hair into her face. She pushed it back with her hand and grinned at Jake. "You serious?"

"Absolutely."

"You've been reading that book, haven't you – the one my folks bought you for Christmas? Yeah, I heard about it."

Jake grinned sheepishly and looked down. "Yeah. Yeah, I've been reading it. But that's not why I feel this way. I've been feeling this way for a long time now, actually."

"I see. I guess that would explain your Trump Card vote."

"I guess so. So, how do you feel about, uh, about how I feel?"

Kaylie looked out at the ocean for a few moments, then back at Jake. "I'm surprisingly okay with it. Except –"

"Except what?"

"Well, I'm liking the idea of spending more time with you – getting closer to you. But I'm still a little, uh, undecided, on the whole 'having a family' thing."

"Really?"

"Yeah – I still have career plans, ya know! Maybe I don't want to settle down and be little miss housewife just yet."

"Well, that little guy in there is the one setting the time table now. And anyway, it wouldn't have to be like that. Either one of us could bring home the bacon. I am determined not to be stuck in this chair forever – not that it would affect my ability to provide. And having a child doesn't have to mean the end of acting for you. Are you sure you're really undecided about having the baby?

"Yeah, I am. I think so, anyway. Maybe. I don't know! Every time I think about it I get a headache. My shrink – Len – he says it's because somewhere inside I already do know what I want, but I'm just not consciously accepting it because it will cause me too much difficulty."

"Then why not just face it? I have. I realize what I want, and I'm okay with it. I want you, the baby, the whole package deal. I'm ready to change my life."

Kaylie fingered the edge of the blanket. She let out a heavy sigh. "All right. Fine. Let's say – for sake of argument – I do want to have the baby, and I do want to be with you, and I do want to raise a family. What good does that do? What does what I want matter? They could still get the show back on the air again, and what I want will be meaningless – subjugated to the will of the voters."

"So, you're afraid to commit because life circumstances may change? Because you are not in total control of your life? Well, guess what? *No one* is. Granted, your situation – or, rather, *our* situation – is unique. But look at me! Not every part of my life is in my control – outside forces have drastically altered my existence – but I'm still me, and I still have my own desires and ambitions, and I am *not* going to let anything stop me."

Kaylie stared out at the ocean again. "How did I let myself get in this position? I'm just so mad at myself and the world – why would you even want to be around a big bloated angry frustrated selfish crybaby?"

"That's not what you are. You're an intelligent, talented, beautiful woman who's in an impossible situation – one that I created. You deserve better. I believe I can give you better than what I've given you so far. The question is, do you want it?"

A tear ran down her cheek. "Jake, I'm just afraid. I'm scared I'll embrace what I want, then I won't be able to have it. They'll take it away."

"They won't," said Jake, scooting closer and putting his arm around her. "We're going to win this thing. People will see reason, and this will all go away. I promise."

She turned to him, their faces just a couple of inches apart. "Really?"

"Yes."

Their faces moved together and their lips met in a warm kiss. The kiss grew stronger as they embraced.

Then Jake's cell rang.

They kept kissing.

It rang again.

Jake broke off the smooch and looked at his phone.

It was Lawrence Klein.

"I gotta take this. It's probably the good news we've been waiting for."

He tapped the screen and put it on speaker.

"Jake Granville."

"*Yeah, Jake, this is Klein. Bad news. The judge lifted the injunction. She ruled against us, Jake. As they say, the show must go on. I'm sorry, man. I tried playing every legal card I know, but we just don't have a case. FBC's lawyers are sharp and tough, and they rule the contracts world. As far as I know, they're planning on resuming shooting as soon as possible.*"

Jake was stunned.

And as he tried to catch his breath, his eyes focused on a white van that was pulling up at the parking lot above the beach. A camera crew jumped out.

"They tracked your cell again," said Jake to Kaylie. He hung up on Klein and slammed his fist into the ground. He gulped hard and looked at Kaylie with clenched jaw and steely resolve in his eyes. "We *will* make it through this. We will."

Kaylie now had tears streaming down her face. She shook her head. "I don't think so. I think this is going to end horribly."

Jake took her hand in his. He looked up at the camera crew as they hustled down the trail towards the beach. "Kaylie – this may be our last private moment for a while. I'm sorry – I'm sorry I can't do this properly, with a ring and all – and we only have a few more seconds, but – will you marry me?"

Kaylie's eyes widened. A look of terror was not the response Jake was hoping for.

She smiled through more tears. "Jake, why don't we wait and see how this turns out? I mean, the show. Before we uh, make any commitments?"

As the cameras arrived at their "private" little picnic spot, Jake winked at Kaylie. He didn't need to tell her that the proposal would be their secret – something FBC would never be able to take away from them.

CHAPTER 47

With the crowd going wild, Troy Tanner took the stage of the newly refurbished James Brown Memorial Theater.

He wore blue jeans, yellow dress shirt and navy sport coat, and about a week's growth of trimmed beard. He also wore his sparkling, signature grin.

"Ladies and gentlemen, welcome to *Canceled*!"

More raucous cheering.

"We are *back*! Reports of our – cancellation – have been greatly exaggerated. In fact, we are more alive than ever. Tonight, we'll have a summary of what you've missed over the winter break in the lives of our stars – including a bombshell from sister Amanda – some recent video from the last few days, onstage interviews with Kaylie and Jake, and of course – the voting. Stick around, we'll be right back – promise!"

Kaylie watched from the Green Room, sitting on the couch, holding Jake's hand. After a two-minute commercial break, Troy was at it again. This time, he was seated on his stool, center stage, bathed in a spotlight.

"Now, before we get on with the show, I want to dispel the rumors, set the record straight about our hiatus. You see, we want *Canceled* to be completely transparent with the American people. We know there was a lot of speculation in the newspapers, the tabloids, the entertainment TV shows, radio talk shows – all over – about the fate of the show, and just what was going on behind the scenes of our absence. And the truth is, we were indeed locked in a legal battle. Now, I'm obviously not at liberty to discuss all the details, for legal reasons. And I don't even know all the details myself. But the fact of the matter is, there were certain forces who were bent on removing us from the air – they wanted to shut us down! But we prevailed! We will not be censored! We will not be canceled!"

The crowd burst out in screams and whistles and clapping.

"And so, here we are," said Troy. "And we are at a critical juncture. Your voting this week will need to be very, very intense, because next week is the end of the second trimester, which means it will be a trump card show. Kaylie herself will hold that trump card, worth two-hundred million votes. Now, here's the twist – it's only worth two hundred million. So – if you, America, can somehow manage to vote enough times, you may still win out over the trump card, in effect trumping the trump. And I issue that to you as a personal challenge! Meanwhile, we've got to get you caught up on the last few weeks. Right after the break."

Kaylie squirmed a little at the thought of next week's show. She was going to be forced to make a decision – and she hated that. She had spent the last few months feeling like the opposite of a control-freak – content to go along with whatever was foisted on her by the American voter. But now, as she was starting to have doubts, mixed feelings, and the murmurings of a "will" somewhere deep inside her, she was actually terrified of having to take a stand one way or the other, and of how much half the country was going to hate her when she defied their will – if it came to that.

The show returned and Troy introduced a pretty weak montage of whatever the editing wizards had been able to piece together from the scant footage recorded since the last real episode of the show.

They did have one piece of video that made a splash – the conversation in the kitchen where the whole family learned that Amanda had been raped and had an abortion. That scene brought an amazing hush to the audience, and they went straight to commercial in silence for added dramatic effect.

After the break, they brought Kaylie and Jake out on stage, where Troy tried his best to get them to open up, and audience members took turns peppering them with questions about Amanda and the last few weeks of camera-free life that they managed to skate around pretty well.

At the end, Troy opened up the voting and closed the episode.

Kaylie was surprised they didn't do a reveal of the last show's vote, from back in December, but Jake explained those results had been scrubbed as part of the legal settlement, and that FBC had clearly decided not to bring it up on-air – probably a wise move. This audience was pretty crazy about making sure their votes counted. Having an entire week's votes erased would've made a lot of people angry, so it was best to not mention it. Fans were just glad to have the show back on the air with new material – better not to open old wounds.

After the show, Kaylie went straight home and climbed into bed.

With the cameras back on, she was really missing her freedom.

She was also missing Jake.

Then she had an idea.

She reached over to her nightstand and picked up her cell. Then she pulled the covers up over her head and after a few minutes began to make quiet snoring sounds.

Then she tapped the screen of her phone and set it to night mode, and started to compose a text message.

Jake, I just thought of a way that we can have private conversations! Late at night, we can do what I'm doing – undercover texting. As long as nobody sees it, nobody will know.

She hit send, and a few minutes later got a response:

Great idea. Just don't let them catch you.

She spent the rest of the night texting back and forth with Jake, like high school kids passing notes. They discussed everything from family to cars to life in Oregon to childhood to Troy Tanner to wedding plans.

By six o'clock, when the night shift traded places with the day crew, Kaylie was exhausted and ready to sleep all morning. But she was also exhilarated, feeling like she'd managed to put one over on her oppressors.

And she felt a world closer to Jake.

CHAPTER 48

After more sleepless nights of Kaylie, Jake and The Bulge in undercover text-fests, followed by sleeping-in that lasted until mid-afternoon, Kaylie dreaded having to return to the FBC studios.

It was like that feeling you get when you have to return to work after a nice long vacation. The feeling that you'd rather be anywhere else, and the silly fantasy floating around your head that somehow you'll be saved, *deus ex machina*, from actually having to go through with it.

But the hour was at hand, and she left her apartment building with her security detail, stepped into the FBC limousine, and did breathing exercises all the way to the studio, trying to stay calm and focused.

She tried to tell herself there was only a couple more months of this, but that really didn't help – she may have been an expert at fooling herself in the past, but she knew there was no certainty at all that could be applied to this show.

From week to week, anything could happen.

It was a form of torture – like being forced to play Russian Roulette, over and over again.

The show went off pretty smoothly, with the standard recaps of her past week – visits in which she was reunited with the other stars – Dr. Cho, Len, Molly – following the hiatus.

Mostly pretty innocuous stuff. Kaylie and Jake had barely communicated outside of the texting over the past week, leaving the editors very little to work with in terms of advancing the plot of their relationship.

That gave Kaylie a little bit of *schadenfreude* satisfaction.

But that little happy feeling inside soon evaporated when it came time for the final segment.

"Welcome back!" shouted Troy. "The moment has arrived – the results from the past week's record-setting vote."

Kaylie sat in an overstuffed armchair next to Troy's stool. At Jake's thoughtful request, Wyatt Sloane had agreed to replace Kaylie's stool to provide her a little more comfort as she got bigger.

A red-head in red heels brought Troy the results envelope.

"America – over the past week, you voted. Masses and masses of you voted. *Canceled* received an unprecedented two-hundred and thirty-six million votes!" He turned to Kaylie. "Kaylie, I would normally ask you to stand, but, in your condition – well, why don't you just stay right where you are."

Kaylie was surprised he didn't stall and go to commercial break. Instead, he held the result page and read off the numbers. "With fifty-one-point-three percent of the vote – a landslide compared to previous votes on this show, which have historically been razor-close – America says: 'Go see Dr. Ian!' That's right, it's time to end this!"

Kaylie felt like she'd been socked in the gut. The crowd went hysterical, jumping to their feet and screaming, cheering, clapping, whistling, and booing.

For a surreal moment, Kaylie imagined she was in the middle of a Roman coliseum, the spectators chanting for her to be eaten by the lions.

Crying out for blood.

Then The Bulge gave her a couple good kicks and she snapped out of it.

The crowd was still yelling, and Troy was trying to get them to shut up for a minute so he could drop his bombshell.

"Okay, okay, okay," he said. "Wait, listen. Wait a minute. Hold on, hold on. Folks, there's something you all need to know. Those keeping track of the weeks at home will know that this – today – represents the *end* of the second trimester. And that, folks, means the second of two trump cards! And this one belongs to Kaylie. Her vote tonight is worth two hundred million votes – enough to cancel out the popular vote, if she so chooses."

Kaylie's head was spinning and she felt a little sick. Her temples throbbed and her breath was shallow.

"And we'll find out if she decides to play that trump card – right after the break."

When they went to commercial, Kaylie took a deep breath.

She closed her eyes and shut out the world around her.

No audience.

No lights.

No crew.

No Troy.

No Mom, Dad, Bruce, Amanda, or Jake.

Just her and The Bulge.

She placed her hand on her belly, felt him kick once more. She caught her breath. And then she smiled softly to herself.

Suddenly, she knew.

The show returned, and Troy popped the question to her.

With confidence, she replied, "Troy, I am going to play the trump card. I'm overturning the vote. I'm keeping the baby."

The resultant chaos in the James Brown Memorial Theater required all of the security personnel to step in and try to control the riot.

Speaking loudly over the din, Troy invited everyone to vote again, assuring them that next week, and from here on out, there would be no more result-reversals. No more trump cards. Just pure democracy. From now on, the fate of Kaylie, the fetus, and the show was in the hands of America.

The broadcast ended, but the noise did not.

As the fans were herded out, Kaylie could see a lot of angry faces and hear some of the individual shouts and jeers – some people cussing out the show's producers, others calling her every name in the book.

It was a little scary to see how emotional these perfect strangers were getting over *her* life. Odd to see how virulently some of them were calling for blood – the blood of her baby.

Kaylie left the stage, got changed in her dressing room, and took the limo home.

That night, she pulled the covers over her head and texted Jake: *Finally, I'm sure. I know what I want. I want it to be the three of us. The answer is YES.*

Jake's response was a Snoopy happy-dancing GIF.

CHAPTER 49

The next two months consisted of week after week of intense trauma for Kaylie, as each vote now represented something entirely different for her: the possible death of the baby she wanted to keep.

Jake's lawyer, Lawrence Klein, was still working to try to do something – anything – to tie the show up in a legal battle until after the due date, but so far, FBC's legal team was prevailing at every turn, managing to stave off any court-ordered ruling to stop the show.

Kaylie desperately wanted to talk with Len about finally settling on a decision regarding the baby, but, per her contract, she was forbidden from doing so. But, based on her new attitude, Len quickly sussed out the truth, and let her know that he knew by having Felicity pass Kaylie a note on her way out from one of her sessions.

It simply read: *Glad it's settled. I'll be rooting for you and the kid.*

Meanwhile, her visits with Dr. Cho were bittersweet. On one hand, she was fascinated to learn about her baby's development, and it warmed her heart to hear each new thing about how he was growing. On the other hand, such knowledge carried with it a deep fear that all this could be taken away on any given week.

Kaylie and Jake were still having late-night text-dates, but not every night anymore. Kaylie needed her rest these days, and just couldn't stay up so late all the time without really feeling it the next day, no matter how much she slept in. Besides, they didn't want FBC to suspect anything was going on.

George, Ellen, Kaylie and Jake began a new routine – each Thursday night after the show they would all meet at George and Ellen's apartment and share a late evening supper. Kaylie really appreciated these meals – a chance to unwind from the stress of the show, surrounded by people who loved and supported her – despite still being on camera.

Of course, Wyatt Sloane saw these meals as a chance to add a new weekly segment to the show. He called it "the Decompression Dinner" and each week it aired at the top of the episode after Troy's introduction.

On set tonight, Kaylie had run into Cynthia Davis, who had been brought on full time as part of the production. She didn't have any new inside reports about the Adams family, since Bruce had shut her out of his life like a slamming door in the face after her first appearance on the show. But she was a resourceful reporter, and she covered other angles of the story, often digging up obscure connections to Kaylie and putting together short packages that aired during the show.

When Kaylie nearly bumped into Cynthia backstage before the show, she nearly hauled off and decked the reporter in a moment of flash anger that came out of nowhere. But she took a deep breath, gave Cynthia an "I wish you were dead" smile, and brushed past her without a word.

Kaylie mentioned it at the decompression dinner that night, and Ellen had said, "Too bad you didn't lay her out – that would've made for some *great TV*." They all had a good laugh at that.

As they were saying their goodbyes for the night, Jake got a call. After a few minutes, he hung up and turned to Kaylie.

"That was Dave. Dave Kohler."

"Dave? What'd he want?"

"He says you and I need to come in – to FBC. He needs to talk to us."

"I thought he was suspended," said George.

"He was. But he's still one of the top dogs, and apparently he and Sloane and Tom Highgate want to talk to us. He said it's important, and that it'll be a camera-free zone."

"This could be very good," said Ellen. "Maybe your lawyer managed to make some headway with them."

"Maybe," said Jake. "But if Lawrence had good news, I think he would've called me. And he'd also need to be at the meeting. So, I dunno. But they want us there now."

"Now? But it's after eleven," said Kaylie, yawning and placing her hand on The Bulge. "It can't wait until morning?"

"Dave said it's urgent. I say we go and find out what it's all about. Come on, you can drive the Cobra."

That was just enough motivation for Kaylie, who smiled and said, "Fine. But this better not take all night."

Within twenty minutes, they were at the FBC offices. Kaylie wheeled Jake through the front doors and into an elevator that took them to the sixteenth floor, and then pushed him to Tom Highgate's office.

"Thanks for coming," said Dave.

Sloane was seated in an armchair across the room, his flowing white hair tied back in a short ponytail, and a hard frown on his face. Tom Highgate sat at his desk in a suit with no tie. Dave had grown a full salt-n-pepper beard since Kaylie had last seen him.

"What's this all about?" asked Jake, pushing his wheels with his hands and positioning himself beside the couch, which Kaylie sat on, right next to him.

"I'll let *you* explain, Dave," said Tom, placing a stick of chewing gum in his mouth.

"Well, long story short," said Dave, standing up to pace the room, "we have a serious problem with the show. It's the voting. One of our IT guys discovered an inconsistency. And the more he dug, the worse it got. It's been going on for the past several weeks – since episode nineteen, when Kaylie played the trump card – the same night we vowed on-air that there would be no further vote-reversals and the results were to be 'pure democracy.' That's when it started."

"When *what* started?" asked Jake sternly.

"The voter fraud. Someone out there is stuffing the ballot box with 'keep the baby' votes. A hacker – a very smart hacker," said Dave, who was visibly sweating. "The results have been altered each week, just enough to put it over the top in favor of keeping the baby. The integrity of the show has been compromised."

"Like this show ever had integrity," Kaylie mumbled under her breath.

"So, why is this *our* problem?" asked Jake. "Why are you talking to us?"

"Because it gets worse. We figured it was some ideological group of rabid pro-lifers somewhere on a crusade to 'save the baby.' We hired an outside IT consulting firm to get to the bottom of it. And they traced the hacks. To a server in Portland, Oregon. Kaylie – it was your brother, Bruce."

"Bruce?" Kaylie yelped. "Ha!" Her hands came together with a smack as she grinned. "You are kidding me!"

"I wouldn't joke about this," Dave said, still completely serious.

Jake quickly put the scenario together. "You need us to stay silent."

"Yes," snapped Tom.

"Then why tell us?" asked Kaylie.

"We shut down Bruce tonight – patched the app's security flaw and doubled down on encryption. We figured it was only a matter of time before he told you what he's been doing. Soon enough, the news would break – via your family's website or through some other channels," said Sloane.

"And we'd rather not have the mess of having your brother arrested," said Tom.

"Arrested?"

"Yes, what he's done is against the law, and under other circumstances he would have to be held accountable," Tom continued. "But it's going to look very bad for us if someone who we have paid to be a guest on the show – your brother – has been acting illegally to perpetuate the existence of the show. Nobody will believe that we didn't put him up to it. There will be accusations of collusion and fraud. All previous weeks' votes will be considered null and void – the audience will lose all faith in the system and quit watching. It'll be a legal and ratings nightmare for the network."

Kaylie felt like saying "So what?" – but she stayed quiet.

"If this gets out, Kaylie, if the show is canceled because of this mess, your contract is void, and you can say goodbye to all the prize money. All of this will have been for nothing," said Sloane.

"And it will destroy your reputation," said Dave. "I know you're trying to get started on a Hollywood career – that would be impossible if this got out. Nobody would ever trust you. And Jake, you would certainly never work in Tinseltown again."

"Bottom line," said Tom, "you stay quiet on this, and we don't press charges. Your brother walks away scot free – no arrest, no trouble at all. You leak it – and we will prosecute Bruce Adams to the fullest extent of the law."

The room fell silent for a few moments while it all sunk in. Bruce had broken the law. He had ensured the safety of the baby for the last several weeks. To Kaylie, that geeky big brother of hers was a hero.

But now she was being threatened.

She knew Bruce wouldn't have done what he did if he wasn't willing to deal with the consequences, but she didn't want anyone in her family to pay the price for her. She made up her mind. She glanced over at Jake and exchanged a meaningful look.

"All right," she said. "I won't talk. But I want assurance – in writing – that you will hold harmless all members of my family, meaning you will not at any time in the future – even after the show is long over – bring any charges for anything."

"Of course," said Tom with the totally insincere smile of someone who hated having terms dictated to him. "We'll have a rider drawn up immediately."

"As long as you're all here," said Sloane, "there's one additional item of business. We have roughly five and a half weeks left until the due date – the show's finale, if we make it that far. We need to really ramp things up, especially with May sweeps coming. So, commencing at six Monday morning, we're going to offer a twenty-four seven 'live' video feed from all crew cameras directly to the app. Viewers will be able to log on any time, night or day, and click on a camera to watch your lives in real-time, unedited. It's unprecedented."

"It's freaking crazy!" shouted Kaylie. "Are you serious?"

"Quite."

Tom smiled. "I like that – I like it a lot. Sloane, I see very good things ahead for you."

"But what about the editing for privacy," asked Kaylie. You can't show me showering and going to the bathroom, getting dressed. It's nuts!"

"When I say *live*," said Sloane, "I of course mean there will be a delay of thirty seconds or so – that way our round-the-clock live production crew will be able to digitize anything too, uh, revealing. There will be appropriate masking of your private parts. No worries."

"So, how will the show work going forward?" asked Dave.

"Same as before," said Sloane. "We'll still produce vignettes for the week, have on-stage interviews, big musical numbers, voting results, the whole nine yards. But now, people will be able to log on and watch everything during the week as well – as it happens. Of course, we'll add non-skippable ads to the free app and offer an ad-free paid version, providing a huge additional revenue stream for FBC."

Tom looked positively giddy, while Kaylie and Jake looked at each other with horror on their faces.

"This will require a contract re-negotiation," said Jake. "This isn't what either of us signed up for. If you want to run it this way, we'll need additional compensation on a daily basis."

Highgate was no idiot – he knew a contract negotiation couldn't be avoided. "How much?"

"Five grand a day. Each."

"Fine. But we don't wait until Monday. Sloane – begin tomorrow."

Sloane grinned and nodded.

Jake put his hand on Kaylie's. "It'll be all right," he said. His face didn't match his words, though.

"Yeah," Kaylie whispered, her other hand on The Bulge. "Just five more weeks, right?"

CHAPTER 50

Kaylie thought back to what Jake had said in the hospital the day they shot the show in his recovery room. Wyatt Sloane was pure slime, and Jake's fears had been borne out: Sloane had turned the show into something even worse than it already was.

Knowing that every moment of the filming was going live to the app (with only a thirty second delay) was almost enough to cause a nervous breakdown for Kaylie.

She felt like an animal in a zoo.

But she had to hand it to Sloane – the effect was incredible. The FBC analytics showed the app use had drastically multiplied, with many users leaving the live cam feature running in the background for hours at a time.

Her life had become a full-time screensaver.

This level of intrusion was exhausting. After two weeks of living under the constant gaze of millions of eyes, Kaylie started to feel some false labor, and made two unexpected but ultimately uneventful trips to the hospital.

Dr. Cho blamed it entirely on her level of stress, and Molly the Midwife stepped up the frequency of her aromatherapy and gentle massage sessions to try to reduce the level of anxiety.

Despite being a good shoulder for Kaylie, Len couldn't help much at this point. She no longer had any misconceptions about her own feelings or inner desires. She knew why she was stressed, but there was nothing that could be done.

Meanwhile, the live-streaming life of Kaylie and Jake had not only driven unbelievable levels of app use through a viral explosion of interest in the show, but it had also had Sloane's desired effect of ramping up viewership on Thursday nights.

The last two weeks had pulled an unprecedented sixty-five ratings share – meaning that, by far, most people in the country were watching *Canceled* instead of something else – in fact, more than anything else combined. The other networks actually seemed to be giving up, airing re-runs in the competing time slot and moving their best new material to other nights. And that, in turn, only pushed *Canceled's* ratings higher.

The number one Google search was "Kaylie Adams." Number two was "Canceled." Fame and glory; stress and misery.

"Be careful what you wish for" was Kaylie's new mantra.

It was now early May, and Kaylie was in her final month. It was also sweeps, and FBC was cleaning up. There was a general high level of electricity in the air whenever Kaylie was at the studio, and the other media were all scrambling to jump on board and ride the coattails of this phenomenon.

In the space of two weeks, Kaylie had appeared on six TV talk shows, four radio shows, and the cover of five major magazines (not counting the tabloids).

Jake was getting similar levels of publicity.

It was exactly the kind of fever-pitch hysterical hype that Jake had dreamed of nearly a year ago when he'd conceived this show.

The vote each week – no longer subject to Bruce's technological tinkering, was remarkably close, and surprisingly to Kaylie, each week the vote to keep the baby won out.

But only by a few thousand votes out of nearly three hundred million. Her baby's future had become a margin of error.

There was now only one more voting week – next Thursday. One week after that was the due date, which could potentially entail either a live birth, or an IDX procedure.

It all hung on next Thursday's vote results.

If it ended with a vote for birth, Kaylie had decided (much to Molly's chagrin) to go with Dr. Cho for the delivery.

Either way, if the vote carried her through to May 20, she was going to find herself lying in a hospital bed on live TV that night. She just didn't know if it would be with Dr. Cho or Dr. Ian at her feet.

And that uncertainty was enough to make her want to break down and cry every day and every night.

Tonight, after the decompression dinner, Kaylie took a deep breath and told herself to pull it together.

Only fourteen more days.

What could happen in fourteen days?

The following Thursday, at the top of the episode, Kaylie discovered the horrifying answer to that question.

The show opened with Troy pulling out a cell phone on stage, and pretending to compose a text message. Then, as a simulation of a text message appeared on the screen behind him, he voiced the words on the screen: "Welcome, folks, to the final voting week of *Canceled*!"

After the ridiculously long cheering died down, Troy said, "You may be wondering what I was doing. I was actually texting my girlfriend. Maybe. You see, it turns out, texting can be kept pretty private. Usually."

Kaylie and Jake, sitting in the Green Room, squeezed each other's hands a little tighter and looked at each other in dread.

"But," Troy went on, "when you've signed up to be on this show – there are no private conversations. There are no private moments. And there are no – private – texts!"

They'd been caught.

"In tonight's special segment, which we'll call 'Pillow Talk,' we'll review what's been going on – undercover. We'll unveil the details of the secret life that Kaylie and Jake have been living, right under our very noses! Tonight, ladies and gentlemen, we will check out a sampling of the text messages that Kaylie and Jake have been trading – a full five *thousand* of them – over the last few weeks. What you see may shock and surprise you. It may enrage you. And it may affect your vote tonight. And we'll dive right into all of that – after the break."

Kaylie was mortified.

Jake said, "It'll be all right. We are almost through with this. Just hang in there."

A tear formed in Kaylie's left eye, and she let it drip out, rather than wipe it away and smudge her makeup.

When the show returned, Troy jumped right into the Pillow Talk segment. It opened with the self-aggrandizing Wyatt Sloane appearing in a pre-produced interview on screen.

"Well, we first started to suspect something a few weeks ago. Our camera crews reported that, at the same time each night, both Ms. Adams and Mr. Granville would disappear under their bedcovers for a while. We speculated on what they may be doing, and then I had an epiphany. We requisitioned the mobile phone records for both of them, and it soon became clear what was going on. So, of course, we retrieved the archived messages from the cell carrier's servers, and produced what you are about to see."

Kaylie looked over at Jake, who was starting to sweat a little on his forehead, above his hard frowning eyes.

The segment then dissolved into a large graphic that simulated a cell phone screen, with words scrolling across and filling the screen.

Their actual words.

A pair of voiceover actors (who sound uncannily like Kaylie and Jake) read the text messages aloud as the words appeared.

The series of messages conveniently omitted any that would reveal Kaylie's decision to keep the baby, and focused mainly on their developing love story. Many were aired out of order for dramatic effect. The final ones illuminated their plans on getting married.

The audience provided a strong reaction.

Troy wrapped it up. "So, there you have it, folks. Our stars had been cheating on you! But, let it never be said that *Canceled* doesn't deliver. Next up, we'll bring out Kaylie and Jake for a conversation. I, for one, am fascinated to hear what they have to say about all this. That's coming up, right after the break. Stick around."

Jake and Kaylie (who was starting to feel like a beached whale) moved to the stage during the commercials.

They were back on air moments later.

"So, what do you two sneaky lovebirds have to say for yourselves?" asked Troy with a giant white grin. He was clean-shaven and wore a well-cut tuxedo tonight. Besides next week's show, this one was the most important of the season for FBC, and he needed to look the part.

"What's there to say?" said Jake. "You caught us. Caught us being human beings. Human beings who've been subjected to conditions that are worse than most hardened prisoners have to deal with. Yeah, yeah, I know. It's all in the contract – you guys can do whatever you want, we waive all rights to privacy. But it still sucks. So, we made a little attempt at circumventing the ironclad controlling grip of the network. And we failed. At least we tried."

His statement got a good response from the crowd. Mostly enthusiastic cheering, just a couple of stray boos.

"And Kaylie?" said Troy.

"What *he* said. Just making an attempt to have some semblance of a real life. Just one little secret we could share – a way to stay sane and cling to a remnant of our humanity, our individuality. So, it didn't work. I have no regrets."

Troy then grilled them with a couple more hard-hitting questions about their midnight rendezvous, but the two deflected pretty well.

"Well, folks, there it is," Troy finally wrapped it up. "And just for those of you with the paid version of the app, we'll be pushing out the whole text message archive to the files section, where you can read through the thousands of exchanges that you missed because of the duplicity of our dynamic duo here. Stay tuned for more."

They went to break, and Kaylie, furious about this latest violation of her privacy, leaned in to Troy to whisper. "Are you guys really showing *all* of the texts online?"

Troy screwed up his face. "Of course not. You know there are quite a few that we can't make available until after the final voting closes – like the ones where you express a clear preference for the outcome of the show."

"I see." Kaylie had had just about enough of this. Her emotions were in flux again, much like at the start of the pregnancy. She felt like going all Jerry Springer and picking up a chair and throwing it into the audience full of sick voyeurs. Instead, she took a few deep breaths and tried to clear her mind.

The show returned, and Troy introduced Cynthia Davis, who in turn introduced a segment where she reported on the *Canceled* phenomenon as it was appearing on the national political and activist scene.

The show had become fully politicized.

Pro-choicers nationwide wanted Kaylie to exercise the Dr. Ian option, in an effort to show solidarity with the reproductive rights movement. They wanted Americans to make a statement and "support freedom of choice for all Americans" while protecting abortion rights as constituted under the landmark *Roe v Wade* decision of

1973. Some interviews with top women's group leaders stated the viewing public "must not capitulate to the anti-choice extremists who want to enslave women."

On the other end of the spectrum, Cynthia's surprisingly balanced report showed marches and vigils around the country, where pro-life supporters were making their big push to "save the baby." In some areas, pro-lifers camped on the steps of government buildings and courthouses. A group of them even staked out an area outside the FBC studio gates, where they ended up clashing with pro-choicers last Sunday.

Kaylie actually found the report fascinating. She also enjoyed being out of the direct spotlight for a few minutes, and she took a little comfort in seeing a face put to the large contingent of people who were ostensibly on her side.

When the report concluded, there was a special musical number by the number one selling pop artist in the country, and then there was just a few minutes left in the show.

After a lengthy break, sponsored by huge Fortune 10 corporations, the show returned.

Troy Tanner then surprised her by handing her a personal-sized birthday cake with baby blue icing. It was her twenty-sixth birthday yesterday – and she had completely forgotten.

She was also surprised her folks had not mentioned her birthday, but figured they were waiting until after all of this was over to celebrate properly.

Troy then announced the past week's vote results – another breathtakingly close tally in favor of life – and ran through his usual "please vote" spiel with more thick drama than ever, and that was it.

Now to wait one full week for the results.

As the studio lights faded, the cake slipped from Kaylie's hands, splatting on the stage as she felt about ready to pass out.

CHAPTER 51

Dave Kohler scratched at his thickening beard as he moved through the hallways of FBC, on his way to Tom Highgate's office.

It was the first time he'd been in the building without a suit on. Tonight he wore jeans, sneakers, and a white t-shirt under a light brown Nike sweat jacket. An FBC ball cap was crammed down over his messy hair. He looked a wreck, but he didn't care.

He didn't care about much anymore.

Not only had his job been taken over – leaving him to sit around and wait for the axe to fall – but he was being eaten alive inside over the deaths he'd caused.

The guilt weighed on him like an anvil across his shoulders, causing him to slouch as he approached Highgate's office door.

Dave was sick of it all. He spent his days wishing he could go back in time and tell himself to *not* hire someone to plant that bomb. And he spent his nights with restless sleep overrun by nightmares of burning homeless zombies chasing him through the James Brown Memorial Theater.

Maybe this meeting, called at short notice, would at least release him from some of his stress by firing him once and for all, so he could move on. At this point, with the ratings Sloane was showing the last few weeks, Dave had no chance of being brought back on in any meaningful capacity – so he'd just as soon be free to get a job somewhere else.

After all, this suspension was without pay.

Dave knocked at Tom's door, then stepped inside.

The lights were low. Tom sat in his usual place behind his desk, his silver checkered tie loosened, sleeves rolled up his forearms, and a short tumbler of scotch in his hand. In the shadows, on the couch, Sloane sat in khakis and a pale blue polo, tying his hair back into a pony tail.

"You uh, wanted to see me?" Dave said, stepping in hesitantly. His entire demeanor was that of a man who'd lost all of his previous confidence.

"Yeah, sit down, Dave," said Tom. His voice came out as an exhausted exhalation. Dave took a seat in an armchair, placing himself at the apex of an isosceles triangle formed by the other two men, as if keeping his distance to protect himself. After Dave sat, Tom said, "Go ahead, Wyatt."

Sloane leaned forward and put his elbows on his knees, clasping his hands. "Dave, here's the thing. We've discovered something very disturbing. See, when we wrangled the cell records of Kaylie and Jake, so we could dig through their text messages and exploit that awesome opportunity for more drama, we also requisitioned the calls."

"I don't understand," said Dave. He could feel a drop of sweat run from his armpit down his side inside his loose shirt.

"Since the Theissen Act took effect, communications providers have been required to archive, for one year, a database of actual calls. All calls. You know, for national security purposes."

"Right, I know that," said Dave.

"Under normal circumstances, those records would only be available to Federal terrorism investigators. But as you know, FBC pulled a few strings to get the text messages released. Anyway, I assigned a team to go through the call records to try to find anything, uh, special, that we might use for the finale episode."

"Uh huh." Dave took his cap off and ran his hand through his hair, then replaced the hat. "And?"

"And we found a call between you and Jake Granville. There was nothing explicit, but we were able to put two and two together."

"About what? You got something to say, Sloane, just say it!"

"We know you had the theater bombed."

Dave's head started spinning. "Ex-excuse me?"

"There's no use denying it," said Tom. "Once we suspected something, we hired someone to investigate, track down some leads, clues – you know – stuff the police couldn't figure out, since they were working with no starting point at all, and we strongly suspected you."

Sloane continued. "She found irrefutable evidence, Dave. It's over."

"I'll take your resignation tonight," said Tom. "And I will be reporting this to the authorities – on Friday."

"Friday? The day after the finale? I see how it is," said Dave.

"We can't derail the biggest event in television history," said Sloane.

357

"Think of it as a favor," said Tom. "For you. You've got seventy-two hours to get a head start – skip town."

Dave vacillated inside between anger, pain, relief, fear, and denial. His face contorted into a tired grimace that showed his inner turmoil. "A favor? Huh. How 'bout this for a favor? You guys forget what you've found, and I'll make sure that the fact the show was subject to several *weeks* of voter fraud is not leaked before the finale!"

"Is that a threat?" boomed Tom.

"It's a negotiation," said Dave.

Tom sighed heavily and took a sip of his scotch. "You're a piece of crap, you know that, Kohler?"

Sadly, Dave knew all too well. "You'd know about crap better than anyone, eh, Tom? So, do we have a deal?"

Tom sat back in his chair and laced his fingers across his ample belly. "No. You feel free to 'leak' whatever you see fit – though I think you'll have a hard time proving anything, or even getting anyone to listen. You haven't been running this show for months. Everyone knows you were forced out. Any discriminating journalist will assume you have an axe to grind, and will have to carefully look into your claims. By the time anyone can go to press with anything, the finale will be over, and none of it will matter. But you're still going to prison, so what would be the point? Like I said, you'll have a three day head start. You should probably get going."

Dave was shocked. He actually thought Tom was going to take the bait and offer him a deal.

Instead, he was just going to screw him straight out.

Dave stood up on weak knees, looking piteously at Tom. Then he flashed a glare at Sloane, who stared back impassively. He shuffled out without a word, his mouth dry and his eyes wet.

CHAPTER 52

May 20. Due date.

And the finale of the show.

For the past thirty-six hours, Kaylie had been having contractions – this little guy was right on time, and ready to make a grand entrance.

If he lived.

Kaylie rested both hands on The Bulge, waiting for Francine to finish helping Jake get ready. She considered that this may very well be her child's birthday – as Dr. Cho would induce if the vote was in favor of life. Kaylie was a little nervous at the prospect of giving birth tonight (on air, at that), but that was nothing up to the pressure she felt regarding the show in general.

Kaylie and Jake had decided to ride to the studios with George and Ellen in an extra-long limousine provided by the network. Her siblings would have their own limo.

For this grand finale episode, FBC was pulling out all the stops and bringing in all the "stars" of the show. Kaylie and Jake would of course be center stage, but also making an appearance would be George, Ellen, Bruce, Amanda, Dr. Cho, Dr. Ian, Molly the Midwife, Len Hamlin, and even Vanessa Baldwin.

A special room had been set up off the Green Room, decked out as a fully functional and self-contained medical facility – a "private" hospital room for Kaylie, where one of two things would happen tonight – based on the voting results – in a very non-private manner.

News outlets had said earlier in the day that FBC was predicting tonight's show would have two hundred and fifty million viewers – more than double those watching the final episode of *M*A*S*H** (the previous record holder) – and get a ninety ratings share. A bold claim, but not out of the question.

Tonight, all the men wore tuxedos, and the women wore the kinds of fine dresses often found on the red carpet at Hollywood events. FBC had actually had a top-name designer create a custom dress for Kaylie that had the effect of accentuating The Bulge while making her look far more sleek and elegant than she felt.

The shimmering blood-red gown flowed like the sails of a Spanish galleon and was matched by a pair of tall heels that Kaylie could barely handle in her current condition – but she made it work.

As with everything else she endured this day, she kept telling herself "just make it through today, that's all you need to do – just one day."

The limo arrived, and instead of bringing them in to the secure entrance, the driver had been instructed to deposit them at the front doors, to allow for a greater fanfare and general mobbing by the paparazzi.

Thankfully, FBC also provided a contingent of about twelve beefy body guards to guide them along the thirty yard red-carpeted walkway from the car to the building.

Cameras flashed, microphones were shoved toward them, and people cheered, screamed and booed as the family made its way inside.

Once within the safe walls of the James Brown Memorial Theater, they were led through several long back corridors to the dressing rooms, where makeup artists awaited them for that special face paint that would ensure the studio lights wouldn't make them all look like ghosts.

Kaylie was the first one ready, so she was escorted to the Green Room ahead of the rest.

When the assistant, a young black-haired girl, opened the door, she screamed and backed out. Kaylie peered inside.

Hanging from the overhead rigging, where studio lighting was affixed to a horizontal scaffold of heavy black bars, was a taut white nylon rope.

At the end of it was Dave Kohler.

The rope was cutting into his neck. His face was pale. His eyes were closed, his body limp, his toes about three inches above the floor. He swung slightly, as if the door opening had brushed him with a gentle breeze.

Kaylie dropped to her knees and felt nausea well up in the back of her throat as she smelled the evidence that Dave had soiled himself in death.

Kaylie turned her head away in time to see the assistant, white-faced, back into Wyatt Sloane and spin around.

"What's the matter with you?" asked Sloane, who could not see into the room from his vantage point.

"It's Dave K-Kohler – he's hanging in the Green Room!"

"Well, tell him to get out of there – we're five minutes from air and can't have him hanging around in there!"

"No! He's *hanging* in there!" said the assistant, her voice breaking as tears started to flow.

Sloane pushed past her and into the Green Room, standing above Kaylie who was still on her knees by the open door. He stared wide eyed and open-mouthed at the swaying corpse. All he could muster was, "Oh – my –"

Pulling himself together, he reached a hand down to help Kaylie to her feet and barked at the assistant, "Call Pokrovsky! Have him bring a team down here – now! We need to get this mess cleaned up – we're four minutes out!"

Sloane led Kaylie out of the Green Room doorway and back into the corridor, cussing under his breath the whole time, muttering something about Dave's utter obnoxiousness in making his last act an attempt to sabotage the show's finale.

Kaylie's head was already abuzz with the anxiety of the finale. Now she was really shaken – she'd just seen a dead man – a man who she knew. She had never particularly liked Dave, but that didn't seem to matter much when she thought of the lifeless human husk in the Green Room. She wondered if he'd had a family.

A man Kaylie assumed was Pokrovsky came running past her with three other guys in overalls, and they scooted into the Green Room murmuring to one another.

Shortly after, Jake came rolling up as Kaylie leaned back against a wall and wiped at her brow. She tried to stand up straight, and placed one hand at the back of her hip to support her straining back muscles.

"What's the matter?" asked Jake. "I saw Pokrovsky scrambling in this direction. Are you okay? Are the contractions getting worse?"

"No, it's not me, I'm fine. It's Dave. He's – he's dead. In there."

"What?" Jake wheeled up to the Green Room doorway just as Pokrovsky and his men were carrying Dave's body out.

"He hanged himself," said Kaylie. "Right there in the Green Room."

"Oh. Oh. Wow. It must've just happened," said Jake. "The production crew would've been in there within the last ten minutes to white balance the cameras. I can't believe it."

He put his head in his hands, cupping his face in his open palms, then rubbing at his eyes with his fingertips.

Kaylie stepped closer and put her hand on his shoulder. "I know he was your friend. I'm so sorry. Why would he do this?"

Jake shook his head slowly, then stopped suddenly and looked up at Kaylie. "I think I know. He'd been, uh, hiding something – a secret he'd confided in me. Something that he felt very guilty about."

"What was it?"

Jake opened his mouth to speak, but then closed it again, thinking.

At that moment, Tracy Smith ran up, clipboard in hand. "Hurry! We need you in the Green Room now! We are under a minute from air!"

Jake and Kaylie moved into the Green Room and got mic'ed up. The booth ran a quick sound check, and Tracy gave the fifteen second cue.

Moments later, the final episode of *Canceled* began with a cold open – Troy Tanner bathed in a spotlight, wearing a white tuxedo. A low drumroll played under his voice. "One woman. A surprise pregnancy. A man. Two doctors. And three hundred and twenty *million* votes. Tonight – it all comes down to what America has decided: an induced live birth, or a live abortion. Either way – *Canceled* will deliver."

The lights came up, the crowd went bananas, and the music soared as the screen dissolved to the CG opening sequence, then returned to a flying boom shot on camera one that drifted quickly over the heads of the packed audience and eventually zoomed to a stop on Troy, who still stood center stage.

"Ladies and gentlemen, welcome to *Canceled*! Our grand finale episode. Folks, this is what we've all been waiting for. America's eyes are on us tonight – as we reach the ultimate conclusion of this journey – a journey that began nine months ago. Let's take a look back."

The screen dissolved quickly to a long vignette that recapped the whole pregnancy – Kaylie's entire experience; from the moment she learned she was pregnant, all the way up to this very day. Of course, these highlights included the gunning down of Jake and his subsequent rehabilitative efforts, the blossoming love story between the two, and last week's text message revelations.

About the only important event not highlighted was Kaylie's grim discovery of Dave Kohler's body just before the show.

After this, there was an unprecedented eleven-minute commercial break, and then Cynthia Davis came onstage to introduce another in-depth "recap" type story that focused on the other members of the Adams family, and their individual journeys over the last nine months.

Another long commercial break, and the show returned.

This time, they brought onstage all the rest of the cast for a round-table discussion of Kaylie – Dr. Jenn Cho, Dr. Ian, Dr. Len Hamlin, Dr. Vanessa Baldwin, and Molly the Midwife. A lively conversation ensued in which each talked about their experiences with Kaylie and their candid thoughts on the show itself. With regard to the pending outcome of the show, each made their own position clear, with the vote evenly split.

Kaylie's OB/GYN, Dr. Cho, stated that she was personally opposed to the baby being terminated.

Dr. Ian said he understood Kaylie's contractual obligations, and was glad to perform the procedure if America decided it should be done.

To Kaylie's surprise (since he'd never committed to a position during their sessions), Len was of the opinion that abortion was just plain wrong and that this show was one more thing that's wrong with America's collective psyche today.

Vanessa strongly disagreed (which was no surprise to Kaylie), repeating her previous boilerplate about freedom of choice, simple procedures, women's rights under the law, and fairness to Kaylie.

Finally, Molly spouted a lengthy and circuitous new age diatribe about the justice of the Universe and the sweetness of innocent babies. The words themselves made little sense, but her stance was clear: Kaylie should be allowed to deliver the baby (naturally, of course).

Another break. At each break, before and after the commercials, the booth took the Green Room camera live, showing Kaylie and Jake waiting anxiously, hand in hand.

The next segment included a man-on-the-street feature, where dozens of people on the streets of cities across America were asked what their vote was this final week, the answers edited together in quick succession, with the verdicts apparently evenly split between "yea" and "nay."

Then there was coverage of the many huge rallies staged in major cities, both in favor of keeping the baby and in favor of termination. The crowds were energetic, carrying picket signs with various strongly-worded (and some humorous) messages.

Forget the Whales – Save the Baby
Democracy of Death
Protect America – Keep the Gene Pool Clean
Put an End to This NOW
It's not a choice, it's a person
What's the Fuss? Pull the Plug!
FBC = Financed By Children
Live Short and Prosper (held by a dude dressed as a Vulcan)
Holocaust ≠ Entertainment
Cancel CANCELED with One Simple Procedure!
Protect America's Least Wanted

A final report in this segment was an interview with two U.S. senators – one from each side of the abortion aisle – who'd come together in a bipartisan effort to cosponsor a bill that would make shows like this illegal in the future. Then they interviewed several other senators who promised to never vote for such a measure, claiming it was a violation of the First Amendment.

Kaylie watched from the Green Room, amazed at how explosive it had all become. When the show had started, she had no idea this would turn into this level of political circus nationwide.

One more break of nearly ten minutes, which included a special news break for local stations trying to localize the story, and then Kaylie and Jake were brought out onstage.

Troy asked them the standard "how are you feeling" gut-check questions, followed up by a couple of softballs about the last week's activities, then announced that the moment had arrived for the final vote results. He then said those results would be shared – right after the break.

Kaylie had read online yesterday that this commercial break had thirty-second spots worth six times the going rate for a Superbowl ad.

The show returned with a split-screen shot of Dr. Cho scrubbing up in a small delivery room back stage, and in similar room, Dr. Ian preparing to perform his procedure.

The view dissolved to the stage, where Troy invited George, Ellen, Bruce and Amanda to stand alongside Kaylie. Kaylie still gripped Jake's hand tightly.

Troy then got right down to business.

"America voted. *Boy*, did they vote. Some statistics: more votes were counted for this decision than for the last two presidential elections *combined*. Sixty-eight percent came in via the paid app, thirty-two percent from the free app. Astounding numbers, astounding."

The crowd was screaming and clapping and waving their hands in the air like crazy people.

"Folks," Troy continued, as the camera panned a row of big-name celebrities in the audience, then switched back to the host, "tonight's results were the closest we have ever had on the show. Out of hundreds of millions of votes, the decision came down to fewer than *two thousand* votes. Unbelievable!"

More cheering from the crowd. Another shot of celebrity guests – different ones this time.

"And now, the results."

A pair of tall young ladies – the supermodel type – one blonde and one brunette – walked across the stage in matching white mini-dresses and high heels. Between them, they carried a small white trunk that was padlocked, and handed it to Troy.

A red-head, dressed like the other two girls, entered from the other side of the stage and approached Troy. She reached into the cleavage visible atop her dress and extracted a golden key, which she handed to Troy.

The three ladies left the stage.

Troy unlocked the box.

He pulled out an envelope, and placed the box on the stage.

The lights dimmed and the crowd hushed as a low drumroll played.

A spotlight fell on Troy Tanner, Kaylie Adams, and the wheelchair-bound Jake Granville.

"Kaylie Adams. America. Your final vote for *Canceled* is as follows." He paused for an excruciating ten full seconds of low drumroll. He shook his head gently as he said, "Kaylie, you're going to go see Dr. Ian. They've voted to terminate!"

The music blasted, the lights came up bright, the crowd roared, and Kaylie staggered back a step, only held up by Jake's firm grip on her hand.

The whole Adams family rushed to her and encircled her in their arms.

They all cried great tears of sadness.

Jake lowered his head into his hands, hiding his face from the camera.

Troy actually looked a little shocked, his face alternating between a plastic smile and a look of mild concern as he looked back and forth between the rabid audience and the devastated family on the stage with him.

After a couple of minutes of this chaotic scene, he brought his microphone to his mouth and announced the big musical act, which would play a three song set while Kaylie was brought back to the special medical room to prepare for the procedure.

A curtain was raised at the back of the stage and the music came on hard while the whole Adams family, and Jake, were escorted off stage and back through the corridors to the med room.

Kaylie changed out of her fancy red dress and into a hospital gown, sobbing the whole time.

Dr. Ian was there in the surgery room to greet her with his gap-toothed grin, as if it was just another day at work for him.

She got up on the table, and a curtain was pulled most of the way around, allowing for her face to remain on camera. Another camera was on Troy, and when the music ended, there was a commercial break, then the show resumed, with Troy speaking.

"Ladies and gentlemen, as you know, this is a prime-time network television first – an *exclusive* event! – a live abortion performed right here on FBC. However, as this is of course a prime-time network television program, there are certain guidelines set out by FCC laws and regulations that prohibit certain things. As such, you will not be seeing Kaylie below the shoulders, in keeping with these laws and regulations."

Kaylie was relieved to hear this. For some reason, she had always thought that if it came to this, that America would be getting a full-frontal shot of her private parts. She should've realized they can't show *that* on TV.

But then she considered that instead, millions of Americans would be watching a close-up of her crying face, a portrait of misery and tragedy, her most private, heart-crushing moment captured live for all to see. Then she half-wished the camera would be pointed at her nether regions instead.

Either way, this was a torturous nightmare. She started to have a sudden bout of anxiety and found herself hyperventilating. Dr. Ian noticed, and quietly administered a mild sedative. She felt her breathing return to normal and everything got slightly blurry as her focus relaxed.

She started to tune everything out, the sounds of the room turning to muffled echoes. She closed her eyes.

She thought of the life that almost was. She tried to console herself with the thought of all that money she'd soon have.

It was no consolation.

But in a few minutes, it would all be over.

Jake watched from the Green Room as Dr. Ian spoke directly to the camera, giving a blow-by-blow explanation of the procedure he was about to perform.

The other family members were there, too.

It broke his heart that Kaylie had to be in there, facing this alone, but as with any medical procedure, only medical personnel were allowed in the surgery.

He held his breath as Dr. Ian ducked into the curtain and did something that could not be seen. He came back out and gave some further explanations. He genuinely seemed to be enjoying himself.

This segment of the show – the second hour of the two-hour finale – seemed to drag on as Jake watched from his wheelchair, unable to do anything but wait.

A commercial-free, uninterrupted segment, it was already twenty-five minutes in when Dr. Ian announced that there was a minor, unexpected complication, and it was going to take longer than normal.

Jake continued to hold his breath, sipping at a glass of cold water, sweating around his hairline and under his shirt.

Behind him, he could hear Ellen weeping from time to time, and George trying to console her.

Bruce and Amanda sat in stunned silence.

Another fifteen minutes later, Dr. Ian emerged from the curtain once more, his gloves covered in blood.

"The procedure is complete," he announced. He still wore a tiny smile. Or maybe his face just looked that way all the time.

A minute later, the curtains were pulled back to reveal Kaylie lying on her back, the covers pulled up to her neck, her belly almost flat.

Tears streamed down her flushed face.

Jake finally let out the breath he'd been holding.

And smiled to himself.

After the show wrapped up with a big preview of next fall's *Death Row: Mercy or Justice* (which had managed to win its legal battle after all), Jake and the family were allowed in to see Kaylie.

No cameras anymore. That part of their life was finally over, for good.

Jake allowed Kaylie's mother and father to hug her and whisper with her and console her, then they stepped back so he had room to roll up to her bedside.

The parents crossed the room to stand with Bruce and Amanda, murmuring and looking like members of a funeral party. Bruce looked like he'd lost more weight than he needed to, and Amanda had streaked mascara lining her cheeks.

Jake leaned close and whispered to Kaylie. "You okay?" he asked.

She smiled weakly. "Yeah, I'm great. What happened? I could've sworn –"

"The baby is doing fine," Jake said. "A little jaundiced, but nothing serious. He's seven pounds thirteen ounces. They have him in a special nursery right next door. Dr. Ian's nurse will bring him in after a few minutes."

"How – how did – it was *you*, wasn't it?"

"I talked to Highgate and Dr. Ian. We made an arrangement. They'd do their 'TV magic' on this – that is, Dr. Ian would induce, deliver, and sneak the baby out through the back of the curtain – then they'd loop the audio so no one would hear the cries of the little guy."

Kaylie stared at Jake, her face a mixture of shock and awe.

"What can I say," Jake continued, "as I once told Dr. Ian, you should never believe everything you see on TV."

"But, how did you get them to agree to this?"

"Well, in exchange for the trickery, I agreed to *not* go public on the voter fraud, *not* go public on the truth about the bombing incident, and *not* go public on the scandalous death of Dave Kohler. I also forfeited my prize money and signed a five-year non-compete. Your money's is still safe, as I couldn't really speak to your contract. I also agreed to keep a certain secret about Highgate – something dark that could end his career – some dirt I had on him and his daughter. Nasty stuff we don't need to talk about."

"What about Dr. Ian?"

"He was easier to convince. When I told him we both wanted to keep the baby, he had a hard time with going against our wishes. And throwing in my Ferrari helped, too."

"But you kept the Cobra, right?"

"Of course – it's your wedding present."

They shared a little laugh. "I just can't believe they went for that deal."

"They had nothing to lose, and I kinda had Highgate over a barrel. Blowing the lid off the behind-the-scenes corruption would damage the network and hurt or sink their careers. And in the end, Highgate simply couldn't let the truth get out about his – uh, you know."

"I don't wanna know."

"And he knew we could get away with the deception. He just had one other stipulation. To ensure nobody ever finds out – we need to split. We need to leave town, never return, and stay out of the public eye."

"Stay out of the public eye? Huh, I can live with that!"

They shared a kiss. "I think we need to tell your family now, before they grieve any more."

Kaylie looked brightly toward her parents and siblings. "Mom, Dad, I have some news."

EPILOGUE

Kaylie stood beside Jake's wheelchair.

Her flowing dress was beautiful, and so was she.

The sparkling water of the scenic Rogue River rolled past just beyond the trees, and the sound of chirping birds could be heard on the fresh, warm summer air that smelled like a bouquet of flowers.

And there was not a TV camera in sight.

Vivaldi played softly, and a small crowd of family and close friends watched, seated in white folding chairs on the trim lawn. The music stopped, and the minister opened his thick black scriptures and began to speak.

Kaylie looked down at Jake in his tux. He looked so handsome. With effort, he wiggled his toes and grinned up at her. Kaylie smiled back, then glanced over at her mom, who held the tiny babe in her arms.

The boy whose name was about to become David George Granville.

David George Granville, America's least wanted.

THE END

Find more books by Michael D. Britton at

www.michaeldbritton.com
www.amazon.com/Michael-D.-Britton/e/B004UW28I6
www.smashwords.com/profile/view/michaeldbritton